Sarasa Nagase

ILLUSTRATION BY

Mai Murasaki

New York

I'M THE VILLAINESS, SO I'M TAMING THE FINAL BOSS, Vol. 4
Sarasa Nagase

Translation by Taylor Engel
Cover art by Mai Murasaki

Yen On
150 West 30th Street, 19th Floor
New York, NY 10001

Visit us at yenpress.com
facebook.com/yenpress
twitter.com/yenpress
yenpress.tumblr.com
instagram.com/yenpress

First Yen On Edition: November 2022
Edited by Yen On Editorial: Emma McClain, Ivan Liang
Designed by Yen Press Design: Andy Swist

Yen On is an imprint of Yen Press, LLC.
The Yen On name and logo are trademarks of Yen Press, LLC.

Library of Congress Cataloging-in-Publication Data
Names: Nagase, Sarasa, author. | Murasaki, Mai, illustrator. | Engel, Taylor, translator.
Title: I'm the villainess, so I'm taming the final boss / Sarasa Nagase ;
illustration by Mai Murasaki ; translation by Taylor Engel.
Other titles: Akuyaku reijou nanode last boss wo kattemimashita. English
Description: First Yen On edition. | New York, NY : Yen On, 2021
Identifiers: LCCN 2021030963 | ISBN 9781975334055 (v. 1 ; trade paperback) |
ISBN 9781975334079 (v. 2 ; trade paperback) | ISBN 9781975334093 (v. 3 ; trade paperback) |
ISBN 9781975334116 (v. 4 ; trade paperback)
Subjects: LCGFT: Fantasy fiction. | Light novels.
Classification: LCC PL873.5.A246 A7913 2021 | DDC 895.63/6—dc23
LC record available at https://lccn.loc.gov/2021030963

ISBNs: 978-1-9753-3411-6 (paperback)
978-1-9753-3412-3 (ebook)

10 9 8 7 6 5 4 3 2 1

LSC-C

Printed in the United States of America

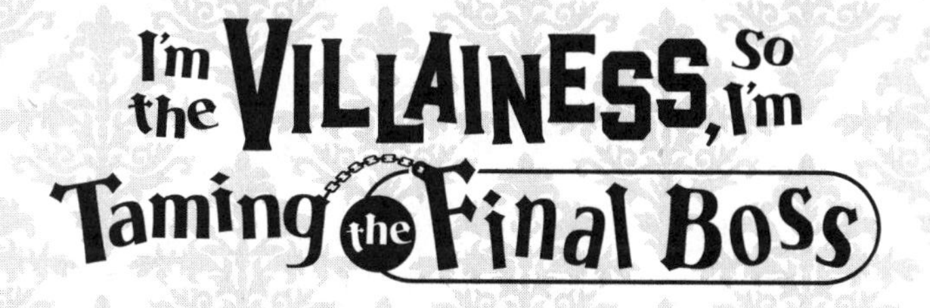

CONTENTS

Claude Jean Ellmeyer
Crown Prince of Imperial Ellmeyer and Aileen's husband.
The final boss of *Regalia of Saints, Demons, and Maidens 1*.
Baal Shah Ashmael
Holy King of the Kingdom of Ashmael and protector of the Daughter of God.
Final boss of *Regalia of Saints, Demons, and Maidens 3*.
Aileen Jean Ellmeyer
A villainess who's remembered her past life. Crown Princess of Imperial Ellmeyer.
I'm the VILLAINESS, So I'm Taming the Final Boss
Character Introductions and Glossary

Ares Emir Ashmael

The main hero of *3*.
Sahra's husband.

Sahra

The main heroine of *3*. The Daughter of God who holds the key to the holy sword's restoration.

Roxane Fusca

The villainess of *3*.
Baal's principal consort.

Lilia Reinoise

The heroine of *Regalia of Saints, Demons, and Maidens 1*. Like Aileen, she's actually reincarnated.

The *otome* game *Regalia of Saints, Demons, and Maidens 3*

According to its founding myth, the Kingdom of Ashmael was created when the Daughter of God received the holy sword and used it to slay the fiend dragon. Water welled up from the sword, creating a fertile land in the desert. Its king is descended from the Daughter of God; he possesses sacred power, and it's impossible to use magic in his kingdom. However, Baal, the current holy king, becomes a consummate tyrant and is possessed by the fiend dragon. The kind General Ares starts a revolution: In cooperation with the Daughter of God, he uses a new holy sword to slay Baal and assumes the holy king's throne—or that's the intended classic route. In this world, the kingdom uses every opportunity to complicate things for the Imperial Ellmeyer, which has a similar founding myth.

✦ Prelude ✦
The Villainess's Departure

The smell of salt hangs in the air, and the water's surface is white with choppy waves. The vast ocean glitters. Seagulls skim over the great passenger ship, making for the bright blue horizon.

"All right, Master Claude. I'll be going."

Resettling her broad-brimmed hat on her head, Aileen looks up at her husband, who's come to see her off. Even when he's glum, his face is rapturously beautiful. He checks with her for the thousandth time: "You insist on going, no matter what?"

"I do. I must demonstrate our sincerity by going in person."

"...Wouldn't it be better if I teleported you there, at least? Even if it is a luxury passenger liner, you are the crown princess. Arbitrarily instructing you to board this ship, instead of sending a personal escort? It's outrageous."

"Let's view it in a positive light. Besides, if we use your power, Master Claude, they may take it as an intentional display of the demons' might. We'll never establish amicable relations that way."

"But if anything were to happen to you—"

"Never fear: Rachel is here, and Serena will guard me. Besides, I have this." Softly, she touches the gleaming band on her left ring finger. It's the ring she hasn't been able to remove since she pledged her eternal love—or rather, the one she always wears. It has been imbued with the demon king's magic, and as long as she has it, the sacred sword within her is an invincible weapon capable of subduing any foe. "Don't worry. I am the second strongest person in the world, after you."

"I wish I could accompany you, but if you're bound for the kingdom of the oracle-princess, where men are forbidden..."

"Why not disguise yourself as a woman and come anyway? With your beauty, Master Claude, you could be the loveliest woman alive."

Claude grimaces. Aileen chuckles a little, then gives her husband a kind smile. He gets surprisingly lonely. "I won't be gone long. Wait for me, if you would."

"According to your logic, I suppose sending demons to guard you won't do, either."

"That's correct. We must show that we aren't plotting to use demons to dominate the world by maneuvering through the Queendom of Hausel."

The day after Claude and Aileen's wedding, an invitation arrived from the Holy Queendom of Hausel, a land that claimed perpetual neutrality. It is an "invitation" in name only; in reality, this will be a court of inquiry. Claude is well aware of this.

"It was bad timing. The fiend dragon appeared in the neighboring Kingdom of Ashmael while my memories were gone... Thanks to that, they suspect I'm plotting an invasion."

Internally, Claude's grumbling nearly makes Aileen break into a cold sweat, but she doesn't let it show. "Well, I will go and explain to them, in no uncertain terms, that their assumption is incorrect!"

"But since I did have amnesia, I'm not entirely certain it isn't my fault."

"You weren't to blame, Master Claude! Besides, the Kingdom of Ashmael and Imperial Ellmeyer have always been at odds with one another. Even my father said that this may be mere fault-finding."

Just as Imperial Ellmeyer had its sacred sword and Maid, so the Kingdom of Ashmael had a founding myth about a Daughter of God and her holy sword. Upon receiving the holy sword, the Daughter of God slew the fiend dragon, and water welled up from the sword, creating a fertile land in the desert. Or so the legend goes.

Roughly a century ago, the Kingdom of Ashmael had abruptly claimed that Ellmeyer's Maid of the Sacred Sword was in fact the Daughter of God, which made Ellmeyer a vassal state to Ashmael. Bridling at their treatment as a subordinate state and this baseless denial of their founding myth, Imperial Ellmeyer had vehemently objected. While they had avoided outright war, the Kingdom of Ashmael had been isolationist to begin with, and diplomatic relations between the two countries had been severed.

Now Ashmael had requested mediation from the Queendom of Hausel on the grounds that the demon king, Ellmeyer's crown prince, had revived the fiend dragon and was attempting to encroach on their sovereign territory.

"They haven't even explained the current situation with the fiend dragon," Aileen continues. "If it weren't for the fact that the Queendom of Hausel is mediating, this wouldn't even merit our attention. It's utterly galling."

"Since our countries have no diplomatic relationship, requesting mediation by a third party is a legitimate approach. It's far better than a sudden declaration of war from Ashmael. War is pointless, and I'd rather avoid it."

The Holy Queendom of Hausel is a pacifist, inviolable, benevolent land. It claims neutrality, is under the protection of a goddess, and has a history of giving aid to countries far and wide. All these things explain its selection as mediator.

Every country respects it, and making an enemy of it would earn them criticism from around the world. They'd find themselves with a host of new problems—everything from diplomatic issues to unease among their own citizens. Conversely, if they can satisfy the Queendom of Hausel, the complaint from Ashmael will end as mere carping.

"True, at the very least, we do want to avoid war. That said, we must not back down."

"Yes, after all, this incident is still suspicious either way... I really am worried. We should send someone el—"

"Goodness, Master Claude! Do you imagine I'll be outdone in the negotiations?"

If so, he's drastically underestimating her. When Aileen glares up at him belligerently, Claude looks troubled. "That isn't what worries me."

"In that case, rest assured and wait. I promise you I'll thrash them within an inch of their lives!"

"If you thrash them, won't we end up with a war on our—?"

"I meant in spirit! They summoned me, you know!"

As the crown princess of Ellmeyer, Aileen is currently the empire's highest-ranking noble lady, as well as the Maid of the Sacred Sword. If she goes as an official representative, she can't possibly return empty-handed. Not even if it means traveling with an individual who's a nuisance of the highest order, constantly spewing a storm of *otome* game terminology—

"Lady Aileen! We'll be setting sail soon."

Coming up behind her, the nuisance embraces her arm. Aileen's face stiffens, but the other girl's smile practically glows.

Her shining eyes gleam more brightly under the clear sky; is that a heroine bonus?

"...Lady Lilia. I'm quite certain I told you to remain with Serena."

"Oh, did you? I'm sorry. The thought of traveling with you makes me so happy that I simply can't sit still!"

Since Claude is present, Aileen smiles at her, and Lilia responds with a charming smile of her own, feigning ignorance.

"We are on our way to a diplomatic engagement. If you forget your manners, you'll bring shame on our nation. You are the fiancée of the second prince. Bear that in mind and behave yourself, please."

"It's all right, Lady Aileen! Things have gotten rather complicated, but the Queendom of Hausel wants me, the true Maid of the Sacred Sword. Why else would they summon me as well? Hee-hee. I'm looking forward to it."

"Looking forward to it? Even though you'll be parted from Prince Cedric for a while?" She gives Lilia a thin smile, and the other girl's expression cools. Peering into her eyes, Aileen whispers. "Let me caution you one more time: Behave yourself, Lady Lilia. All right? If you don't, I'll have such an intense urge to tell Prince Cedric that I'll truly regret the fact that men are forbidden at our destination."

"......"

"Besides, it would be awful if the spell on your neck were to activate, wouldn't it? Particularly the cleanup afterward."

"..........."

Lilia is silent, but she hasn't flinched. That thin smile is still on her lips, and crackling sparks fly between the two of them. Claude, who's watching, murmurs. "...If men are forbidden, there's no possibility that you'll come back with more lackeys. I suppose that's something."

"? Did you say something, Master Claude?"

"No, it was nothing... You are my wife. I'll leave this in your hands."

Since he put it like that, she'd have to give it her very best. Throwing her shoulders back, Aileen nods. "Yes, you may count on me."

"Once you've arrived safely, send me a letter. After that, I want you to write me once each day."

"...Wouldn't it be enough to write only in an emergency?" Claude's epistolary talents make it difficult to come up with responses, and she tries to put him off with a smile.

However, he promptly comes back with an alternate proposal. "Would twice a day be better?"

"O-once a week."

"I'd gladly accept one every hour."

"Very well, once a day it is! Communication is the key to success, after all!"

It looks as if she's compromised, when in fact she's given in to Claude's original demand. However, if she ends up souring the demon king's mood, the weather will be a problem. She can't have him causing a storm that might keep the ship from leaving port.

When Aileen gives in, the corners of Claude's lips relax into a smile. "That will do, then. If anything happens, summon me at once. I may be the next emperor now, but I am also your husband."

"I-I'm aware of that."

They haven't yet been married for a month, and she still isn't used to claiming him as her spouse. Feeling rather embarrassed,

Aileen begins to lower her gaze, but Claude raises her chin with his fingertips.

As his shadow falls across her face, she hastily closes her eyes. Aileen is so nervous she can feel the tips of her eyelashes trembling. Where will his lips fall? On her forehead, her cheeks, her eyelids? Or perhaps on her own lips, which, despite their marriage, he has yet to kiss?

We are already man and wife, you know! Come, Master Claude, steel yourself and take the plunge— The atmosphere is rather lacking here, but that's all right! It's better than staying as we are, never truly becoming husband and wife!

But contrary to Aileen's internal enthusiasm, Claude's lips land gently on her forehead.

"......"

"Be careful, Aileen. I love you."

"...Y-yes. I...love you...as well."

In response, the demon king gives her a sweet, melting smile, then vanishes.

She's never doubted his love, but her shoulders slump. Putting a hand to her forehead, she sighs.

"......"

"Lady Aileen, tell me, is it true? Have you and Master Claude still not consummated your mar—?"

"Unless you want to die this instant, be quiet."

Lilia is currently being treated as a criminal, imprisoned under guard along with Cedric. Since the Queendom of Hausel requested her presence as well, they've been compelled to grant her permission to go out. In exchange, a spell has been cast on her neck, in lieu of a bomb.

Since it is a spell, it won't be spotted easily. However, if Aileen sends the merest trace of Claude's magic into it from her wedding ring, the merciless spell will send Lilia's head flying.

That said, Lilia calls herself "the player," and is treating this world as if it were a game. Perhaps even her own death doesn't feel real to her: She's completely unperturbed. "But the demon king was very fast about that sort of thing in the game, you know. There were still images in the fan discs." As Lilia reveals information nobody wants, Aileen turns on her heel, leaving her. Lilia follows. "Could it be that your womanly charms leave him cold? That couldn't be, could it, Lady Aileen. Not when you're my very favorite character. Oh, or perhaps the main game's 'All Ages' rating is still in effect? If that's true, then you'll never, ever—"

"Don't talk about that. People will think you're a lunatic."

"Oh, yes. The business about the *otome* game was our little secret, wasn't it?" Lilia says cheerfully. Aileen has given up trying to understand this side of her. "Still, I didn't expect that. To think you'd intentionally go with me to a country that serves as the stage for the game. Even though everything about the scenario is sure to give me the advantage."

"That's no reason for the crown princess to run from a diplomatic mission. Besides, this is a different era."

"Hee-hee. That's true. I'm sure it won't end so quietly, though. Not when the Maid of the Sacred Sword is going." Without specifying which of them she means, Lilia overtakes Aileen, then twirls around to face her. "Don't look so grim. I just know we'll get to enjoy the game again. That's why, just this once, I'll behave for you."

"Even with a bomb around your neck?"

"Oh, this is nothing. Considering the game's plot, there's no way I'd die now."

Stepping lightly, Lilia boards the ship ahead of Aileen. Fighting back a sigh, Aileen follows. Serena, her guard, materializes from who-knows-where and falls in behind her. Rachel, her lady-in-waiting, has had their luggage loaded onto the ship, and she greets Aileen with a bow. "Lady Aileen, let me show you to your cabin."

"Thank you, Rachel... Serena, I insist that you cooperate with me this time. If you don't, I'll have you marry Auguste."

"What kind of a threat is that?"

"My, my. Don't tell me you've tripped a flag? This late in the game?" Lilia's mutter seems to perplex Rachel and Serena. The woman is disregarding the warning Aileen literally just gave her. When she glares at her, Lilia smiles, putting her index finger to her lips in a charming gesture. "I know. Our little secret, correct?"

"...Ignore her. Let's focus on reaching the Queendom of Hausel safely... In order to avoid a marital crisis, among other things."

Serena frowns. "What marital crisis? Don't tell me..."

"The secret art of the Holy Queendom of Hausel."

Serena looks patently disgusted. Beside her, Lilia's eyes widen. "Lady Aileen, you can't mean you're after *that*, can you?"

"Don't be ridiculous. My goal is diplomacy, the avoidance of war. However, since we're headed there anyway, I may as well try for two birds with one stone!"

Men are forbidden in the Holy Queendom of Hausel. However, while it may sound like a celibate nation, that isn't the case. In order to rapidly seduce men and beget children, they have a wanton, sophisticated secret art that's more than a match for any aphrodisiac or lovemaking technique.

It had been part of the scenario in the game, and in reality, it was an open secret, whispered about as if it were true. Some said that the reason the Queendom never lacked for money was the steady stream of visitors from around the world who came to pay for a chance to experience that art in the flesh.

If Aileen had it, even the demon king would surely yield to her.

And really, so what if their first night hadn't gone as planned? Her husband is practically carnality in human form, and he hasn't even kissed his new wife, let alone made a move on her— What is he thinking?!

"Just you wait, Master Claude...! When I get back, I swear I'll make our first night together a success!"

"Lady Aileen, I sympathize, but you're being very loud."

"This is ludicrous..."

"...Hee-hee, hee-hee-hee-hee-hee, you truly are magnificent, Lady Aileen!"

No matter how Lilia laughs at her, her resolve remains unshaken. A whistle blows, and the ship sets sail.

A bright future of conjugal bliss is sure to be waiting for her at the end of this journey.

Out on deck, Aileen laughs dauntlessly into a headwind, until a strong gust buffets her and nearly knocks her down.

✦ First Act ✦
The Villainess Insists on Standing Out

Alucato, the capital of Imperial Ellmeyer. Its castle is a symbol of its abundance and the pride of its citizens, with alabaster stairways and sun-drenched crystal corridors. Its blue spires can be seen from anywhere in the city, and its silver bells toll the hours. In a corner of the imperial castle—or rather, behind that castle, in the older keep that stands in the depths of a dark, eerie forest, a meeting is underway.

"I've summoned you here for one simple reason: There's a matter I would like your help with."

Claude may be the imperial castle's effective master now, but he's also the demon king of the old castle. As he speaks, he scans the faces assembled at the conference room's round table.

Starting from the right, there's the third son of an upstart count, the president of a middle-class newspaper, and a doctor, a botanist, and an architect-cum-artist, all from the lower class. Every title, rank, and occupation are more eclectic than the next. However, they are all equal executives of the Oberon Trading Firm, an organization created by his wife.

Since she is its president, even though Claude is her husband, he isn't in any position to use these men. He also feels that such boundaries should be clearly defined.

The executives probably understand that as well. They seem puzzled.

"Us? Help the demon king?"

Isaac, the third son of Count Lombard, grumbles that he can't see this going anywhere good. He is Claude's wife's right-hand man and an extremely clever adviser.

Claude nods. "That's right. I don't want Aileen to know."

"Oh, gotcha. Are you planning some sort of surprise for Miss Aileen while she's away?" Jasper speaks up cheerfully, trying to dispel the rather awkward atmosphere. The president of the *Varie Newspaper* is older than the rest, and skilled at gathering information.

Respectfully, Claude corrects him. "Aileen isn't a 'miss' any-more. She's my wife."

"Your wife, hmm? Yes, on paper, that's true." Smirking, Luc mutters in a way that's perfectly audible. He's a brilliant doc-tor who graduated from university despite being born in the fifth layer, the capital's poorest district. He's definitely the one who sent an uncalled-for concoction to Claude on his wedding night.

"...As long as it won't hurt Aileen, let's hear it," Quartz says quietly. The young botanist is Luc's childhood friend from the fifth layer and a fellow university graduate. His black eye patch seems significant, but that's not what interests Claude.

"As long as it's fun, count me in. Are we making an ice castle this time?" Denis asks, flashing a cheerful smile. He may be the youngest member of this group, but he's a genius who can make anything. Having Denis on his side is reassuring. Keeping his eyes on Denis, Claude shakes his head.

"No, it's more urgent than an ice castle. A moment ago, one of you said we were husband and wife 'on paper,' correct? It's about that."

"Oh, count me out. I don't want to hear th—"

"I want you to develop safeguards for my real first night with Aileen."

"What 'real first night'?! Aaaaargh, I told myself I wasn't gonna make any snappy comebacks..." Isaac, the one who'd immediately tried to make a break for it, clutches his head.

Claude nods mildly. "I see. You'll gladly undertake the challenge, then? That's great news."

"At what point in this conversation did you hear that?!"

"That's unexpected," Claude says. "I never took you for the type who'd want to waste time. Not that I have anything against taking this nice and slow."

"...Young master Isaac. The demon king's already decided that we're helping him," Jasper sighs.

"Yeah, but come on, like we could just say 'okay'? You know it's gonna be a pain in the butt." Isaac crosses his arms, prepared to fight this to the bitter end.

Beside him, Luc smiles calmly. "The demon king himself, asking us for help. That's quite pathetic, isn't it."

"Yes, I am the demon king. In other words, even if I rip off a human limb or two for no particular reason, the fact that I'm letting the human continue living is quite merciful enough, don't you think?"

There's no response.

Satisfied with the ensuing silence, Claude settles deeper into his chair and recrosses his legs. "All right, on to the main topic. The truth is, I haven't been doing well lately."

"You mean in the head, don't you? Mm, yes, I see."

Before Luc has quite finished speaking, the vase of flowers on the table explodes. After watching one of the shards graze Luc's cheek, Claude sighs. "My magic is unstable. If I let my guard down even slightly, this happens."

"Uh, that was completely on purpose..."

"Perish the thought. Incidentally, sometimes all the air disappears from rooms, so be careful what you say."

"Seriously, you're doing that on purpose, right?!"

"If I attempt to touch Aileen while I'm like this, and my heart races, I'll cause a cataclysmic earthquake. That's what's troubling me."

Everyone looks at him.

Isaac speaks up, looking rather dubious. "...Wait, that's what you're worried about? That your magic is unstable?"

"Isn't that what I've been telling you?"

"So that's why you've been avoiding Lady Aileen." Denis looks as though everything suddenly makes sense to him. At that, finally, Isaac and the rest turn serious.

Jasper picks up his fountain pen. "Uh, so... You're saying you genuinely aren't doing well. In the magic department, right?"

"That's right. I want you to investigate the cause and find a way to improve my condition."

"You can't be telling us to make you a medicine that will correct the state of your magic." Luc's eyes widen. Claude nods.

Quartz frowns. "...Magic isn't our field. You should ask the mage."

"I will have Elefas and the rest of the Levi tribe help, of course. You may use Walt and Kyle as test subjects."

"Don't sell out your subordinates... I think you're treating the Levi tribe worse than the last guys did. If they hit you with some weird spell and you get amnesia again, don't come crying to me."

"I'm in trouble, so there's no help for it."

"Do you have any ideas about this?" Luc asks. "Such as what may have caused you to lose control over your magic, for example?"

Claude shakes his head. "Not a thing. I suspect it's an aftereffect of losing my magic when I had amnesia, but that's all I can think of."

Isaac gives a long sigh and tilts his head back, gazing at the ceiling. "First you lose your memories and your magic, and now your magic's gone haywire...?"

"I'm sorry. I know it's a nuisance. However, if you help me, I'm sure this will be resolved in no time."

"Look, nobody's said we'll help you yet. Don't just decide—"

"If my magic gets out of control, I may transform into a demon. Just think how sad Aileen will be if I lose my humanity."

The others flinch. Their reactions are simultaneously funny and anything but. Claude goes on matter-of-factly. "It would be best to clear this up before Aileen returns. If she finds out about it, there's no telling what she'll do."

"—I'm with you all the way on that."

"Then you'll help me, won't you?"

The only response is silence. He can force them, but if he does, there's no telling when they might sell him out. The important thing is sincerity. Resting his elbows on the table, he decides to spill his heart to them. "Being unable to make love to Aileen is sheer anguish."

"As far as we're concerned, it serves you right."

"Luc... He's not feeling well. Be a little considerate..."

"Every night, Aileen stays up late, waiting for me to finish work. I've seen her fidget as she tries to bring up the subject herself. Every time I choose to go to bed, she looks dejected."

"H-hey, whoa, hearing a young fellow brag about his girl is real rough on this old guy—"

Jasper's reproach is swallowed up by a slight tremor. Denis looks around curiously. "...Did anybody else feel that?"

"I want you to understand how much effort it's taking me to stay rational, even as we speak."

Claude closes his eyes, thinking of his beloved bride. When she'd slept like a log on their first night, the sadness had cut him like a knife, and he'd begun plotting ways to get back at her later. However, Aileen had been so sweet and pathetic that it had blown the idea right out of his mind.

Watching her try to tempt him into their bedchamber, even though she couldn't have been comfortable doing it. Seeing her brood over what it would take to make him yield, how to get him to touch her... But it would be dangerous to sleep with her right now. He knows this. And yet his feelings can't keep up.

The world begins to shudder and shake. He can't keep his thoughts to himself any longer.

"How can a husband be completely unable to touch his wife?! What is this madness...?!"

"Agh, agh, agh, earthquake! It's an earthquake!"

"I-is this the demon king's doing?!"

"It makes no sense. Is it my fault, because my heart races over a single kiss? I love my wife, that's all. I'm not doing anything wrong. Or is Aileen to blame, because she tempts me? No, she's just being adorable...!"

"Calm down, would you? What an infernal nuisance...!"

"...Should we maybe call his adviser?"

"I'm finished. I can't take it anymore... Every night is hell... If this is what the world's like, then I might as well—"

"Okay! Okay, we give, we'll help you! Just don't destroy the world!!"

At Isaac's shout, the clattering chairs and table go still. Only the chandelier keeps swinging. Claude elegantly recrosses his legs, resting his chin in his hand. "I see. That's a relief. The world's continued existence depends on your efforts. Give it your best."

"...Isn't this a bit hasty, Master Isaac?" Luc's gaze is chilly.

Isaac sighs. "Considering how much work it would take to shut down Aileen if she went on another rampage, it's more or less the same magnitude. Luc and Quartz, you work with Elefas and the Levi tribe to improve the demon king's symptoms. I want the old guy to check into magic-related illnesses and similar stuff. Denis, you and I will stick with our usual duties for now—"

"Milord! You're there, aren't you?! Great, he's there, grab him!"

"Huh?"

While Isaac is still issuing orders, the door behind him bursts open and three figures dash in. As Claude scowls, wondering what's going on, a rope coils around him and his chair several times, binding them together before pulling tight. Walt and Kyle are holding its ends.

Those are his guards, all right: That was a superhuman feat. While Claude casually admires their handiwork, magic emits from the rope, which has some sort of pattern drawn onto it. The magic is coming from Elefas; he's turned his palm toward Claude.

Isaac and the others look stunned. Evidently, they have nothing to do with this.

In that case, the only possible mastermind is Claude's own adviser. Speaking of, the man has come to stand right in front of him, pushing Isaac out of the way.

"A binding spell, hmm? What is this about, Keith?"

"Master Claude. I need you to stay calm and listen to me."

"You'd tie me up just to get me to listen to you? What do you think your master is, anyway?"

"A demon king who's far too free-spirited for his own good......... We've received a report that Lady Aileen's ship has gone missing."

With a clatter, Isaac starts to his feet. Looking straight into Claude's wide eyes, Keith continues, speaking plainly. "They say the ship was attacked by pirates, but we don't have any details ye— Master Claude!"

"Let me go...!"

He strains to tear the magic rope apart, and it crackles ferociously, constricting him. The kickback from his unstable magic turns into a blast that rips through the room.

The rope holds. Even if Claude isn't in the best condition, that's impressive. *Tsk*ing in irritation, he glares at the three who are helping Keith with this binding spell. "Walt, Kyle, Elefas...! Whose side are you on?"

"Yours—yaugh! Quit amplifying your magic and please calm down! Elefas, we're not going to get blown to bits, are we?!"

"It's all right. I'm holding him back, so I'll be the first to go."

"Doesn't that mean it's not all right...?!"

"—Master Claude. You are the next emperor. You have that position because of Lady Aileen's tireless efforts."

At Keith's quiet voice, Claude looks up. His attendant knows him better than anyone, and even when magical energy rips through the room, he addresses his master with an unwavering gaze. "Conduct yourself in a way that will not embarrass her, please."

"……"

When he stops straining, the wind subsides. Relieved, Walt, Kyle, and Elefas let the tension drain from their shoulders. The others—who've either been clinging to the table or have ducked for cover—carefully turn his way.

Letting out a long breath, Claude growls an order. "…Continue your report, Keith."

"I'm told the source of the report was a kraken that was near the scene. Possibly because of your irregular condition, informing you directly wasn't an option, so the message went to Almond instead. According to that report, Lady Aileen's ship was attacked by pirates, then vanished."

"…It vanished?"

"Yes. The entire ship, abruptly, as if spirited away. Apparently Lady Aileen told the kraken 'It's dangerous here, get away'—Walt, Kyle, Elefas!"

Keith's warning comes too late. Taking advantage of the trio's lapsed attention, Claude snaps his fingers and turns the magic rope to dust. Rising to his feet, he smiles at Keith. "Unlike you, it seems these three don't understand me yet."

"…It certainly looks that way. I'll give them a thorough lecture later."

"There's something I want to check on. I'll return in ten minutes."

His worrywart adviser relents with a sigh. Though it barely counts as approval, Claude takes that as a sign to go ahead and teleports himself to the ocean where the kraken is.

"The next emperor," hmm?

His magic is already unstable, and the worry and unease are making his heart pound. Doing everything he can to calm down,

Claude opens his eyes. A bright blue expanse of ocean and sky spreads out before him. A large shadow comes up right beneath his feet, then begins to glide forward, as if guiding him. Claude follows the shadow over the water.

Before long, it surfaces. The demon is an enormous, slimy squid—a kraken. Apparently, this is where the attack took place.

There isn't a soul in sight. Only the wide blue ocean.

Claude speaks to the kraken. "I hear you tried to help Aileen. That was very brave of you. Are you hurt?"

The demon silently confirms that nothing happened to them. Claude closes his eyes.

All trace of the ring is also gone.

He infused the wedding ring he gave Aileen with his magic. In theory, it should be possible to track the presence of that magic, but the trail also ends here, very abruptly.

The ring can be drained. If Aileen cloaks the sacred sword in magic, the rate of consumption is so ferocious that it probably wouldn't last an hour.

He doesn't see any traces of a fierce battle here, though.

"Do you know why Aileen told you to run?"

The kraken's huge body contracts in apparent distress. It was because sacred power was used, or so they tell him.

"Don't let it concern you. You did well. If sacred power was involved, it was far too dangerous for you and your kind. You should steer clear of it. Yes, if you hear anything else, tell me." He strokes the kraken, who looks pleased. Shyly, the demon sinks back under the water.

Left on his own above the ocean, Claude sighs, gazing up at the blue sky.

Sacred power, hmm? That must be how the entire ship disappeared.

If anyone could do that, it would be... Well, if she's merely disappeared along with the ship, she's probably safe. That still leaves the question of what in the world has she been dragged into this time.

Claude decides to begin methodically. Investigating the pirates comes first. He'll also need to deal with the Queendom of Hausel, which Aileen was supposed to visit. Unless he takes political concerns into consideration, even though Aileen is a victim, she may be accused of neglecting the duties of a crown princess.

And because sacred power is involved, Claude is loath to ask the demons for assistance. He'll need human help for this. That means relying on all the pawns Aileen's collected to date.

"...The next emperor, hmm? What a nuisance."

However, that is the person she had wanted Claude Jean Ellmeyer to be.

Let me reexamine the situation carefully, she thinks.

Why did this happen? It can't be because I carelessly spoke to him earlier, can it?

"Earlier" had been shortly before those insolent pirates attacked the luxury liner.

"By the way, haven't you broken up with what's-his-name, that Isaac fellow, yet?"

Since they had the chance, Aileen had decided that they should all have lunch in the shipboard restaurant, which was one of the vessel's most showcased amenities. Rachel had tried to refuse on the grounds that she was a lady-in-waiting; however, Serena had taken a seat with no reservations whatsoever, so she'd compromised by sitting next to Aileen. Then, as they were relishing their fish meunière, Serena had broached the topic with Rachel.

Rachel smiled, sticking her fork into the plump, steaming white fish. "I wasn't involved with Isaac to begin with."

"What? What's this? It can't be— You're a villainess, but you've tripped a romance flag with a mob cha— Mmph!"

"Lady Lilia, you simply *must* try this delicious bread." Shoving a whole roll into Lilia's mouth to shut her up, Aileen cleared her throat pointedly before continuing. "And what about you, Serena? How goes it with Auguste? Not only did you skip the dinner, but I hear you stood him up for your date together. He waited ten hours for you."

"You know that wasn't a date. Even the dinner was with the former student council; the boys had fun on their own. It'll serve them right if none of them ever manages to get married."

"What, you kept him waiting for ten hours? I wonder what that did to his affection level— Mrgl!"

"These apples are splendid as well, Lady Lilia... You really aren't honest about your feelings, are you, Serena."

"...What are you trying to say?"

"All four former student council members are prime real estate. Better than Prince Cedric," Aileen said firmly, her eyes shining.

Serena looked disgusted. "You're saying that right in front of Lady Lilia, while she tries to eat an apple whole?"

"Someone who's trying to become her fiancé's mistress is capable of far greater tact, I see."

"A mistress? Cedric's? ...What, Serena?" Apparently, Lilia had managed to down the apple surprisingly quickly. She was quite a skilled eater. Thinking about what to stuff in her mouth next, Aileen became curious about where this conversation might head and watched the pair out of the corner of her eye.

Giving a triumphant smirk, Serena took a wedge of grapefruit. "That's right. He said if I lent him a hand, he'd make me his mistress."

"If you pull that off, I'd be impressed." Lilia was smiling, and Serena looked rather deflated. However, as Lilia slowly let her eyes return to the food, Aileen realized that she wasn't smiling one little bit. Her lips moved slightly, spitting out a short remark. All she caught was "Pathetic love interest doesn't know his place."

...I wonder whether Prince Cedric will get what he wants. Auguste, too.

Why was it that all the game's heroines felt increasing hatred for its heroes? Catching herself, Aileen sighed, shaking her head. She, at least, should refrain from basing her thoughts on the game's plot. "Really, I think you're all making this unnecessarily complicated. You simply have to snag an eligible gentleman, then domesticate him to suit your preferences."

"Whatever you do, you mustn't say that to Prince Claude, Lady Aileen."

"Master Claude is an exception. He's accomplished with both pen and sword, he's handsome, and while he may be a bit too much of a free spirit, that side of him is rather endearing. He's chivalrous, kind, and tolerant. I know of no man who's more perfect... If I had to name a flaw, perhaps his face is a bit too indecent."

"And then there's you, in a chaste marriage with such a man."

Serena's sneer jolted Aileen out of her rapture, unable to reply.

Rachel, who'd finished eating, dabbed at her lips with a napkin and admonished them. "This isn't a proper lunchtime conversation, you two."

"So that All Ages rating really is— Mggh!"

"Lady Lilia, this pie is also magnificent— Whoa, that's too fast! Don't just swallow it, chew first!"

"Hey, you. Woman."

Abruptly, she heard a man's voice, and a shadow fell over her.

Irked at being hailed so brusquely, Aileen slowly turned to look at the shadow's owner. "Are you addressing me? ...Can I help you?"

"Show me that ring you've got on."

As she scowled, he snatched up her left hand, yanking her out of her chair. Aileen glared at him. "You're being incredibly rude. At least introduce yourself—"

The man had been standing with his back to the light, and the moment she saw him clearly, she fell silent.

He was wearing the dress of a foreign land. The hand that had caught her, the entire arm, his shoulders, chest, and neck were all exposed, but he was well-muscled, with no extraneous flesh. The outline of his face, the straight bridge of his nose, his thin lips—all his features were even and pleasant. His bright, dazzling hair put gold to shame, and the almond shape of his eyes gave them a fierce look that underscored his wild, masculine beauty.

What was really striking were his tranquil violet eyes—the same color as Lilia's. If the game's scenario held true here, they were proof that he possessed holy power. However, none of these things were what had made Aileen gulp.

His face and form were just like a certain piece of art from the game.

Serena, her guard, had half risen from her chair, and Rachel fully stood to rebuke him. "Stop that at once. She is—"

"Be quiet, Rachel… Lady Lilia."

She felt apologetic toward Rachel, but Lilia was the only one who could confirm this. Lilia looked blank at first, but then, seeing the face of the man who'd caught Aileen's hand, she flashed a little smile. Putting a finger to her lips, she motioned for Serena and Rachel to get behind her.

Even under guard with a bomb around her neck, Lilia was the fiancée of the second prince of Ellmeyer. After Aileen, the crown princess, she possessed the highest rank here. From behind Aileen, she spoke in her usual artless way. "Are we by any chance in the presence of the noble Baal Shah Ashmael?"

"What, you know of us?"

His easy acknowledgment made Aileen's breath catch. He was from the Kingdom of Ashmael, of all places. The very nation they were at odds with. Knowing the purpose of their journey, Rachel and Serena, too, froze in surprise.

What's more, he wasn't simply *from* Ashmael…

"Then we really mustn't abandon you. After all, the holy king is merciful."

"Master Baal, we are technically traveling incognito."

At the sight of the figure who emerged from behind Baal, Aileen nearly felt dizzy. What sort of punishment was this? Sure enough, Lilia spoke up, sounding delighted. "Goodness, General Ares! You are General Ares, the Kingdom of Ashmael's celebrated god of war, correct?!"

The young man sported black hair and bronze skin. His shapely eyebrows came together in a frown. Since he'd mentioned being incognito, he probably didn't want them making too much of a fuss about this. Pretending she hadn't noticed, Lilia continued; on this particular occasion, Aileen was grateful for that audacity. "What brings you aboard this vessel? Is it official business of some sort? This ship is bound for the Queendom of Hausel, you know. Won't you be sent back just as soon as we land, since you aren't women?"

"Erm— Miss, could you be quiet?"

"It's fine, Ares. Never mind that, look at this woman's ring. We were right: It is cursed."

"What?" Aileen frowned.

Gazing at her wedding ring as if it were something dreadful, the man covered his mouth. "A monstrous grudge resides within it. The thing is brimming with obsession."

"......"

"We've never seen such a vindictive cursed object before. We're impressed you've managed to keep your wits about you, woman."

Aileen was trembling with indignation. Behind her, Lilia, Serena, and even Rachel were fighting back laughter. *"Cursed object"...? This wedding ring is infused with Master Claude's love, surely...maybe...I'm fairly certain!*

Forcing herself to assume his expression had been based in his awe at the immensity of Claude's magic, Aileen smiled. "I—I am perfectly sane. Release my hand, won't you?"

"We can't do that. Unless we purify this thing soon, it will call down disaster. Our meeting must have been fate: We'll break the curse for you."

"Excuse me? —Wait, no!"

He plucked the ring from her finger. According to Claude, the ring could never be removed. So Aileen wouldn't lose it, of course—certainly not because it was cursed.

He neutralized Master Claude's magic...?!

However, there was nothing strange about that. Nothing at all, when you considered this man's background. On the other hand, that meant he would share many similarities with the character in the game, meaning…

…If we involve ourselves with him and get dragged into more trouble when we're already fielding a diplomatic incident, we'll have a catastrophe on our hands! I have to take back my ring and get away from—

The man's hand closed around her wedding ring. There was a sizzle and a puff of smoke: The magic had dispersed. Grimacing, the man opened his hand, revealing a burn-like mark.

"Master Baal, you're hurt…!"

"Don't worry about it, Ares. It'll heal right up. More importantly, woman, where did you get that ring?"

"It's—"

Out of nowhere, there was an earsplitting boom, and the ship listed to one side. The tables and chairs began to slide across the deck, and screams mingled with the sounds of shattering china and glass.

Rachel hastily tugged on Aileen's hand. "Lady Aileen, this way…!"

"What is this? An accident? —No, of course it isn't. Hey, where do you think you're going?! You come here!" Serena caught Lilia by the scruff of the neck.

The man cut in front of the two of them, muttering, "Pirates? That wasn't on the schedule."

Below them, several sailors had brought a pirate ship right up alongside the passenger liner and were attempting to board. They were armed with large swords and what appeared to be firearms, and they were very obviously hostile.

This was a luxury vessel transporting important passengers

to the Queendom of Hausel. Although men could travel as far as the port, the majority of the guards were women. On top of that, the kidnapping of even one young noblewoman would become a major incident.

"Serena, lend me your sword. You evacuate the ship along with Lady Lilia and Rachel. Protect them."

"You can't possibly be planning to fight pirates." The man was looking at her, arms crossed, as if he was going to stand by and watch. She sidled away from him.

"Please don't trouble yourself with me. Hurry and run—"

Before she'd finished her sentence, the ship listed dramatically again. This time, she heard screams from the pirates, as well.

The water's surface bulged, and a white limb with rows of suckers emerged—a squid. The tentacle began dexterously snatching up the pirates and tossing them into the ocean.

"It's a demon!"

"A kraken's attacking! Run...!"

"Lady Aileen, that's..."

"I'll make it stop," Aileen answered tersely and leaped down to the upper deck. The kraken hadn't come to attack humans, but to save Aileen, the demon king's wife. That much was certain when a tentacle smashed the plank that connected the pirate ship to the passenger vessel before lobbing the pirate craft into the distance.

...But the humans on the chaotic passenger ship probably wouldn't pick up on those things. Not only that, but someone who was very bad news happened to be on board.

On the pitching, rolling deck, amid the screams and yells, Aileen shouted at the shadowy shape in the ocean. "Kraken! Enough, I'm fine. Get away from he—"

"And now a demon attacks, hmm? We may have hit the jackpot this time."

The voice was very close to her, and Aileen turned. The man had come up behind her before she had even realized. "You don't shrink from pirates or demons. And then there's this cursed ring."

"—Return that, if you would!"

The ring shone between the man's thumb and index finger. She put out her hand for it, but someone caught it. It was the guard, the man known as "the god of war." Aileen knew his face.

"This ring is important to you, is it? ...Interesting. I'd expect no less from a woman selected by the Queendom of Hausel. You should prove useful."

"What?"

The man snapped his fingers. It was the same gesture Claude used.

Immediately, Aileen screamed at the kraken in the water behind her. "Run! You mustn't come any closer—!"

"You women should consider it an honor. As you wished, we've come to carry you off."

As the man shouted, light enveloped him, and he rose into the air, arms still folded. That power was the polar opposite of Claude's. "Today you enter the harem of Holy King Ashmael! Offer up your sacred power to us, in the service of defeating the fiend dragon!"

He roared with laughter, and Aileen's vision warped. It was just like Claude's forced teleportation: She was being dragged in.

Holy power that would turn demons to dust enveloped the ship, lifting it out of the water. Assailed by the sensation of being spun in all directions, Aileen and the others fainted— And that's the last thing she can recall.

Once more, Aileen looks around the place where she's awakened.

A long, high wall encloses a circular area of bare sand. Weapons are propped carelessly against the wall, and there are two sets of iron double doors, one directly in front of her and the other behind her. Other than that, the place is bleak and barren. It looks a bit like an arena.

However, the group that's been confined in this space, with its swirling clouds of dust, is made up entirely of women.

Some are wearing cotton dresses, while others are clothed in fine gowns like Aileen's. The colors of their skin vary, as do their social standings and origins. Aside from the fact that all are women, they seem to have nothing else in common. Aileen's only guess is that they had probably all been passengers on the ship.

"...I still don't understand. Why did this happen...?!"

"Seems like we were kidnapped, ship and all. That aside, it's hot. Where are we?"

Serena, who'd been the first to wake up, is fanning her face with her hands. When Aileen doesn't answer her, Lilia does, even though she's just opened her eyes.

"Say, Lady Aileen, isn't this—?"

"You hold your tongue, or I'll shove sand in your mouth!"

"Lady Aileen!"

Rachel awakened at almost the same time as Aileen and gone to speak with the women around them. Now she's returned, out of breath. "Th-this is awful. When I asked the others, they told me this is the Kingdom of Ashmael, and that all the women here are intended for the royal harem— Lady Aileen?!"

Aileen has fallen to her knees. Lilia's face lights up. "I knew it. We're in Ashmael! In other words, Game 3—"

"I told you to hold your ton—"

A gong sounds, sending a tremor through the air. At the same time, cheers go up from the far side of the wall. There are spectators in the fan-shaped seating area beyond the wall, looking down over the arena. They're all men, with turbaned heads and long kaftans. All of them wear jewels and fine clothes.

"...What is this? Are they going to auction off the abductees?" Serena mutters, sounding disgusted.

Rachel speaks up anxiously. "Lady Aileen. Let's tell them who we are. They'll never get away with this."

"Why not summon a demon instead? Then we can just leave."

"...I can't. If this is truly the Kingdom of Ashmael, I can't summon demons." Rachel and Serena blink at her. Aileen goes on, bitterly, "Ashmael is protected by the holy king's barrier. By sacred power. It negates all magic and spells. Demons can't get in."

"...E-even so, Lady Aileen, you're..."

"Rachel, think. Why were we summoned by the Queendom of Hausel?"

Because the Kingdom of Ashmael suspects Imperial Ellmeyer of inciting the fiend dragon and plotting to invade them.

Rachel gasps, covering her mouth. Serena lowers her voice. "In other words...we're smack in the middle of enemy territory?"

"If they find out that Lady Aileen is the crown princess...!"

The crown princess of a country suspected of plotting an invasion, and the fiancée of said country's second prince. At best, they'd be hostages. At worst, their severed heads would make a fine declaration of war. No doubt their guard and lady-in-waiting would be killed immediately.

Apparently, she doesn't even need to say it. Rachel's face turns pale, and Serena falls silent. The only one smiling is Lilia.

The gong sounds again. In the midst of thunderous applause and cheers, a man assumes the highest seat—the same one who stole her wedding ring on the ship.

"Silence. Some of you may never see us again, so we'll introduce ourself."

The man is wearing a long kaftan decorated with precious stones, and his face is very familiar to Aileen. He's the one and only person permitted to sit in the very back, surrounded by stone pillars and protected by guards.

"Our name is Baal Shah Ashmael. We are Ashmael's holy king."

The Kingdom of Ashmael is a country that boasts defenses no demon can set foot in, ruled by a king who wields holy power as a matter of course. The name of its ruler is Baal Shah Ashmael.

He is the master of the harem, the holy king—and the one who will someday be possessed by the fiend dragon and destroy the Kingdom of Ashmael: the final boss of *Regalia of Saints, Demons, and Maidens 3*.

If someone told Aileen they had memories of their past life, she'd initially doubt their sanity. Her position is a tricky one, though: She has personal experience with such things, so she couldn't completely write them off either.

That said, if she explained that this is the world of an *otome* game that she played in her past life, *Regalia of Saints, Demons, and Maidens*, the possibility that anyone would believe her was very slim. At present, no one understands. The only one with whom she has memories in common is Lilia Reinoise, a dangerous character and self-styled "player" who is entertaining herself with this world as if it were still a mere game.

Even if it were a game, it isn't possible to save or play through it multiple times. The hands of the clock march ruthlessly onward, and there is no going back and doing things over again. Most of all, since Aileen should already have died in the game, she's able to state one thing categorically:

This is not a game, but real life. Her life.

"You have earned the opportunity to enter our harem. Consider yourselves honored."

And so, no matter how unhappy she is with this development, she can't hurl the game against the wall.

"Hah!" Serena sneers quietly. Her gaze is fixed. "Fine words from a kidnapper. What does he think he's talking about?"

"I couldn't agree with you more, but Serena, do nothing to make yourself stand out. Behave. That goes for the rest of you as well."

"However, obviously, we cannot accept all of you. If you win our favor, you may become the mother of our heir. We must select someone suitable. Therefore, to begin with, we will measure your strength of character."

Baal looks down at them from the dais, resting his chin on one palm. Then he lightly raises a hand. A gong sounds three times.

Aileen and the others brace themselves. With an unpleasant noise, the iron doors directly under Baal's seat slowly open. From the pitch blackness beyond them, an enormous, transparent, viscous *something* emerges. The color inside its body isn't quite red, blue, or green. Is it a...tentacle?

Slime drips from the tip, and several woman shriek and back away.

"It may look like a monster, but it's a holy item. It melts away magic and exposes the truth of whoever it touches." The women's fright seems to amuse Baal; there's laughter in his voice. "Sacred power won't harm humans. If you are genuinely aligned with what is holy, there's no need to run."

He can say whatever he likes, but the writhing mass that's slipped out through the iron door is thoroughly monstrous. It has no arms, no legs, and no trunk, but there's an eye inside its body. It glares this way and that, looking down on the women appraisingly. The slime it drips with every move makes it appear to be salivating.

"L-Lady Aileen. What should we do?"

"There's really no question. We can't stand out, so we'll have to run for it. Let's slip through that door before it closes."

She jerks her chin at the door from which the cyclopean monstrosity emerged. Rachel and Serena nod, but Lilia pouts, looking dissatisfied. "This is the harem selection event, isn't it? Since we're here, let's take it on, Lady Aileen. You and I could pass easily, I'm sure of it."

"What's the point of passing it?! Would you focus on reality already?!"

"Granted, the slime will melt your clothes away," announces Baal, "but that's merely entertainment."

In other words: If that thing catches them, they'll be stripped naked in front of all these people. *Don't tell me... Is that why the audience is here?!*

Baal's offhand comment could easily have made a sheltered young noblewoman faint on the spot. "As you will be part of our harem, you belong to us. If we say something should be so, you have no right to refuse. Let that be your first lesson."

He snaps his fingers.

All at once, the mass expands to either side like a net, falling on them from above. The women scream, and the spectators cheer. Serena yells: "This looks pretty harmful to me! What do we do?!"

"...For now, run! The door up ahead is still open—"

"Noooooo!!"

A woman who's been caught right off the bat is raised high into the air. Poised to make a run for the door, Aileen looks back.

The girl is a noblewoman about Aileen's age. She's desperately holding her skirt down so that it won't flip, but the holy item is melting her clothes away wherever it clings to her. Aileen hears her plead tearfully. "Somebody, anybody, help me! Help—!"

Vulgar catcalls, whistles, and guffaws rise from the crowd.

Something in Aileen snaps.

"Lady Aileen...!"

If she shows them the sacred sword, they'll realize who she is. She's still conscious of that, just barely, so she snatches up one of the blades that are lying around and kicks the ground with a high-heeled shoe, springing into action.

Holy items are made of sacred power, and only sacred power can destroy them.

There's a flash, and the young noblewoman falls to the ground. The piece Aileen has severed from the holy item crumbles into sand and disappears.

"Ah, ah, ah..."

"Everyone get back against the walls!"

Aileen's voice rips through both the heckling and the screams. The cry makes the damaged holy item freeze as if it's daunted. Some of the women who've been chosen for this spectacle clutch at their heads with tears in their eyes, while others are already trapped and wailing, but every one of them looks at Aileen.

"I shall protect you." Getting a better grip on her sword,

Aileen dashes off to rescue the next victim. "Serena, Rachel, lead the others!"

"A-all right— This way, everyone! Hurry!"

"First you say we're running, then you say you'll fight. Make up your mind..."

Despite the sudden change of plans, Rachel and Serena follow her instructions. Aileen's eyes are fixed on the holy item. Watching her profile, Lilia breaks into a thin smile.

"Yes, that's the spirit. After all, you are the protagonist, Lady Aileen."

Baal blinks at the unexpected turn of events in the arena. Then he slaps his knee. "—It's the woman who had that cursed ring! This is getting interesting, Ares."

"Your Majesty... As I've said many times before, this selection is in poor taste."

"We can't just take women the Queendom of Hausel sends us as is."

"Selfishness again. You're taking this too far."

His retainer admonishes him with a sour expression, but that's nothing new. Letting the man's words go in one ear and out the other, Baal props his chin on one hand, observing.

The woman is taking great, sweeping slashes at the holy item with her sword, catching other women who were about to be engulfed and dragging them out through the gaps she's carved. With every rescue, her slime-spattered clothes are growing more and more ragged, but she pays them no heed.

A second girl is gathering the rescued women and leading them away. She seems powerless, but she's running around energetically, her soft hair streaming behind her. She lends her hands or her shoulders to the rescued women, stepping on the wriggling fragments of the holy item with no hesitation. A third figure stands in front of the group gathered by the wall, fending off the holy item as efficiently as possible. She doesn't look enthusiastic about it, but she is protecting them. Probably.

"There are a lot of promising candidates this time."

"...The three who are attacking the holy item, you mean?"

"No, four. See that woman there? A situation like this, and she's smiling."

Following Baal's finger, Ares looks at the woman, then frowns. "Are you sure the fear hasn't unsettled her mind...?"

"You're wrong. Watch closely. The holy item is avoiding her. She may have even greater potential than Sahra."

"Impossible. It must be coincidence."

"Even if it is, her luck is excellent. That's reason enough. The best prospect is the woman who's actively fighting the holy item."

Even the item seems to have identified her as its enemy: The selection has become a one-on-one battle.

Although this event has been held several times before, this particular development is a first, and the spectators are in an uproar. Even if they are camouflage, the vulgar audience has always disgusted Baal, but he can understand their excitement now.

The holy item's weak point is its eye. However, that eye is hidden in the very depths of its springy body. She could carve away its flesh until the eye is within reach of her sword, but the thing is enormous. There's no telling how much she'll be able to accomplish with a woman's physical strength.

"Which do you think will win, Ares?"

"The holy item has a long and distinguished history. There's no way she could destroy it. Even Sahra only kept it at bay. I'll give the signal to retrieve the item. It's about time in any case."

"Wait. We want to see what the woman does."

"Not this again. Quit stalling. The holy king himself, adding more women to his harem in hopes of finding one who'll replace Sahra...! There is no one who could replace her."

Baal shoots him a glance, but Ares doesn't seem to realize he's misspoken. Not only that, he gives the king an accusing, straightforward glare. "Let's ask the Queendom of Hausel for support, not mediation. Then we should openly declare war and swiftly subdue the fiend dragon, and the demon king backing it. We have the holy sword and the Daughter of God on our side, after all."

Ares's counsel is drowned out by cheers.

Ares turns back. His eyes widen, and Baal's jaw drops.

With one brilliant downward slash, the woman has cleaved the holy item in two. The item crumbles from the top down, melting away in a swirling gust of wind.

Even as the resulting blast of air hits him in the face, Baal bursts out laughing. "—She did it! The woman won! She destroyed the holy item! Well done. We'll have to reward her."

"Your Majesty!"

Ares's urgent shout and a metallic clash of swords echo at the same time, from somewhere very close.

It's almost as if the woman rode the whirlwind up from the arena: She's come right up to Baal and thrust her sword at him. Ares responds quickly and knocks her blade away.

However, even though she's been disarmed, the woman isn't the least bit rattled. On the contrary, she stalks over to him and whips up her right hand. Baal doesn't stop her from bringing it down.

A dry slap rings out. The electrified audience goes dead silent.

"Making a spectacle of women like that... What abominable taste."

"Wretch of a woman! You are in the presence of this nation's holy king...!"

"And a foolish king he is! Any woman who joins your harem will be your wife, correct? If you want a truly splendid woman for a wife, then become a proper king first!"

It's been a very long time since anyone gave him such a thorough tongue-lashing.

Smiling thinly at the dull pain in his cheek, Baal gazes back at the woman. Her eyes are blazing with anger, and instead of shrinking from his gaze, she issues another demand. "And return my ring."

"...Oh, the ring? That cursed one. Hmm. We don't know where it went."

"First you steal it, and then...!"

Her eyes glitter with fury, and she's beautiful. He realizes he's smiling. "—Interesting. We like you."

At that remark, everyone freezes up. Even the woman frowns, but that's trivial.

"Woman, if I recall, your name was—Aileen. That's what the others called you."

Abruptly, the woman seems disconcerted. Her gaze begins to wander, and she backs away. He gets to his feet, following her.

A woman with enough sacred power to defeat a holy item. All that holy power, plus a cursed ring with an enormous quantity of demonic magic. The name Aileen.

He knows of exactly one woman who might fit all those conditions.

The crown princess of the neighboring country who's said to have married the demon king, despite possessing the sacred sword.

We've picked up something very good here… Or so we'd like to think, but if she was on the ship the Queendom of Hausel provided, then this is no laughing matter.

She's a disaster waiting to happen. They'd go this far to pit him against the demon king? The idea disgusts him.

Now then, how should I shut her up?

He's surrounded by enemies, and the one woman he thought he could open up to has married another man. Baal looks down at Aileen, fighting the urge to burst out laughing. "We've made up our mind. We will make you our consort."

"Excuse me?!"

"Your Majesty! Even if she does have holy power, making her your consort out of nowhere is—"

"We will hear no objections. That's an order."

Ares puts a hand to his forehead, apparently fighting a dizzy spell. The woman looks even more anxious. "I—I refuse!" she shouts.

"You must know you have no right. We are the king."

"—That's right, the ring! You saw the ring; I know you did! I'm already married!!"

"I see. You love your husband, hmm? Then I'm sure you wouldn't want him killed." He's backed the woman up against the wall. Catching her chin, he pulls her in so close he can feel her breath, then he whispers. At this distance, no one will overhear them. "Don't worry. At this point, we are the only one who knows who you are. The citizens of this country are appallingly ignorant of other nations' circumstances."

"…Wh-what are you talking about?"

"Aileen Jean Ellmeyer," he says softly, and the woman freezes. "It isn't a bad offer. Just behave and become our consort."

"Wha...whatever for?"

"Understand that you're in no position to ask questions like that. Or would you like to test it? We could take you hostage and see how the demon king reacts." Hearing her gulp, Baal chuckles. "Don't imagine he could beat us, though. We are the holy king: In our presence, even the demon king is simply human, and if we have the holy sword, he's mere dust. We can torment your husband to death. Now, what will you do?"

The woman scowls at him, but the threat has apparently gotten through to her. She's silent, her clenched fists trembling. That means she'll obey. Unless she wants the demon king killed, she has no choice.

Still, does she really consider the demon king her husband? Is the woman insane?

Could it be the influence of that cursed ring? Just as the possibility distracts him, she lashes out at his solar plexus. He catches her fist before it connects, then gazes into the woman's eyes at point-blank range.

They are blue jewels, blazing with quiet anger, and they speak eloquently of her love.

"I'll make you regret treating my husband like dirt."

Her words are so bold no one would think she was being threatened.

He's stunned. Gradually, exhilaration wells up inside him. To bystanders, it may look as if they're whispering sweet nothings to each other. The thought amuses him even more, and he laughs out loud.

"Your Majesty?"

"It's nothing, Ares. Give Aileen the Sea Palace, and install her in the harem. From this moment on, she is a high-ranking consort. Our favorite."

At Baal's order, Ares and everyone else bow their heads and kneel.

Only the new favorite doesn't bow. This strikes him as hilarious.

✦ Second Act ✦
For a Villainess, Two-Timing Is Child's Play

"I *will* make that man cry…!"

Aileen has been shown to a room with the words, "As of today, this is your home." The moment she's inside, she flings a cushion embroidered with gold thread with all her might. Then she smiles.

Her clothes, which fasten at the front, are made of a thin fabric and don't leave much to the imagination. The indigo of the outer robe complements her eyes. It's also the color denoting the high-ranking consort who has won the king's favor. Sandals peek from beneath her inner robe, which is made of white silk. Earrings with blue jewels, fashioned in an unfamiliar shape, jingle softly below her ears. The costume of a foreign land. And these rooms of gold and marble are the Sea Palace. It's a corner of the harem, where the royal consorts are housed.

This is a harem, a place where women vie with one another for the king's affection. Why has she been given a consort's palace in a place like this? She, the crown princess of Imperial Ellmeyer, wife of the demon king— It's all the holy king's fault. No matter how many times she turns the thought over in her mind, her anger refuses to die down.

"He treated my husband like trash…! Even a simple attempt on his life would have been unforgivable, so how dare that man brazenly— And on top of that, he threatens me? Hee-hee, hee-hee-hee-hee-hee-hee-hee."

"What are you talking about? You were the one who got careless. Dashing out there, fighting, slapping the king; could you make yourself any more obvious? You're just lucky he didn't have you executed."

Serena has made herself completely at home: She's lying on her stomach, hugging a cushion to her chest, and her long, slender limbs are sheathed in silk gauze. "I'm not thrilled about being your lady-in-waiting, but the Kingdom of Ashmael is rich. Maybe I'll hunt for a husband here."

"You've adapted way too quickly, and you're being far too idle! If you're a lady-in-waiting, emulate Rachel and get to work!"

"My real job is guarding you and keeping an eye on 'Lady' Lilia, isn't it? I can't very well leave my post."

"I see you're as skilled at hairsplitting as ever…!"

"Never mind that, this woman's still laughing."

Serena deflects the conversation to Lilia, who has her face buried in a cushion; she's been laughing the whole time. At the sound of her name, Lilia finally sits up and turns toward them. She looks as if she couldn't possibly be enjoying herself more. "Well, I mean… I can't help it. Lady Aileen never disappoints. Two-timing the demon king with the holy king…!"

"Don't say it like that! What will people think?! I'm leaving this place at once…!"

"How, exactly? They've set guards on us," Serena warns her shortly.

When Aileen glances at the open window, Serena rolls over languidly and adds, "Just so you know, there's no escaping a place like this with a group this size and no plan, especially when we don't know our way around. The sacred sword won't work on humans, remember?"

Aileen is confident in her skills, but she's only able to display extraordinary strength by borrowing the power of the sacred sword. She may be unrivaled against demons, but she'd be at a disadvantage surrounded by humans, let alone trained soldiers.

"I know that. Let's calm down— I will calmly and most assuredly make him cry."

"That sounds like the opposite of calm..."

"Hee-hee! It's all right, Serena. I expect we're the ones with the most information regarding the current state of this country, and how it will change." Lilia stops laughing and resettles herself, smiling faintly.

Serena eyes her, unnerved. "What, is this another of your prophesies? Those are incredibly fishy."

"Just ignore her. Lady Lilia believes she's somebody special, poor thing."

"Lady Aileen. I apologize for the delay. It's late, but I've brought your luncheon."

There's a knock at the door, and Rachel comes in, pushing a meal cart. Through the open door, Aileen can see men standing guard. Serena was right.

When they see Rachel begin to serve lunch, both Serena and Lilia stop lazing around and get up. The room's table isn't large, but it's the perfect size for conversing in whispers.

"Did you learn anything?"

"Yes. Most of the women from that ship have been taken into the harem as ladies-in-waiting attendants. That seems to have been the plan all along, and no one is grumbling about it."

"What do you mean, 'that was the plan'? Nobody told me about it." Serena sounds extremely skeptical.

Rachel sets plates meant for tasting for poison in front of Serena. Lilia is technically a princess, so it made sense to serve her, but Aileen had wondered why she'd silently served Serena as well; apparently, she intends to make her the food taster.

"That's true for me as well. Do you suppose we boarded the wrong ship somehow?"

On that note, Baal had said something concerning. *He said the Queendom of Hausel had planned this... Have we fallen into their trap? But who did they intend to trap, us or him?*

Sighing, Aileen picks up one of the dishes. "Let's set that aside for now. None of the food is poisoned, Serena, so you may relax and eat."

"You'd better be sure about that."

"I am. The sacred sword isn't reacting to it... And Rachel? Is it true that the fiend dragon has revived?"

"Yes. About three months ago, they say black rain fell. According to tradition, that's a sign of the fiend dragon's return. However, the Daughter of God is here, so no one is worried."

"...Did you learn the name of this Daughter of God?"

"She's called Lady Sahra."

The name rings a bell, and Aileen sighs. Beside her, Lilia is giggling quietly.

"What about the holy sword?"

"Nothing but rumors: The Daughter of God has it, or the holy king is keeping it somewhere safe."

Still, if the fiend dragon has revived, then the game is underway.

"Anything that's happened twice will happen again, hmm...?"

"That's right."

Although Lilia's brief agreement irritates her, Aileen has no choice but to steel herself.

The Kingdom of Ashmael, the stage of *Regalia of Saints, Demons, and Maidens 3*, is located to the southeast of Imperial Ellmeyer, across a shipping canal. In the game's chronology, it seems to follow Game 2, falling either between the first two fan discs or immediately after the second one. And that is where the timeline happens to be in reality as well.

I did have a bad feeling about this. Ever since I heard them mention the fiend dragon, the Daughter of God, and the holy sword...

Set in Ashmael's harem, the story of Game 3 echoes the legend of the holy sword and the Daughter of God, and it's set in motion by the fiend dragon's resurrection.

The game begins when the heroine, who was sold to the harem as a maid, meets the hero. She possesses the power to heal. Even as she's troubled by conflicts in this garden of a thousand royal beauties and her forbidden love with a man who isn't the king, her sacred power gradually develops, until at last she awakens as the Daughter of God. At that point, she is able to repair the holy sword, the one weapon that can seal the fiend dragon. Once resurrected, the fiend dragon possesses the holy king, and he commits all manner of atrocities. She seals the king and the dragon together, starts a revolution with the hero, and retakes the kingdom. That is how the story generally proceeds on every route.

First, she'll need to compare this foreknowledge to the actual situation.

As she slowly works on her lunch, Aileen turns to her lady-in-waiting. "Rachel. How much do you know of the Kingdom of Ashmael?"

"Its territory is almost entirely desert. However, thanks to the holy water which wells up from the sword, it possesses water in abundance."

Holy water was a miraculous substance: If one drop fell to the sand, it would become a pond. According to legend, it began to flow from the holy sword when the fiend dragon was sealed.

"I hear sacred stone is quarried here as well, but the kingdom is insular, and we do not get much information about it. Diplomatic relations with Imperial Ellmeyer have been severed for ages, ever since the countries disagreed about the interpretation of their founding legends. At present, they suspect us of invading their territory by resurrecting the fiend dragon, and although the Queendom of Hausel is mediating, relations continue to deteriorate."

"So this place has a holy sword and a Daughter of God? Considering the fact that you two are Maids of the Sacred Sword, I doubt this Daughter of God is anyone decent."

"Lady Serena, please refrain from being rude to Lady Aileen."

"But they're basically the same thing, aren't they?"

Serena has the right idea. If they hadn't been similar, Ashmael would probably never have accused their country of fraud.

With her knowledge of the game, however, she can state with confidence that they are not the same.

"There are a few differences. The Daughter of God's sacred power is the power to heal. Instead of slaying demons, it seals them. In contrast, the Maid of the Sacred Sword purifies and destroys them."

"Huh... Well, healing's a foreign concept to you people anyway. You're basically all about destruction."

"Lady Serena."

"It's fine, Rachel. Offense is the best defense, after all. A second difference is that, unlike the sacred sword, the holy sword physically exists. That means it can degrade. The fiend dragon revives because the holy sword has grown old and lost its power. Unless the Daughter of God repairs it, it can't manifest its true power. In other words, the Daughter of God doesn't wield the sword, she heals it."

Even though Aileen has declared that the food is safe, Rachel is forcing Serena to taste it for poison, and Serena glares at her. "You mean if the Daughter of God fixes the holy sword, anybody can use it?"

"That's right. Since it is a physical weapon."

"Don't people fight over it, then?"

"The actual holy sword is sealed on sacred ground along with the fiend dragon. That means no one can use it unless the Daughter of God removes it from that spot. Besides, while it isn't a problem if the Daughter of God continues to repair it, the sword doesn't retain its power for very long."

Rachel, who's finished serving all the food and retreated to stand behind Aileen, looks puzzled. "Then you mean anyone who uses the holy sword must also have the Daughter of God to repair it?"

"That's right. There's one other major difference between the holy sword and the sacred sword: The holy sword works on humans." That is the biggest reason Aileen has yielded to Baal's threat. "The fiend dragon possesses humans and uses their power. The holy sword exists to slay it, so of course it's able to affect humans."

"Huh...? Then this whole resurrection of the fiend dragon doesn't mean an actual dragon's going to attack?"

"Just think of it this way: The resurrection of the fiend dragon basically creates a second demon king." Lilia has begun talking without permission, and Aileen glares at her. However, Lilia looks her right in the eye and continues undaunted. "In other words, the holy sword that seals the fiend dragon can kill the demon king as well. That's what you're worried about, isn't it, Lady Aileen?"

"Don't drop spoilers. Anyway, listen, you two. Lady Lilia is a peculiar person."

"I know. You mean she's like you, right? It doesn't bother me at all."

Serena's remark stuns her.

Rachel is indignant. "You're wrong, Lady Serena. Lady Aileen is much more incredible!"

"Was that an attempt to defend me, Rachel?!"

"The holy sword is said to be a copy of the sacred sword created by the Queendom of Hausel. However, since it was forged by human hands, it ended up as a sacred weapon capable of harming them as well. A sloppy explanation, yet oddly persuasive."

"I told you, no spoilers! At any rate, since the holy sword is dangerous to Master Claude, we can't oppose them carelessly. It would be absolutely awful if the holy king were to use it. We'd have no means of defense. That said, if we simply try to run without a plan, that alone will get us executed for adultery..."

The conversation has suddenly taken a dangerous turn, and both Rachel and Serena look shocked.

In Ellmeyer, the emperor may have multiple consorts, but there is no harem where thousands of beauties vie for his favor. That probably makes the concept difficult to understand. Playing it safe, Aileen puts it in simple terms for them. "This harem exists to pass on the blood of the holy king. Bearing a child who carries his blood outside the harem, or conceiving one who does not within the harem, are both grave crimes with implications for national stability. That's why, with a few exceptions, all men who are employed here have had to part with a certain vital part of their anatomy. They're known as eunuchs."

"...'Had to part with'? Wait, you mean...?"

"This place prioritizes the creation of a holy king above all else," Rachel says, summarizing efficiently.

Aileen nods, sighing. "In exchange, even a simple court attendant who has no rank may become the king's consort, if he beds her. That makes competition among the women all the fiercer, but— Serena, if you develop any misguided ambitions, I'll tell Auguste."

"I'm free to do as I please, and anyway, why would you bring up Auguste?!"

"Because he's the one who's least likely to give up on you."

Depending on one's point of view, that might be quite romantic, but Serena looks dejected.

"If you try to become the king's favorite, and then war breaks out with Ellmeyer, we'll have to dispose of you at once, on suspicion of being a spy. Is that clear, Serena?"

"Enough. Fine... Although I'd rather not hear it from someone who's already the king's consort."

That dig hits a nerve, but Aileen pretends she hasn't heard it and issues another warning. "You as well, Lady Lilia."

"Don't worry. You are my favorite character, Lady Aileen."

There's no point in Aileen saying that isn't what she meant. There's no telling what this woman may do, and keeping her in check is going to be the most difficult hurdle. Bracing herself, Aileen resumes her explanation. "At any rate, the real problem is the holy sword. That's why we'll steal it and take it back to Imperial Ellmeyer with us."

The other three freeze up. Aileen continues, her expression composed. "That way, they won't be able to start a war, and we'll have protected Master Claude. It will solve everything."

There's a short silence. Then Lilia bursts out laughing, while Serena scowls at her and yells, "Are you an idiot?! The holy sword is this country's lifeline! Stealing it would be heinous!"

"Goodness, as long as they sign a diplomatic treaty, I don't mind returning it to them. I'll have it mounted on a stand that won't allow it to be drawn without a key. Denis will build one for me. We shall keep the key, of course."

"That's a threat! Besides, if you take their holy sword, what happens to their water?! The water comes from the sword, right?!"

"The holy water has accumulated in lakes, traveled underground, and created ponds all over. A single drop is enough to form a pond, after all. What they have will last them more than a decade. Besides, they've kidnapped the crown princess. We can't let that go unpunished. Don't you agree, Rachel?"

"When you put it that way, you do have a point... All right. So we'll simply take the holy sword back with us," Rachel agrees, straight-faced. Her lady-in-waiting really couldn't be more reliable.

They nod at each other, and then Aileen smiles at Serena, whose expression has stiffened. "This is a fine example of diplomacy. You strewed uncut demon snuff all over and destroyed Misha Academy; I don't want a woman like that telling me I'm heinous. I am currently modeling my actions on that reckless dynamism of yours."

"You never stop needling people, do you...?! And you! Just how long are you planning to laugh?!"

"W-well, I mean, steal the...the holy sword, and take it home... There's no route where... You're amazing, Lady Aileen. I never thought of that...!" Lilia is hugging her stomach; she's laughing so hard she's wheezing. She straightens, wiping tears from the corners of her eyes. "Th-that sounds quite entertaining. V-very well. We'll steal...the holy sword...!" She seems to find that particularly amusing, and she bursts into laughter again.

Aileen gazes at her with eyes that have lost some of their enthusiasm. *I'll have to be careful. This woman is exceptional. I don't think she could repair the holy sword, but she may make it her own.*

The game set in the Kingdom of Ashmael is *Regalia of Saints, Maidens, and Demons 3*. In other words, Lilia is merely the protagonist of a previous installment. However, even in another country, the name and existence of the Maid of the Sacred Sword continue to influence the game. The scenario of Game 3 may not have much to do with the Maid, but Aileen can't afford to get careless.

"For the moment, then, we're in agreement on our plan of action."

"No we're not! Are you seriously going through with this?"

"Of course I am. If you're against it, then propose an alternate plan."

Serena's eyebrows come down as far as they'll go, and then she mutters, "I'd rather find a powerful man, wrap him around my little finger, and have him arrange our way out of here..."

"As far as information gathering is concerned, that could work. Proposal accepted. But keep it to a level that won't upset Auguste."

"As I said, why Auguste?!"

Because you react like that. But Aileen doesn't say it. Instead, she gives her an additional warning. "Listen, mention the name of Imperial Ellmeyer only as a last resort. I don't know what the holy king is thinking, but gathering information comes first. I swear I'll protect Master Claude to the end and make that man cry!"

"In that case, Lady Aileen, let's meet with the heroine Sahra first. We need to grasp the current state of both the fiend dragon and the holy sword, or we won't know what stage the game is at."

"If the sword hasn't been repaired yet, we could always break it... But if we're using it as a bargaining chip, it would be better if it remained usable. Let's boost her parameters quickly and have her fix it! It doesn't matter who she romances; there are no bad faces or titles here."

"Let's make it Ares. He is the main hero, and he's relatively easy to conquer."

"But the villainess Roxane appears on that route!"

The arrival of the villainess will almost certainly complicate matters. Aileen herself was once known as a villainess, but that was then, and this is now.

As Aileen argues with the dissatisfied Lilia, Serena speaks up from behind them, sounding exasperated. "...I have no idea what you're talking about, but you two seem surprisingly close."

"Don't even joke about that! I'm simply requesting her help out of necessity!"

"Consort Aileen, are you there?"

A voice calls from the other side of the door, and everyone falls silent. It's Ares.

"His Majesty summons you to take tea with him. Your presence is requested in the central garden immediately."

Aileen exhales. When she signals Rachel with a glance, her outstanding lady-in-waiting promptly begins to get her cosmetics and clothing in order. Beside her, even Lilia begins to fidget. "This can't be the tea party event, can it? Oh, what should I do?"

"As you have been told time and time again, Lady Lilia, I will not tolerate any arbitrary action on your part. Don't forget you have a bomb around your neck."

"Are you testing me, Lady Aileen? The barrier cast by the holy king cancels out every sort of magic there is. I know full well that the spell cast on me is gone." Lilia puts a hand to her throat.

Serena, who's been listening in, looks aghast. "Wait just a minute. This woman's free...?!"

"That's right. I will cooperate, though. After all, I doubt I'll have another opportunity to join forces with Lady Aileen. Rachel, I'd like you to redo my hair as well."

"What?"

"I'm currently Lady Aileen's lady-in-waiting. I must look the part, mustn't I?!" Lilia clings to Rachel's arm, coaxing her like an ordinary young noblewoman.

Serena is watching them as if the sight is deeply unsettling. Aileen turns to her. "Serena. Don't take your eyes off Lady Lilia. She is most definitely not our ally."

"...I'll do what I can. Getting kidnapped with this group was rotten luck."

"No, that's not true. In a way, it's reassuring." Aileen and Lilia are the only ones who are aware of it, but both Rachel and Serena were deeply tied to the game series as well. It should be possible for them to throw a wrench into its works. "Behave yourself and help us out this time. Our current situation really is rather desperate."

"...Fine. Besides, I might get to see your face when word gets around that you've had an affair a month into your marriage."

Serena's last taunt makes Aileen freeze up.

She'd let her anger take over so she wouldn't have to think about it, but once she does begin to think, she breaks out in a cold sweat. Even if she was forced into it under threat of violence, Aileen has become another man's consort.

If she explains, she has no doubt Claude will understand that there was no alternative. However, it wouldn't be surprising if half the world were covered in ice before she managed to explain everything.

What she fears most is that Claude may come to the Kingdom of Ashmael in search of her.

I'll conduct this romance at top speed. I need to leave this place before Master Claude finds out.

She can't ask her husband for help in a country whose holy sword could harm him. As his wife, it would be unforgivable.

So please, Master Claude, just this once, be a bumbling, incompetent husband who can't find his wife!

This is, of course, to protect him from the holy sword. Not because Aileen is deathly afraid he'll find out she's a consort. She could never be scared of her kind husband. No, never.

With Serena and Lilia joining Rachel as her ladies-in-waiting, Aileen follows Ares. She walks carefully, confirming the locations of buildings and paths. Every time she spots a background from the game, she almost sighs.

In contrast, Lilia seems to be in a terrific mood. Almost

immediately, she asks Aileen, "What will we do if it's the tea party event?"

The "tea party" event occurs in the initial stage of the game. Having entered the harem as a maid, the heroine is ordered to wait at table, and she ends up spilling tea. Since she goes on to form a relationship with the character who gets splashed, it serves as a love interest selection.

"They're already calling the heroine the Daughter of God. An early event like that will be long over."

"But there's no guarantee that Sahra is on Ares's route. Though I do think it would be entertaining to romance him."

"—Did you just say Sahra?" Abruptly, Ares stops and turns back slightly.

Aileen responds before Lilia can say anything. "Yes, we're told that she is the Daughter of God. What sort of person is she?"

When she tries to sound him out, Ares glares at her.

Ares is a military general and the son of the previous holy king's younger brother, which makes him Baal's cousin. While he doesn't manifest holy power, he has both popular support and the right to inherit the throne. He frequents the harem on a regular basis, with Baal's permission. In the game, he's the main hero, and he gradually grows repulsed by the king's tyrannical behavior and the way he kidnaps women for his harem.

On the Ares route, he ultimately starts a revolution. He and the Daughter of God defeat Baal, whose mind has been taken over by the fiend dragon. He is then given the holy sword and becomes the new holy king.

Among other things, Game 3 is the tale of a revolution that topples a wicked ruler. Learning what Ares thinks of Sahra, and of Baal, will be an excellent way to grasp how far the game has progressed.

"She is a woman with the sacred power to heal, chosen by God. She isn't like any of you."

"My… You seem to know a lot about her."

"Of course I do. She is my wife."

Aileen stops in her tracks. "Your wife?"

"That's right. Consort Aileen, tea will be held in that pavilion over there."

Before she's managed to get her thoughts in order, she finds herself confronted with a foreign landscape.

Planned waterways have been designed to look like small brooks, and the sound of their murmuring envelops the garden. Stone bridges and paths are surrounded by verdant lawns and great trees. In a desert country, such luxury is possible only because water is abundant here.

A marble pavilion sits in its center. It's surrounded by more channels of water, and bridges lead to it from the four cardinal directions, linking it to the harem and the quarters known as "palaces."

She knows this because she's seen that exact view as a still image in the game.

No, forget about that. Did he just say "wife"?

Her eyes go to Lilia. Lilia is also blinking, stunned. Apparently, Aileen wasn't hearing things.

"Um, General Ares. About what you just mentioned…"

"Roxane, why are you the only one here?"

Ares has set off toward the pavilion, and when Aileen hears what he says, her mind freezes up again.

She can see a lone figure in the pavilion, on the other side of a small bridge.

Roxane Fusca, the villainess of *Regalia of Saints, Demons, and Maidens 3*. She's a beautiful girl, with translucent porcelain skin, pale silver hair, and cold eyes. She is from the house of Fusca, a distinguished family in Ashmael, and she was betrothed to Ares at birth.

A true aristocrat, she deals with the lowborn heroine harshly. As the game progresses, she torments her in ways unique to a harem—trying to kill Sahra with poison and informing Baal of her relationship with Ares in an attempt to get her executed—and she even secretly colludes with the fiend dragon.

However, she gets the standard ending: Her various machinations are denounced by Ares and the heroine, and her engagement is dissolved.

"Where is His Majesty? Don't tell me..." Ares seems anxious.

In contrast, Roxane responds so quietly that her doll-like face doesn't move at all. "He heard that Sahra was in the harem kitchens and went to fetch her."

"For the love of...!" Ares *tsk*s in mingled irritation and disbelief. He turns to Aileen again. "Wait here. I'll go retrieve His Majesty."

"...Yes, but first, who is the lady?" Aileen needs confirmation. That's all she intends the question to be, but Ares nods, then says something preposterous.

"Queen Roxane. She is King Baal's principal consort."

"?!"

There's no telling what Ares has thought of Aileen's astonishment. He turns to Roxane and introduces her rapidly. "Roxane, this is Aileen; she's a new high-ranking consort."

"I know of her. After all, as principal consort, the harem is under my jurisdiction."

Roxane speaks indifferently, and Ares's expression sours. "Don't think that means you can throw your weight around... Chat with each other for a little while. Consort Aileen, Roxane is the holy king's official wife. She outranks you—or rather, she is the highest-ranking consort of all. Be careful: The woman has driven many consorts from the harem."

Dropping that remark, and without giving anyone a chance to respond, Ares starts to walk quickly back the way they've just come.

...Huh? What did he just say? The holy king's official wife? —She isn't Ares's fiancée?!

When she glances at Lilia again, she is standing with her mouth hanging open. That means Aileen hasn't misremembered.

Reality doesn't match the game's plot.

"...If you're curious about Lady Sahra, you may follow him," Roxane says, in a voice as thin and soft as rain. She won't even look them in the eye. "It isn't pleasant to see you standing there in a daze."

"You heard her. Lady Aileen, let's go."

Clearly excited, Lilia is the first to turn on her heel. Aileen hastily follows her. Serena and Rachel are bewildered, but they exchange glances and go along with them.

"But where are we going?"

"To the harem kitchens, obviously. They're this way."

"How do you even know that...? You really are crazy..."

Serena seems creeped out, but Lilia tells her it's a secret and leads the way. Her confident steps impress even Aileen. Lilia has played this game in depth as well.

And now, when the difference between reality and the game is so immense, that may prove helpful.

A voice as lovely as a songbird's breaks her train of thought. "Master Baal! I'm sorry, I was supposed to come to you..."

Harem maids have bowed their heads, stepping aside to clear a path. Here, where only the underservants go, the nation's king is laughing.

"Be at ease. We suspected you'd be haunting the kitchens. You may be married, but you're still a hard worker, Sahra."

At the sound of that name, Aileen stops, fixing her eyes on the girl in the distance.

Sahra! It's her, the heroine of Game 3...!

Sunlight filters through the silky, lustrous pink hair that falls to her shoulders. Her large violet eyes and rosebud lips hold a mischievous smile. Clouds of aromatic steam rise from the large pot she's carrying. Apparently, she's been cooking. That's right: In the game, Sahra first worked as a cook. As she smiles at Baal, her long, canary-yellow kaftan sways.

Hmm? She's wearing canary yellow? But the harem attendants are supposed to wear light green...

Upon closer inspection, she sees that the cut of Sahra's clothes is different as well. No, more than that— She had heard the word *married* just now, hadn't she? As she's thinking, Ares abruptly emerges from the bushes beside her.

"Sahra! You're here again... And you, Your Majesty! I asked you to wait in the central garden!"

"What, Ares, did you get lost again? You're late."

"I don't know my way around the harem...!"

With a cheerful laugh, Baal turns back to bronze-skinned Ares. When Sahra sees him, her face lights up. "Ares! Look, it came out well! I thought I'd serve it to all of you."

"You're no longer a servant. Why would you come here to use the kitchens...?!"

"I-I'm sorry. I'm less likely to get lost here than in the palace."

"Ares, Ares. It's fine. We've told Sahra she may return to the harem whenever she likes."

There's no room for Aileen or the others to break into their cheerful conversation.

A soft voice reaches her ears. "He's the same as ever." It's one of the attendants who are standing with bowed heads.

"His Majesty still has feelings for Lady Sahra, doesn't he?" responds another.

"Even though he allowed her to leave and marry General Ares?"

"Only because he couldn't fight with the general over a woman. After all, as His Majesty's cousin, General Ares has the right to inherit the throne. He relinquished his claim to keep the kingdom from being torn in two."

There are times when women's gossip is the best source of information. Aileen compares what she's hearing to her game knowledge, putting it in order.

"I heard that King Baal and General Ares arranged it together, as a way to protect Lady Sahra."

"Mm, yes, perhaps. When General Ares married Lady Sahra, he presented Lady Roxane, his own fiancée, to His Majesty. Everyone says it's because Lady Roxane was infatuated with General Ares: They're keeping a close eye on her to ensure she doesn't harm Lady Sahra."

"I heard that Lady Roxane negotiated with King Baal: Provided he made her his principal consort, she wouldn't hold a grudge against Lady Sahra for stealing General Ares."

Like Aileen, Serena has been listening in, and she's starting to look rather disturbed. "Oof... Roxane? Isn't she the consort we just met? Talk about sordid."

"It does sound that way... Granted, it's not exactly unusual, but..." Rachel looks troubled.

True, it's rather common for two men to fight over a woman. Even in the game, depending on affection levels, that sort of event occasionally occurred. However, Aileen's attention is elsewhere. *Wait just a minute. If Sahra really is married, then that means...*

Ares is the main hero, and his route is the so-called standard route. If Sahra has married him, she's achieved the ending where his affection level is as high as possible. In other words, she's finished romancing him.

But Baal is the final boss on the Ares route, and he's still holy king. On top of that, the villainess Roxane has simply had her engagement broken. Not only has she not been executed, she's Baal's official wife...?

From the moment she heard of the fiend dragon's resurrection, Aileen knew the game was entering its second half, but she'd never dreamed it was already over.

"Oh? Your Majesty. Who are they...?"

"Ah, our new consort and her ladies-in-waiting."

"I knew it! You're Miss Aileen, then?" Sahra comes running up to her with a smile. Her innocent manner is a good fit for a heroine. "Ares says you destroyed the holy item!"

"Sahra. I told you, that holy item was quite old and worn. It was only coincidence that it broke."

"I know that. The fiend dragon isn't the only thing threatening the country right now, though. Our neighbor, Imperial Ellmeyer, has fallen to the demon king... We can't count on the Maid of the Sacred Sword, but my power alone may not be enough to protect the kingdom. I'll need everyone's help. I'd like you to lend me your strength."

Smiling, Aileen listens without moving so much as an eyebrow. The other girl squeezes her hand. "Everyone says I'm the Daughter of God, but please just call me Sahra. There's no need for formalities. Let's be friends."

"...Yes, Lady Sahra." Aileen is being formal in spite of the request, and Sahra's eyes widen. However, she promptly smiles as though that was what she expected would happen. She probably thinks Aileen is just being reserved.

When Sahra calls for everyone to come along, Ares follows her, looking relieved in a weary sort of way, and Baal follows him. When he passes in front of Aileen, Baal leans forward slightly and whispers, "The moment you hurt Sahra, you will cease to be useful. Watch yourself."

"I have no reason to hurt her."

"The Daughter of God must be an eyesore to you, Maid of the Sacred Sword. The holy sword is in her hands."

"Oh, then you mean it hasn't been repaired yet?"

Baal's eyes widen slightly. Then he offers her a smile that doesn't go past his lips. "Who can say? ...We don't dislike clever women."

Deftly dodging her question, he strides away. Aileen exhales heavily, watching the trio's receding backs. Sahra beams at Baal with a pure, innocent smile, and he returns it with one of his own.

...Is he a fool? She's someone else's wife.

However, thanks to her former fiancé, she's seen a man lose his head for love before, so she isn't really surprised.

"'We can't count on the Maid of the Sacred Sword,' she says. She's only the heroine of a sequel. I sense no respect for past installments," Lilia says, coming up beside her. This is the woman who taught Aileen how pathetic and foolish men could be when they went mad for love. "It looks as if we won't be able to simply boost Sahra's parameters, snatch the holy sword and be done with it, Lady Aileen."

"That's how it always is. Don't tell me you've lost your nerve."

"Of course not. I am the player, you know."

"As long as you're confident, that's all that matters. Let's go."

Ignorance is a crime: Unwittingly, the Daughter of God has made enemies of two Maids of the Sacred Sword.

Her first priority is information. Aileen must learn why neither the final boss nor the fiend dragon have been vanquished, even though the Ares route has reached its conclusion.

I can't sense any trace of the fiend dragon in the holy king, either. I have no idea what's happening here...

Depending on the situation, they may have to revise their plan to take the holy sword.

"Sahra says she's baked a snack for us. Replace both the sweets and the tea, Roxane."

"...Yes, Your Majesty. Let us have black tea, then."

No sooner have they returned to the pavilion than Baal gives an arrogant order. Acknowledging it, Roxane sets to work. When she sees this, Sahra is flustered. "What? But the sweets here already are quite wonderful as they are..."

"They're just ready-made stuff. They could never equal something you prepared yourself. Besides, we aren't throwing them away, we're bestowing them on others. No doubt someone will enjoy them."

"I-in that case… Miss Roxane, I'm sorry. You were the one who brought these, weren't you…?"

"Don't fret over that; it's Roxane's duty. Come, Sahra, sit down. We'll listen to your complaints about Ares."

Baal's casual tone makes Ares grimace. "Your Majesty…"

"No you don't, Ares. You're our guard. Just watch your dear wife talk with us from there."

Sahra's smiling wryly. Ares sighs in resignation. The mood among the three of them is tranquil.

Frankly, though, this is unpleasant. Especially General Ares's attitude. Proudly watching another man fawn over his own wife…

Either his self-confidence is incredible, or he unconsciously considers the holy king beneath him.

But she's the most unsettling one.

Aileen steals a glance at Roxane. The woman is setting out tea and sweets in an impassive, businesslike way.

The role of hosting tea parties falls to the wife, the mistress of the house, and so what Baal is saying isn't outrageous in and of itself. However, Roxane looks less like a wife and more like a lady-in-waiting or a simple maid. Her face is perfectly expressionless, and she works efficiently, hardly speaking at all.

"Um… Lady Aileen. May I assist Lady Roxane…?" As someone gradually becoming a genuine lady-in-waiting, Rachel can't take this anymore.

Aileen shakes her head slightly. "Watch and wait, Rachel."

"But if we let this situation stand, it will reflect on you as well."

"I'm aware of that."

Even Serena looks uncomfortable. Lilia is wearing a smile bursting with curiosity, but she's out of step with this world's common sense anyway, so she isn't a good reference.

There's no shortage of comments I'd like to make here, but observation comes first. Gather information.

As Aileen is thinking this, Lilia suddenly approaches the service cart. "I'll help you! —Eek! I'm so sorry, General Ares!"

"Oh, erm, it's nothing."

Aileen turns around, clenching her fists. She'd like to compliment herself for not hauling the woman up by her bodice and shaking her.

Apologizing meekly, Lilia blots at the hem of Ares's tea-drenched clothes. Aileen has seen this exact sight in artwork for the tea party event. If Sahra had been the one to spill the tea instead of Lilia, it would have been identical to the game. But Lilia's the one who spilled it.

Don't tell me she's trying to trip a flag for the Ares route!

The tea party event is a route fork early in the game. Lilia just might manage to make it happen.

As Aileen's trying to decide whether or not to stop her, Baal's laugh rings out. "What's this, Ares? That's an oddly familiar scene. Who'd have thought you'd get splashed with tea twice... Now, who was the insolent maid who did it last?"

"St-stop it, Master Baal. I am sorry about that, you know..."

This new information makes her anger at Lilia evaporate.

"Come to think of it, that was how you two met. It hasn't yet been a year, and still that takes us back."

"Hee-hee. You're nothing like you were then, though, and neither is Master Ares. Or rather, Master Ares was kind then as well, but..." Sahra blushes, and Ares smiles back at her, rather self-consciously. They're in a world of their own.

This rose-colored atmosphere is incredibly awkward, but even as her expression stiffens, Aileen's mind races. *In other words, she pulled off the tea party event, and they got married. Why, the game's already over and done with! She's awakened as the Daughter of God, and yet she's managed to get through her wedding without the final boss appearing... Did any such ending exist?! And even the villainess's denunciation event— Her engagement may have been broken, but I'm hesitant to call this "being condemned."*

She looks over at the seat next to her own. Roxane is drinking tea as mechanically as a clockwork doll.

It sounds like her engagement to Ares was indeed dissolved, but she's become the principal consort of Holy King Baal. She's married into the purple. It doesn't sound as if she's been vilified at all—though she doesn't look particularly happy, either.

Perhaps I should ignore the game's plot entirely...?

As she's puzzling over her thoughts, Aileen hears a clamor of voices.

"Lady Sahra! Thank you for your invitation!"

"Oh, it's you!"

As the group crosses the bridge to the pavilion, Sahra rises from her chair, beckoning them over. The fact they're harem women is obvious at a glance: Their faces are all lovely in different ways, and they're dressed in fine silks. Even the bows they offer to Baal are beautifully executed. Since none of them are escorted by ladies-in-waiting, they must be low-ranking consorts and not very wealthy.

The thing that concerns her is that every one of them is dressed in red.

Wasn't red a color only the principal consort was permitted to wear...?

Just as Aileen has been given the Sea Palace, as the king's official wife, Roxane will have been granted the Sun Palace.

That palace's symbolic color is red, of course. As a matter of fact, Roxane's clothes are a deep pomegranate hue.

Even without official restrictions, it's customary to avoid wearing clothes in the same color as the most noble woman in the room. High society in Imperial Ellmeyer observes that rule as well. In flouting it so blatantly, these women could very well be picking a fight.

And yet none of the newcomers have gone pale. They're laughing with Sahra as if they're enjoying themselves.

"It's been so long! How have you been?" asks Sahra

"Quite well, thank you. You look well, too, Lady Sahra; that's wonderful to see."

"Listen to you: 'Lady Sahra'! You could just call me Sahra like you used to, you know."

"We mustn't. You're the wife of General Ares, and the Daughter of God who will save this kingdom."

"Hey, Sahra, what's this about? Now you're summoning our consorts? Are you more popular than we are? And you, the ones who let yourselves be summoned: We weren't told about this." Baal sounds as if he's sulking. There's no possible way he hasn't noticed the color issue. He doesn't point it out, though; he just keeps chatting with Sahra.

"Well, Master Baal, you would have said they couldn't come. That harem custom wouldn't allow it. That's why I asked them quietly!"

"Still, preparations must be made for these things. Look, there aren't enough chairs."

"Oh, you're right."

"Good grief. Roxane!"

Baal calls her name without even looking at her. Roxane responds, then does as she's told. As Aileen clenches her fists, struggling against some emotion welling up inside her, one of the low-ranking consorts addresses her casually.

"You're Lady Aileen, aren't you? I hear you were made a high-ranking consort by special decision, because of your great sacred power."

"Do help Lady Sahra, please," chimes in another. "Thank you so much."

"Lady Roxane comes from a distinguished family, the only one in Ashmael to engage in diplomacy. However, in terms of sacred power, they are rather… She is a very accomplished woman, quite knowledgeable about history, but in times like these, well…"

"Still, even if she did have sacred power, what good would it do her without the holy king's favor?"

"Fortunately, such ridiculous disputes hold no interest for me."

When Roxane firmly cuts them off, the lower-ranking consorts' furtive smiles vanish. It doesn't take them long to recover, though. One of them says she's obtained an unusual type of sugar and begins to add it to the tea, passing it around.

"I shall keep this." Rachel reaches over and stays the consort's hand. If they were acquaintances or had been introduced by a third party, this would be rude. However, as a lady-in-waiting, it's only natural for her to be on her guard against poison.

The consort seems a little irritated, but she obediently hands the sugar over to Rachel. Having witnessed this exchange, Baal laughs. "You'll have to forgive her. She's just been sent to us as a bride from a foreign land, and she doesn't fully trust us yet."

"A foreign land! I see. I'd love to hear about it!"

As she listens absently to Sahra and Baal, Aileen sees the

lower-ranking consort reach toward Roxane's tea. No one stops her. Even though the king's principal consort might be poisoned.

No, as a matter of fact, what she's just dropped into the tea is—

That wasn't sugar! It can't be...sand? What? But wasn't that from an event where the villainess bullied the heroine?!

"Lady Roxane. Please, go on. Drink."

Baal can't see the woman's malicious jeer. Just as Aileen begins to rise to her feet, Roxane drains her teacup without pausing to breathe.

Then, looking unperturbed, she gives her thoughts on it. "I am the principal consort. Anything you present to me should be at least a little higher quality than this."

Her attitude stuns not only Aileen, but the lower-ranking consort who set her up.

Roxane dabs elegantly at her lips. She must be fully aware that the lower consorts hold her in contempt, and that her husband pays absolutely no attention to her.

However, despite her situation, she has demonstrated that it will take more than this to crush her spirits.

Her pride brings a slow smile to Aileen's lips. She's seen something refreshing, and she's beginning to enjoy herself— *Yes. Stirring them up may not be a bad idea.*

Ares scowls. "Roxane. Being the principal consort doesn't excuse arrogan—"

"Gracious, Lady Roxane! You needn't say it like that." Intentionally interrupting the rebuke, Aileen emits a musical laugh. "She must not have known which sugar would go with the tea. She may have mistakenly substituted sand. That's hardly fit for human consumption, is it? —Rachel, take it away."

"Yes, milady," Rachel says, clearing the tea away. Sahra looks blank, but the lower-ranking consorts are another matter entirely. They flush bright red, growing angry.

"A-after she took the trouble to prepare that...!"

"Who on earth do you think you are?! You've only just arrived!"

"C-calm down, everyone... Um, umm, Miss Aileen."

"—Lady Sahra, wasn't it?"

"Oh yes," the girl says, sitting up straighter.

Aileen gives her a smile. "Leave my presence, insolent one."

"Huh?"

Sahra looks as though she's never heard those words in her life. Aileen repeats herself, slowly. "I told you to leave. Are your ears as weak as your mind?"

As she'd anticipated, Ares flies into a fury. "Wha—? Woman! Sahra is the Daughter of God! What are you saying...?!"

"What am I saying? It's merely common sense. Or am I to believe that the status of a high-ranking consort in this kingdom is so low that the wife of a mere retainer—even if he is the holy king's cousin—may refer to her so casually?"

Since Aileen is a high-ranking consort and Ares is of royal blood, there may not be much difference in rank between the two of them, but she definitely outranks Sahra.

Ares is making no attempt to hide his anger. His fists are trembling, and even Serena steps in front of Aileen, joining Rachel. Lilia is desperately choking back laughter. Surprisingly, Baal seems to have chosen to stand by and watch.

Sahra looks troubled by the volatile atmosphere. "Ah, umm, I didn't mean..."

"Sahra is His Majesty's honored guest. She is also the wife of

General Ares. More than anything, she is the Daughter of God, and vital to this kingdom." Roxane fixes quiet eyes on Aileen. "I will not tolerate impertinence."

"However, if this sort of thing happens at a tea party hosted by the principal consort—a woman of the house of Fusca, which handles this nation's diplomacy—the future seems rather bleak, does it not?"

One of Roxane's eyebrows rises. It's the first human gesture Aileen's seen from her.

"I will bear that in mind, as a bit of nonsense from a consort of unknown origin."

Roxane has accepted her challenge squarely. Aileen smiles back at her. "That's reassuring. I believe you and I will be able to have a decent conversation."

"Do you? One can only hope we will find a topic in common to discuss."

"As proof of our friendship, I'll have fresh tea made for you. Rachel, bring something that will not embarrass Lady Roxane."

"I shall look forward to it."

Aileen's smile never falters. Roxane's responses are cool. The people who were indignant just a moment before are hanging back, watching the situation unfold.

Baal shrugs. "So this is how women fight, is it? Bloodcurdling. Well, the thought that you are fighting over us is pleasant… Hey, why did you fall silent?"

Even after Rachel has finished pouring the tea, the silence continues to expand. Baal shoots a sidelong glance at Roxane, then *tsk*s in irritation.

The fact Aileen isn't responding to Baal is only natural, but it's surprising that Roxane has adopted the same attitude.

Does this mean her end goal was simply to marry into the purple? Or does she still have feelings for Ares...?

Is that why Baal's spitefulness doesn't seem to bother her?

"Sahra. Just look at how cold our wives are. Console us, would you?"

"N-never mind that, Master Baal. The others have a matter they would like to discuss with you. Please listen to them. That's why I invited them today!"

For some reason, Sahra has taken the reins. However, if Baal agrees, no one will be able to object.

"Very well. We'll hear it."

"They say a ghost has begun to haunt the harem recently. I'm told it's the same one I saw, long ago."

At the word *ghost*, Aileen turns to listen. Behind her, so does Lilia. They're probably thinking the same thing.

That's the "ghost" event, the encounter with the previous Daughter of God... It's happening again?

It's an event that must occur in order for the heroine to awaken as the Daughter of God. Would something so important happen multiple times?

"Oh, now that you mention it, there was a commotion about a ghost sighting before, wasn't there?"

"Unlike then, this time I have a bad feeling about it. There's something I'd like to see for myself, but—"

"No, Sahra. Demonic power grows stronger at night. You are the first one the fiend dragon would target."

"...As you can see, Ares won't let me. Now, though, we have Miss Aileen in the harem. You will help, won't you?"

It *is* the "ghost" event. Aileen wants to look into it, but on an emotional level, she doesn't want to meekly accept Sahra's request.

She acts as if it's only natural for everyone to serve her. I don't like that attitude! ...Even if I'm not that much different.

However, the others have begun to move the conversation along without her.

"What a wonderful idea! If Lady Aileen resolves it, we won't need to worry."

"Besides, Lady Sahra is busy with her prayers regarding the fiend dragon and the demon king's subjugation."

"Consort Aileen. This is an honor. You should accept."

Ares speaks as if he's settled the matter. It makes her consider dashing her tea over him, but just then, a dignified voice rings out. "Don't force her. As the Daughter of God, this is a task Lady Sahra should perform."

Ares gives Roxane a sour look. "Weren't you listening? It would be dangerous for Sahra."

"Then why not refrain from subjugating the demon king as well? If war breaks out, you won't be able to give Lady Sahra preferential treatment."

Aileen blinks, startled.

However, Sahra seems to have been surprised by something else. "'Preferential treatment'?" She looks blank.

Ares raises his voice protectively. "You just want to get rid of her!"

"I am saying that, if she claims to be the Daughter of God, she should have commensurate obligations. Subjugating the fiend dragon is one thing, but subjugating the demon king means starting a war with Ellmeyer. People will kill one another. I do not believe that Lady Sahra can bear that responsibility."

"As long as we win, it won't matter. Roxane, this is sophistry masquerading as a sound argument. You simply want to get in

Sahra's way. You fear you and your family will lose influence, since you don't have the power to fight."

"That isn't..."

"Oh, and another thing: I hear you've been finding fault with women sent from the Queendom of Hausel and running them out of the harem. They have nowhere else to go. How can you be so cruel? Are you still in the habit of tormenting women you don't care for?"

"...The harem is under my jurisdiction. General though you are, you have no right to order—"

"Roxane, be quiet."

Baal shuts her down, coldly and abruptly, and she falls silent. Ares looks triumphant. The low-ranking consorts snicker at the fact that Roxane's been taken down a peg, while Sahra seems troubled.

...I wonder what his aim was there.

Had Baal shut Roxane up because her excuses annoyed him, or had he cut her off with intentional coldness, to keep her from further reproach? Their relationship is difficult to read. Neither even attempts to meet the other's eyes.

As she's watching them and thinking, Baal's gaze shifts to her. "Well then, Aileen. The conversation drifted a bit, but that's how things stand. You'll do it, won't you?"

"...I will. On the condition that Lady Roxane, who has authority over the harem, orders it." The others' eyes widen. Having scored a hit of her own, Aileen smiles. "Unfortunately, I don't intend to work for Lady Sahra's sake."

Everyone else freezes up. In contrast, Roxane draws her eyebrows together. "...And yet if I order it, you'll accept?"

"Yes. After all, if I were to defy the principal consort, I might lose my rank." The prevailing mood is that it's only natural to work gladly for the Daughter of God, and that subjugating the demon king is a just cause. In the midst of that, Roxane is holding her head high, refusing to be swayed by public opinion. She doesn't mind helping a woman like that look good. "Besides, there's no one else who can do it, is there?"

The lower-ranking consorts almost speak up then. However, if they say that she's wrong, the job will fall either to Sahra or to them. Seeing this, Roxane turns to face her squarely. "Please handle it, then. Do nothing reckless."

The others look as if this doesn't sit right with them, but Aileen accepts, her expression composed.

Desert nights are cold. Wrapped in a warm cape, Aileen looks up at the dark sky. Her white breath turns the stars misty.

"Why would a ghost turn up in a country where demons don't?" muses Lilia. "That seems weird."

"Probably because ghosts aren't demons," Aileen answers. "Don't worry about little things like that. Rachel and Serena, you circle around to the right. Lady Lilia and I will patrol from the left. If you see anything, either run away or scream and alert us before attempting to deal with it yourselves. Is that clear?"

Rachel nods obediently, then drags the grumbling Serena away. After she watches them go, Aileen sets off. Rather than circling in the opposite direction however, she pushes her way into the forest in front of her.

Far from objecting, Lilia follows her cheerfully. She knows.

If this is the event, the ghost will appear in the consecrated area adjacent to the lake of holy water. In the actual event, the heroine is summoned to that spot, but it will be faster if they just go there to begin with.

"Lady Aileen, do you think she'll be there? The ghost—the previous Daughter of God."

"That's what we're on our way to find out."

The lake of holy water lies in the depths of the harem's forest. A shrine at its center houses the holy sword. However, since it is consecrated ground, anyone who lacks sacred power will lose their way before they reach it. Being able to reach the lake is the first test any potential Daughter of God must pass

The event itself is apparently over...but we'll be able to confirm whether the holy sword is there or not.

Just then, the view abruptly opens up.

The lake is so wide and still it's hard to believe it's located in a desert. Its surface reflects the twinkling stars and crescent moon like a mirror. There is no ghost, which is disappointing. "We reached it without any trouble..."

"Of course we did. You and I are in what's commonly known as 'cheat mode,' Lady Aileen. Even if we can't repair the holy sword, the intensity of our sacred power should get us through all the conditional events easily."

"Let's go at once and see whether that sword is there."

There's a shrine in the very center of the lake. The holy sword should be inside it.

Aileen takes a step into the oddly bright lake, creating a widening ring of ripples. Her feet don't get wet. Instead, she walks over the water's surface, reaching the shrine in no time at all.

She sets her hand on the shrine's door, which is made of sacred stone. When it detects her power, light races through its cracks, and the entire shrine dissolves and vanishes.

Then all that's left is the timeworn holy sword—or that's how it should be, but...

"It isn't here."

Looking at the now-empty surface of the lake, Aileen sighs. Lilia, who's been watching from behind her, puts a finger to her chin. "Then she's played through to the part where she takes the holy sword from the hallowed ground. I wonder where she's keeping it. In the game, the ceremony to repair the sword is held quite soon after she removes it; then they go right into battle against the fiend dragon, so there's no mention of where it was stored."

"—Lady Lilia. I really don't want to ask, but I'm going to: I'd like your opinion." In the middle of the shining lake, Aileen turns to face Lilia. "What do you think of this situation?"

"Goodness! Hee-hee. Who would ever have thought you'd talk about the game with me, Lady Aileen? I'm so glad." Aileen suspects the other girl will be evasive, but Lilia gives her a proper response. "People are calling Sahra the Daughter of God, but her parameters aren't high enough. I doubt the holy sword has been repaired."

It's a levelheaded answer. Aileen sighs. "Agreed... I can't sense that sort of power from her."

"They're only treating her as the Daughter of God because she removed the holy sword. It does look as if she's managed to make her romantic conquests, though, so the conditions should be in place. She simply needs to complete the remaining awakening events."

"Do you think she can, as things stand?"

She was only with them for an hour or so, but both Baal and Ares were terribly overprotective. No matter what approach is used, the events that trigger the Daughter of God's awakening tend to be dangerous. If she's surrounded by people like them, even attempting the events will be difficult. And in any case, Sahra doesn't seem inclined to do so.

Leaving aside their methods, both Lilia and Serena had been proactive enough to do something about their situations on their own. As Aileen's feeling keenly aware of just how helpful that was, one of those heroines makes an outrageous proposal. "In that case, you and I should romance Ares and Baal."

"...Huh?"

"That way, they'll stop being so overprotective. You're Baal's consort, so you work on him. I'll go steal Ares!"

"Wait just a minute! I'm Master Claude's wife; romancing another man isn't—"

"You can't do it?" Lilia closes in on her. Her eyes are sparkling brightly. "Just look at the enormous soft spot he has for the hero-ine, even now. If you romance Baal while he's still the holy king, he's sure to grant your every wish. You'll even be able to save the demon king..."

"I-I'm not falling for that! Do you have any idea how angr— I mean, how hurt Master Claude would be?!"

"Aww. Don't ruin our fun." Lilia puffs out her cheeks, sulking.

Shooting her a sidelong glare, Aileen crosses her arms. "You have the right idea, though. Those two are far too blind where Sahra is concerned; we'll have to open their eyes a bit. Ares in particular puts too much faith in the Daughter of God. If there's a successful revolution and he becomes king, it's going to be a headache."

He's sure to attack Imperial Ellmeyer without giving them any room to negotiate, then turn the holy sword on Claude.

"Do you want to adjust the situation so that Baal remains holy king?"

"Let's see… It does look like he still has enough discretion to refrain from a relationship in order to keep the kingdom from being torn in two."

"In that case, isn't romancing him the only way? On the Baal route, even when he's taken over by the fiend dragon, the power of his love for the heroine protects him. He's treated as a hero who tried to seal the fiend dragon inside himself, and he remains the holy king to the end."

The conversation's come full circle. Aileen frowns, muttering to herself, before coming up with a desperate plan. "That's it! He already has a principal consort. Let's have Lady Roxane provide the power of love!" As she's saying it, the plan strikes her as surprisingly ingenious.

But Lilia's eyes are cold. "You'd assign the final boss to a villainess? This isn't you and the demon king… All talk of the game aside, that couple is completely ignoring each other."

"That simply goes to show they're on each other's mind. There is a way. Even I was treated coldly by Master Claude at first… My, this plan may actually be rather good."

"Perhaps. If everyone were as brazen as you are."

"Don't be rude. We'll just have to help out! Honestly… Were Ares and Baal always such pushovers?"

"Gracious, Lady Aileen. All love interest characters are like that." Turning on her heel, Lilia sets off toward the shore.

Following her, Aileen suggests a possibility. "Could Sahra be conducting her romances based on the same sort of memories you and I have?"

"I really doubt it. No heroine would put herself in such an inane situation if she were self-aware."

"Why? Her situation isn't that bad. She's managed to marry Ares."

"—Oh, perhaps you don't understand, since you're a villainess." A gust of wind sends ripples across the lake. "She is the heroine, remember? Her success is guaranteed. Why let that slip through her fingers? If I were her, I'd hurry and defeat the fiend dragon, successfully lead that revolution, and take over the kingdom myself."

"...I don't think everyone's as bursting with ambition as you are."

"If she has no ambition, then why do you suppose she carries herself like a superior to the principal consort, behaves as if she owns the harem, and has both her husband and the holy king waiting on her hand and foot?"

"She may just be innocent. The way you used to be."

Lilia reaches the edge of the lake, stepping lightly, then turns. "I don't believe I ever made you serve me at table, Lady Aileen. From start to finish, that heroine acted as if it was right and proper for everyone to treat her as if she were above the villainess."

The low-ranking consorts had picked up on her attitude, and that had created this bizarre hierarchy.

"...True. On that point, you're correct."

"I'm glad you see it. Anyway, from now—"

Lilia stops in the middle of her sentence. Aileen also stiffens, staring at a spot on the lake.

Right in the middle, where the shrine had been, a woman stands listlessly. Her feet float above the water, and yet she casts no shadow. Lilia shrugs. "You and I really are cheaters. Too bad we can't just become Daughters of God."

"—...that...girl."

A cracked voice drifts over to them on the wind. The woman's eyes are hollow, and every time she speaks, waves rise on the lake.

"Tell...that girl—...king is..."

"The king?"

Did she mean the holy king? Aileen frowns. *In the event, she tells you about the fiend dragon's resurrection and the holy sword...*

"—coming. As it is now, the holy sword can't win aga..."

"...Lady Aileen. This isn't what she says in the game."

"Aaah... Coming... He comes...!" The woman clutches her head as if she's frightened. Whipped up by her unease, the wind grows fiercer, building to a storm. Standing her ground, Aileen shouts. "What exactly is coming?! If you have something to say, speak clearly!"

"The demon king."

Aileen freezes up.

Half-crazed, the previous Daughter of God screams. Her words are a prophecy. *"The demon king comes! Tell that girl to make haste and restore the holy sword...!"*

"......"

"Ohhh God, my God... The world will be destroyed... I beg you, protect us!"

Clasping her hands as if in prayer, the woman vanishes. Immediately the wind dies, the lake stills, and silence falls.

"....................."

"That's the demon king for you. He's already on his way."

"—That wasn't like the event at all, was it?! She didn't even mention the fiend dragon."

"Probably because the demon king is coming, don't you think?

The demon king outranks the dragon. Oh, so that's why she came to deliver a second warning."

"Do you suppose 'that girl' is Sahra?"

"I wonder when he'll get here. In a day? Two days? What do you think?"

"Be quiet!" Aileen shouts. Clutching her head, she crouches down at the edge of the lake. "He's already located me...?! It's too soon! It hasn't even been a week since I disappeared!!"

"That's the power of love. Ever since the other day, the demon king has earned my respect in that department."

"Don't! A love that you find impressive sounds terrifying! At any rate, we've learned that the holy sword hasn't been repaired yet. If Master Claude is coming, what should our first priority—?"

Abruptly, her vision warps, and the lake vanishes. As if time has rolled back, the forest they passed through earlier is right in front of them again. This is where they parted with Rachel and Serena.

The event has ended. Feeling rather dissatisfied, Aileen has just gotten to her feet when she hears a woman's ear-piercing scream.

Lilia murmurs, puzzled. "Was that Sahra?"

"But she shouldn't be in the harem... In any case, let's go!"

Aileen takes off at a run. Lilia follows her, looking perplexed. "The heroine, attacked in the harem at night... That happens after the 'ghost' event, doesn't it? But the actual event is over already. What's going on?"

"Never mind, just run! If it's the fiend dragon, Rachel and Serena are in danger!"

The scream hadn't sounded too far away, and as expected, it

isn't long before they see several human figures and hear the clash of swords.

"—Rachel! You're all right?!"

"I—I am. But Lady Serena and General Ares...!"

Rachel, who has an arm around Sahra's shoulders, directs her attention to Serena with a glance. Serena has just kicked an armed man and sent him flying. Beside her, Ares rams another man, stunning him. The fact that all the men are dressed like eunuchs makes Aileen frown. "Don't tell me there's been a rebellion..."

"N no. They were all at work tending the lamps when they suddenly growled and attacked."

"...Why is Lady Sahra here?"

"She says she was accompanying Master Ares on his patrol, since he doesn't know his way around the harem."

"He stopped her from going out at night, and then brought her along?!"

"I-it's the fiend dragon," says Sahra. Like Rachel, Sahra is standing a little ways from the action. Her face is dead white. "I-it really does control humans... What should I...? Ares...!"

"Argh, what a nuisance! What are these people? I thought this place was haunted by a ghost, not by these—!" Serena is irritated; she hits their assailants hard, but even when their eyes roll back in their heads, they get right back up. Aileen places her hands on the ground. Dealing with this situation comes first.

Sacred sword.

She shifts her attention from the stone-floored corridor to the ground below the fallen humans. The sacred sword won't work on them, but she can dispel the magic that clings to them.

For a brief moment, a gust of wind blows up from the floor, and then the eunuchs begin collapsing as if they've been drugged.

A step behind Aileen, Lilia smiles. "I'd expect no less of you, Lady Aileen. Although these are hardly worthy opponents."

"Ares!"

Ares is scanning the now-silent corridor when Sahra runs to him and throws her arms around him, clinging. Wiping her brow, Serena turns back to Aileen. "You should've come help us sooner."

"You are the one who's supposed to guard me, remember? ...Did this commotion break out with no warning?"

"Yes. Except I think I smelled demon snuff, just for a moment."

"Demon snuff? But that's strictly controlled by the church."

"Don't ask me. I only said I smelled it."

Since the Kingdom of Ashmael had no demons, it didn't see any value in kowtowing to the church. Their mutual dislike was notorious. More to the point, it was hard to imagine a nation this insular acquiring demon snuff on its own.

Still... If someone had that, they could lure the fiend dragon...

But the dragon's resurrection was already public knowledge in this country, and even the Daughter of God was here. Why would anyone need to lure it out, if not to slay it?

Brooding, Aileen comes up beside Ares. "Do you happen to know anything about this incident?"

If reality mimics the game, this man is plotting to usurp the throne from Baal.

Ares answers indifferently. "Of course not. I can guess, but... What did Sahra say?"

"...That it was the work of the fiend dragon."

"That settles it, then. Imagine allowing the fiend dragon to invade the harem... The principal consort has blundered."

"Lady Roxane?" Aileen frowns; she hadn't expected that accusation.

Ares snorts. "She rejected my proposal on the dubious grounds that the harem was under her jurisdiction and wouldn't let me make any security recommendations. Now this happens. What would you call that, if not a blunder?"

"...Lady Roxane is your former fiancée, but she doesn't trust you."

"She's probably holding a grudge over the broken engagement. She's proud... I did my best by her, though."

"Your best?"

"That's right. She couldn't have become principal consort if I hadn't allowed it. She's ungrateful, and on top of that, she flaunts it as if it was a personal achievement. She has no idea."

Aileen's fingers tighten around her upper arms. She doesn't know Roxane well enough to deny any of this. However, the man's attitude toward his former fiancée is his true nature. She's certain of that.

"In the first place, the fiend dragon is active again, and I am a general. In a situation like this, no place should be beyond my reach. Surely King Baal won't complain. Putting that aside, I thank you for your help. I'll take care of the rest; you may go now. I'm sure you don't want to draw baseless suspicion to yourself."

"Whatever do you mean?"

"You're one of Roxane's supporters, aren't you? Although I can't see why." Quietly, Ares looks down at Aileen. "There's a rumor that her grudge against Sahra is so great she's secretly communicating with the fiend dragon."

"......"

"Whatever the consequences, they're no concern of mine. But know that I will not forgive anyone who harms Sahra."

With that, Ares puts an arm around Sahra's trembling shoulders and calls for someone to come tend to the fallen eunuchs.

The area is suddenly bustling with activity, and Rachel calls to her softly. "Lady Aileen. We'll stand out here."

"...Yes, you're right. Let's withdraw for now. There's something I must take steps against, and quickly."

"What, did something else happen?"

"Lady Lilia. I'm adopting your plan... We'll avert that civil war."

Lilia looks stunned. Then she smirks. "Hee-hee. I admire the way you deny the game yet continue to make use of it, Lady Aileen."

"Only if that is how reality stands... May I leave the information gathering to you?"

"Gracious, who do you think you're talking to?" Lilia's smile is so dauntless it's unsettling. She had never thought the woman would seem reassuringly reliable. Not that she'll let her off the leash entirely, of course.

"Serena, you accompany Lady Lilia. I'll pay you a special allowance."

"—Fine. I plan to squeeze you dry."

"Rachel, you're with me. Hurry. There's no time."

Aileen turns on her heel. Behind her, Lilia claps her hands together lightly. "Very true. After all, the demon king will be here soon."

Oh, that's right.

Instantly, Aileen freezes up. As if urging her on, a gust of wind that's stronger than usual blusters into the night sky.

Auguste is poking at the fire when the sound of a small sneeze makes him look up. "Demon King, are you cold?"

"No, I'm fine. I'm sure Aileen is waiting for me to rescue her."

"Don't get sappy when we're right in the middle of the desert..." With a disgusted look, Isaac hands him a hot medicinal tisane. He may not talk like it, but he's good at looking after people.

"Thanks. Only I don't want to drink this."

"Look, just down it in one go. It's medicine Luc and Quartz sent with us so we could do something about your haywire magic."

"That's stopped now that we're here. It won't be a problem."

They're inside the holy king's barrier, and the magic that was causing the trouble has been silenced, so Claude is in perfect shape. Granted, it does mean he's now no different from an ordinary human... As that thought crosses his mind, two elongated shadows appear in the moonlight that streams through the mouth of the cave. It's Cedric and his man.

"We've returned, Brother. It went well. We'll be given an audience in the next few days."

"I see. Good work, Cedric. And, uh—" Who was this again? Claude ponders the answer, but the young man gets angry before he can remember.

"I'm Marcus Cowell, Your Highness! Would you remember it already...?!"

"Oh, that's right. My apologies. For some reason, I can't get you to stick in my memory."

"Ha! Man, if the next emperor finds you forgettable, the house of Cowell is done for." Isaac's sneer irks Marcus, and invisible sparks fly between them.

Auguste hastily breaks in. "E-easy, easy. Here, drink this and settle down, um..."

"I just said it's Marcus Cowell! Are you patronizing me because you belong to the Holy Knights...?!"

"Huh? Are the Holy Knights that big a deal?!"

Auguste is genuinely startled, and Marcus's lips tremble.

Looking as if he's lost the urge to fight, Isaac mutters, "This is just tedious. Seriously, why would you choose this crew to infiltrate Ashmael...?"

"Isn't it easier to work together if we each have a clear objective?"

Isaac is worried about Rachel, Auguste is worried about Serena, and Cedric and the other young man are worried about Lilia. When there's something they want to save, people are willing to put up with a certain amount of discomfort.

"Besides, I'm using Elefas as a body double to hide my absence. It won't look natural if Keith, Walt, and Kyle aren't with him. I had to leave the demons in James's care, so I couldn't take him, either. On top of that, the members of the Oberon Trading Firm aren't suited to rough work." By process of elimination, he'd been left with this group.

Isaac snorts. "That doesn't mean we need those two. Who knows when they'll sell us out?"

"What are you saying? Cedric's a good boy. Long ago, he came to me and asked if I could use magic to cover up the fact that he'd wet the bed."

"Brother! There's absolutely no need to bring that up...!"

"True, he did get a little rebellious once, and denigrated me for being the demon king. Even then, though, when I helped him practice his swordsmanship a little, he quickly broke into tears and apologized. Deep down, he's straightforward and meek. Besides, this time around, there's no better bait than Cedric."

"Bait, huh…? Okay, it's pretty clear which of you two is boss…" Isaac shoots a pitying glance at Cedric, who's visibly flagging, his hands planted on the wall.

"At any rate, we'll be in Ashmael's royal capital soon. Let's all try to get along."

The Kingdom of Ashmael and the Queendom of Hausel were the only countries the demon king's magic couldn't touch. Even though a ship had vanished, the Queendom of Hausel's messenger insisted that there had been no such accident, or indeed any ship to begin with, and that the crown princess must have run away. At that point, Jasper had brought word that the Kingdom of Ashmael's royal harem had acquired quite a lot of women recently.

That was enough to make Claude choose Ashmael as his destination. After that, he'd simply tasked Jasper and the rest of the Oberon Trading Firm with making the arrangements.

Even if he knew where Aileen was, the Kingdom of Ashmael was protected by its holy king and sacred barrier, and the demon king would be powerless to intervene. Or that must have been the plan, though Claude still isn't sure who is behind this. What he does know is that he will outfox them.

Or rather, he's going to reclaim his wife, who will definitely not be behaving herself in the harem.

"I'm sure Aileen is waiting for me there. Let's all do our best when we arrive. Cedric, Isaac, Auguste—" He falters again.

Unable to take it any longer, the young man drops to his knees. "Marcus Cowell! How many times do I have to tell you…!"

"Oh— It's okay, Marx, I remember!"

"N-no, that's—"

"Hang in there, Maracas." Even that final jab from Isaac can't bring the young man back to his feet. Cedric, who silently offers his friend a medicinal tisane, really is a good boy.

✦ Third Act ✦
The Villainess Pushes People's Buttons Without Blinking

The Kingdom of Ashmael and Imperial Ellmeyer had been founded at roughly the same time. A glance at the history book's table of contents shows Aileen their history also begins with the legend of the holy sword and the Daughter of God.

"The holy sword purified the land which the fiend dragon's poison had defiled. Holy water welled up, and the nation came into being..."

Confirming that the real-life legends match the game, she returns the elementary history book to the shelf. The library is crammed full of books all the way to the ceiling, and it's quiet. Rachel is waiting for her at the entrance, but Lilia and Serena are acting separately.

It's been three days since the attack... The next condition for the Daughter of God's awakening is the uproar over the fiend dragon's summoning, which is a prelude to the "condemnation of the villainess" event. In the game, the event occurs because Roxane is unable to give up on Ares and has been communicating secretly with the dragon. I wonder what will happen in real life...

Even if reality proves to be different, it's very possible that a slightly changed event will occur and retrace the path of the story. That's happened before.

After running a finger across the spines of the books on the shelf, she picks up a history book written in the old tongue. Her thoughts break off for a moment as she scans the words.

"'The royal family of Ashmael is of the bloodline of the Daughter of God, and children with sacred power are born unto them. In order that their blood should not die out, the institute of the harem was established…' Hmm. Their history is the complete opposite of Ellmeyer's."

Ellmeyer's imperial family also carries the blood of the Maid of the Sacred Sword, but her power hasn't stayed with them in the same way. On the contrary, the legends said that their line would produce the demon king.

"Say, aren't you curious? About why the demon king was born into the imperial family, for example, when they're supposed to be descended from the Maid of the Sacred Sword."

"You can read that book?"

A voice speaks above her, and she looks up. Baal is floating there. He descends, alighting at an intersection between the bookshelves. "Perhaps we should have expected as much from Ellmeyer's crown princess, but who'd have thought you could read our ancient tongue?"

"You're making too much of it. This is merely the product of education."

It had been several centuries since the Queendom of Hausel standardized the language and units of measurement. However, in earlier eras, every nation had its own language, and these were now referred to as "old tongues." Aileen can read the old tongues because they were drummed into her as part of her education as crown princess: She would need them when conducting diplomacy and concluding contracts.

"All I can do is read them. My third older brother can speak the ancient languages of every country as if they were his mother tongue. He can even write treaties in them."

"Oh-ho. That's impressive. Would that we had such talent in our kingdom."

"Ever since another nation kidnapped a prince of Ashmael in a bid to gain its holy power, the kingdom has essentially isolated itself from the rest of the world. You'd wish for such a thing, despite all that?"

"Ah, you were aware— Still, without stimulation from the outside world, we'll rot from within." Coming to stand beside her, Baal takes the book from Aileen and flips through it.

"...Are you considering future diplomatic exchange with other nations?"

"That's right. To that end, we've welcomed women from a variety of lands into our harem."

"By kidnapping them?"

"Hmm. From your perspective, it was kidnapping, I suppose." He speaks as if that isn't the case for the others. Darting a sidelong glance at his face, for the first time, she realizes he's pale. "Either way, it's a triviality. Now that the demon king's poised to become Ellmeyer's next emperor, everyone wants a connection to the holy king. This is our chance." He doesn't seem to be aware of his pallor, though. He's excited about his work. "The fools are considering going to war with Imperial Ellmeyer. But if we are with them, they can win without fighting at all. We've also obtained a trump card in you. There are any number of ways to—"

"Hold out your hand."

"What?"

This is shaping up to be a bother, so she reaches out and takes his hand. Sure enough, it's cold. However, judging from the fact he teleported here, he must be totally oblivious.

Sighing, she sends holy power into him through their joined

hands. Baal looks startled, but he lets her do as she pleases. Before long, his hand grows warmer and his color improves, so she releases him.

"...Oh, that's right. You are the bearer of the sacred sword."

"You've only just remembered? Isn't that why you made me your consort?"

"We didn't think you'd catch on."

She bites back a sarcastic response to that last remark and his wry smile. "...Are you sleeping properly? The fiend dragon's power is stronger at night. You aren't pushing yourself, are you?"

"What, does our bedchamber interest you?" He laughs and brushes her off. If life is imitating the game, though, he'll be struggling to keep the fiend dragon in check at night.

Come to think of it, she hasn't heard anything about evening visits to his bedchamber, even though such matters are what interest the harem most. It's likely he hasn't summoned any consorts.

We don't know where the holy sword is. Under the circumstances, it won't do to have him collapse on us... If Ares becomes king now, it's going to be a problem.

Her motto is "Once resolved, don't hesitate." Still holding the book, she takes his hand again, tugging him along with her. "Hey. What's this? Where are we going?"

"Never mind, just follow me. There, sit down right here." She seats herself in the shade of a tree just outside the library and pats the soft lawn beside her. "Go on, lie down."

"Why?"

"You haven't been sleeping. It's broad daylight, and even if the fiend dragon goes on a rampage, I'll be here to restrain it. Relax and sleep."

"...You expect us to believe you? You, the demon king's wife?"

"If resurrecting the fiend dragon is my true goal, I'd hardly have any reason to share my power with you."

Her actions should carry more weight than her title, but Baal still doesn't seem quite convinced. "That's...true, but you have no reason to help us."

"You are a troublesome man, aren't you?"

"Troublesome?! What about us is troublesome?!"

Case in point, she thinks privately. But since it's a bother, she gives in quickly. "Very well. If you want a reason, you shall have one: You said you wouldn't start a war with Imperial Ellmeyer. That is my reason."

"We told you we wouldn't need to. The demon king can't beat us."

"But you're restraining the others, aren't you? Both General Ares and Lady Sahra are determined to go to war."

Sahra is already known as the Daughter of God. She has retrieved the holy sword, and omens point to the fiend dragon's resurrection. However, because this man is king, they haven't attacked Ellmeyer. He's used Claude's life to threaten her, and she won't forgive him for it, but she's compelled to acknowledge that much. "And so, until a better king comes along, I will be your ally."

"...You feel we are preferable to Ares?"

"Unfortunately, yes."

He examines her as if he's eyeing a rare beast. It's quite rude. "What is that look for?"

"...Never mind. Are you implying...that Ellmeyer doesn't intend to fight with us?"

"When you kidnapped me, I was on my way to a diplomatic conference with the goal of averting a war."

"You were, were you...?"

He gives a deep sigh. She isn't dense enough to miss its meaning.

"It sounds as if there really is something behind all this. Is it possible that you brought me here by mistake, or perhaps due to a trap of some sort?"

If he was considering diplomacy, not war, he would never have kidnapped the crown princess.

The mastermind would be someone who wanted to use the kidnapping to set Imperial Ellmeyer and the Kingdom of Ashmael firmly against each other.

"Do you think we would tell you so easily?"

"In that case, I insist that you sleep. It will be a downright nuisance if you collapse."

Baal doesn't move. With a smile, Aileen slowly balls her hand into a fist. "Or would it be quicker if I struck you?"

"Woman... Isn't there a slightly more seductive way to put it?"

"Why should I have to be seductive for you? I'll kick you."

Grumbling something sarcastic about women who hit and kick, Baal finally lowers himself to the lawn, then lies back in the shade. He doesn't close his eyes, though. Instead, he keeps looking up at the sky.

"...We can't sleep. Sing us a lullaby."

"You aren't a child. Don't be spoiled. Hurry up and go to sleep."

"Woman, you have no concept of restraint or how to create the proper atmosphere."

"Then allow me to speak without restraint: If I were you, I'd give up on that woman," she says, opening the book on her lap. Baal shoots her a glare, but she thrusts the truth at him mercilessly. "She is another man's wife."

"...You speak as if it were so simple. You can't know how it felt when we stepped aside."

"Yes, I can. I've done it myself."

He looks startled. Her history is rather notorious, even in other lands, but apparently the tales haven't penetrated this isolated kingdom.

"You...have done the same? *You?*"

"Yes. Devoting yourself to someone who doesn't love you and pays you no heed is a waste of time. I decided to move on quickly."

"We must look rather ridiculous in your eyes, then." Maybe he feels something like kinship toward her, now that he knows they have that experience in common: Baal gives a self-mocking smile, without attempting to save face. "You may laugh and tell us we're an embarrassment. We'll allow it this once."

"I wouldn't laugh at that. It simply shows how serious you were. Besides—I might have been the same."

If it hadn't been for the memories of her past life and the death flag, she might have clung to Cedric desperately. Exactly as Aileen had in the game.

"...You won't laugh, hmm? Even though you say we should give up on her."

"Well, really, you're the one who's suffering because you aren't able to."

She hears him gulp, but pretends she hasn't.

"...Sometimes we feel as if the jealousy may drive us mad. What about us wasn't good enough?" He covers his forehead with his arms, hiding his face, and she isn't in the habit of peeking. "We know everyone secretly finds it comical. That they're laughing at us. That they compare us with Ares. Everything he says is straightforward. If they say we became king just because our sacred power was greater, and that he isn't like us, they're probably right. What rebuttal is there?"

She gives a brief murmur of assent, just to show she's listening.

"However, we must appear as if we aren't bothered by it. We are the king."

This must be the same sort of loneliness that Claude bears. There's only one thing Aileen can say in response. "I told you I was your ally, remember?"

"...You are a thoroughly peculiar woman..."

"And you're quite rude."

"However, we like strong women."

"Being liked by you would be problematic."

When she cuts him down with a grimace, Baal bursts into quiet laughter. "You're so cold. Well, that's more refreshing anyway."

She can't help but give it a little thought: Baal can't give up completely because Sahra leads him on. Aileen doesn't know whether it's intentional or by accident, but the girl's artlessness and the way she relies on him probably get his hopes up.

And in my case, I was completely disillusioned.

It's difficult. She considers giving him a kind word or two, but when she looks over, Baal is breathing peacefully. He's fallen asleep.

Sighing, she returns her eyes to the book. She took it from library without permission. Thinking she'll have to borrow it officially later, she casually glances at the card in the back of the volume. Her eyes widen.

The book is an academic text, a detailed account of the history and culture of Imperial Ellmeyer. It's in the old tongue, and was written before the "impostor" conflict. Its content is quite different from modern versions, but it's more accurate. It contains the knowledge one must learn if one is considering diplomacy.

"...I'm sure you will be able to love again as well."

Only one person has borrowed the book previously: Roxane Fusca.

Beside him, under the blinding sun, the demon king shivers. He can't possibly be cold, can he? The training ground where they've been ordered to assemble is swarming with new guardsmen, and it's so hot he wouldn't be surprised to see heat mirages. Auguste himself is soaked with sweat.

"Um, don't tell me... Do you have a cold, sir?"

"No... I'm merely shaking with anticipation... I feel as if someone has trod on a very sore spot indeed."

What? That sounds scary. And so, instead of asking for details, he opts to change the subject. "I'm glad they hired us, aren't you? What a relief."

"Yes. I'd never taken a test before, and I was nervous. Do you think I did all right?"

"You were perfect!"

Claude responds with a nod. Relieved, Auguste looks down at the sword he's only just gotten permission to carry. It has the national crest of Ashmael engraved on it.

As soon as they entered the Kingdom of Ashmael, they'd begun gathering information.

Apparently, the fiend dragon had been resurrected, but the Daughter of God had already appeared, and the town was abuzz with talk that they'd be able to defeat the demon king as well. The reputation of the general and his wife had been particularly impressive. The Daughter of God had married a general named Ares; people said she was the fairest of the fair and that he was a holy general. Prints depicting the couple had been selling like hotcakes in the marketplace.

They'd heard a few rumors about the holy king as well. He was in some sort of love triangle; it had sounded like quite the sordid mess. His poor reputation was also concerning. People said he was a spineless man who wouldn't issue the order to subjugate the demon king because he didn't want to give Ares the chance to triumph, while some even speculated he'd already been possessed by the fiend dragon.

...The masses must believe the Daughter of God can defeat the demon king...

The rumors about Ellmeyer were rather dubious as well. People whispered that it was a pitiful country that had fallen to the demon king, and all because they'd believed in an impostor like the Maid of the Sacred Sword— Basically, it was the target of mockery. Auguste wasn't all that patriotic, and even he'd winced. Cedric and Marcus had been quietly furious.

However, in all those rumors, they'd heard nothing about Ellmeyer's crown princess, the second prince's fiancée, or their servants. In other words, if Aileen and the others were here, it wasn't public knowledge yet.

Once they had a good grasp of the situation, Isaac had assigned various jobs.

The fiend dragon had appeared in the harem and attempted to attack the Daughter of God, and so they were recruiting new guards. Since it was a temporary position, applicants weren't required to be eunuchs. (When Isaac had told him about the eunuch system, Auguste had quaked in his boots.) Claude and Auguste had applied, and would attempt to at least find out whether Aileen and the others were in the harem.

Cedric and Marcus were acting separately. Isaac hadn't wanted to let them go off unattended, but Claude had ultimately decided to allow it. Auguste didn't know exactly what they were doing, but Claude had breezily declared, "Cedric is a good boy, so he won't betray us. Since he is my younger brother, there's also no way he could fail." *It must be tough to have the demon king as your big brother,* he'd thought, sympathizing with Cedric: either betrayal or failure would mean death.

Isaac had said he wasn't skilled enough with a sword to be a guard, and he didn't plan to help Cedric and Marcus, so he was working on his own. He'd said that civil war might break out, so he was going to put some safeguards in place. Auguste had no idea how he'd reached that conclusion, but if Isaac said that was the case, it probably was, so he'd just do what he could.

That is to say, he'd infiltrate the harem, gather information, and babysit—or rather, "guard"—the demon king. Even without magic, Claude is plenty strong, so Auguste hadn't thought he'd need guarding. However, he's learned something very thoroughly on this journey: The demon king absolutely does need a guard, or rather, a caretaker. Apparently, the man can't even dress himself.

"Hey, are you the one who cornered General Ares during the selection trial, then turned down a direct request from Lady Sahra to be her guard?"

"...Who's Sahra?"

Then there's his complete lack of worldly wisdom, and the fact he genuinely sees no one but Aileen.

"What did you just say?!"

"Excuse him, please, he has an illness that keeps him from remembering names!" Auguste breaks in, hastily and loudly, stepping forward to shield Claude from multiple pairs of eyes.

Oblivious to Auguste's efforts, Claude frowns, his handsome eyebrows drawing together. "I remember the names of people who bear remem—"

"Oh, look, there's a really rare bird over there!"

"? Where?"

Diverting the demon king's attention to the sky so he won't say anything uncalled for, Auguste hastily turns back to the other man. This isn't the first time he's had to resort to such tricks, and he's starting to get used to it. "I'm sorry. We really haven't been here long. We didn't know what Lady Sahra looked like. He turned down that fantastic offer without realizing what he was doing, and he's regretting it now."

"...Really...?"

"Look at him just staring into space. He might not seem like it, but it shocked him."

As Claude gazes at the sky, his beautiful profile seems melancholy by default. Being handsome is useful.

"I see... Well, if you didn't know, uh... That was bad luck."

"You said it. Argh! You know we'll never get another chance

like that," he laments in an exaggerated way, and the other man gives him a wry smile. Apparently he's won his pity.

"Well, Lady Sahra is a kind woman. She'll forgive him."

"Make sure you don't do anything rude next time, you hear?"

"We know. We'll do our very best, for Lady Sahra's sake!" Over the past few days, he's learned that he can win most people over by saying this.

The man is smiling when he leaves, and Auguste sighs in relief. Abruptly, he remembers Walt and Kyle. He'd assumed guard duty would be a walk in the park for those two, and at this point, he feels like he owes them an apology.

"Auguste. I don't see the bird."

"Oh, maybe it flew off somewhere."

"I see. That's a shame."

"You'll be able to see it again." This conversation is giving him flashbacks to the time he looked after children at a care home. "All right, they'll be showing us around the harem soon. Let's go, Master...uh, Clau... Claw."

Auguste has a whole lot of trouble with what to call him. However, thanks to that, Claude forgets all about what just happened.

"Right," Claude replies. "I'll slip away somewhere in the middle, so you take the tour."

But now he's said something preposterous.

"But if they notice you've slipped out and decide to keep an eye on you, it'll make it harder to maneuver later."

"They're already keeping an eye on me. I came in first at the selection trial. My final opponent may have lost, but apparently he was a general, and now the Daughter of God or whatever knows what I look like." He does have a handle on what's important... Although he's started making risky comments again like, "Who would have thought a general would be so weak...?"

Master Claude was fighting with his left hand, after all.

Auguste had fought seriously, but he'd lost. They may have acknowledged his skill, but he didn't stand out.

"Besides, if Aileen is in the harem, standing out would be better."

"That's...true, but if she isn't there, won't it backfire?"

"If she's not here, then we don't need to be here, and there's no problem."

His assessment of the situation is efficient as well. Granted, he doesn't have a shred of the caution a future emperor should have, but... *Well, it's not as if we're here to dutifully guard the harem anyway.*

Meanwhile, Auguste himself has a careless personality. The real problem, then, is that there's nobody to stop them.

"All right! Then I'll take the tour and do whatever seems appropriate."

"Yes, do. I'm counting on you."

"From what I hear, the harem's really big. Please don't push yourself."

"It's fine. Aileen and I are bound by fate. We're sure to meet."

He has no idea where that confidence is coming from, but if the demon king says so, then it's probably true.

Or maybe thinking it's true is what's important.

...I hope Serena's not getting up to anything...

They stop chatting, fall in line as instructed, and enter the harem.

A garden of women, where the victor is she who wins the

king's favor. Auguste has a very bad feeling about Serena being in a place like that.

I bet she's conning somebody. She just seems like a regular pretty girl if you don't really know her... Maybe Ailey would stop her. Besides, as a rule, I guess there aren't any men except the king here. No need to worry too much, then.

There's no telling what's reassuring about that, but he's managed to persuade himself, and he follows the rest of the line. The demon king is already nowhere to be seen. That was fast.

The harem is laced with little man-made brooks and overflowing with lush greenery. In the middle of the desert, it seems like paradise. In the distance, he can hear the merry voices of women playing in the water. Even as maids in long, pale green kaftans gracefully clear the way, they gaze at the new guards with open curiosity.

Every girl is lovely, and Auguste feels like turning tail and running. As the guards' eyes wander uneasily, a voice calls to them from the head of the group. It's General Ares, the one who's decided to place guards in the harem.

"Listen up: Your job is to protect the harem from the fiend dragon. And remember, all the women here are the king's wives. Don't even dream of fraternizing."

"Yes, sir," they chorus.

But didn't the general marry a girl from the harem?

It's odd that no one is calling him out on it. According to word on the street, the man offered his own fiancée as a form of equivalent exchange, but Auguste doesn't hear anyone pitying the fiancée, either. Apparently, she became the principal consort, but that doesn't necessarily mean she's happy.

Exactly: That's why Auguste is going to stop Serena. Obtaining rank without being loved is sure to be lonely.

Just as that thought occurs to him, he catches a glimpse of long silver hair.

"General Ares! Are these the gentlemen who are going to be guarding the harem?"

"Ah, Serena."

"If you don't mind, I'll show them around in your place. Lady Sahra seems lonely; please go to her."

Serena turns around. Her long, slender limbs are clothed in the costume of this country. Her kaftan is ultramarine. Both the color and cut of the garment are different from what the crowds of harem maids they've been passing are wearing. Even if he isn't familiar with the customs of the harem, he understands that Serena has been given a special rank, and it shocks him.

"I see; Sahra is... Hmm. I don't mind leaving it to you, but you're not frightened?"

"I'm all right. Even you acknowledge my skills, General Ares."

Not only that, but she's oddly friendly with Ares. Even the sulky pout she's wearing is cute.

She's just the way she was during her days at Misha Academy. If he doesn't watch how she behaves to the people around her, compare, and think calmly, he'll get the wrong idea. So she looks this cute to those on the outside? —No, that's not right, either.

"Okay. If you would, then. Don't push yourself, though."

"I won't."

She's capable of agreeing obediently... Even though she always looks at Auguste coldly, as if he's a caterpillar.

No, come on, she's just pretending to be like that. What's the point of letting it shock you?!

On that thought, he looks up. Serena has just seen Ares off, and when she turns around, their eyes meet.

Hers widen. For some reason, she drops her gaze, then lifts it to his face again. Her expression is pitying and a little repulsed. She mouths the words silently: "Don't tell me— Did they cut yours off?"

With that, Auguste is down for the count. As first greetings go, it's more than he can handle.

According to the demon king, if your fates are linked, you'll meet again. If that's true, their fates must be ill-starred.

✦

✦

By the time Aileen's finished reading the library book, Baal has awakened.

He only slept for about an hour, but it seems he slept well. He stretches, looking refreshed. When Rachel comes to find Aileen, he has her bring him some snacks, eats them, then goes back to work. Apparently, some new guards are scheduled to stop by the harem and introduce themselves, so he's going to perform a surprise inspection.

"Ares may be commanding them, but we are still allowing men into the harem. We need to keep them in check."

That's what he says, but when she thinks of the game's developments, it feels as though Ares has bolstered his personal forces. From the fact that Baal chose the phrase "keep them in check," he seems to have picked up on that as well.

Ares has grown arrogant. Still, opposing him right now would be a poor move. It's frustrating, but we'll have to handle him by being evasive... We have far too few allies.

Baal thanks Aileen, pushing his half-eaten piece of fruit against her lips and telling her he'll share it with her. He even says that he'll have her attend him in his bedchamber, as a reward. It seems he's begun to trust her a little. If he wants to sleep, he could just be honest and ask for that. The man is tiresome to the last.

"Still, we may have established a little room to negotiate now— What is it, Rachel?"

Her lady in waiting has completed the procedures for borrowing the book, but she's acting rather strange. They're on a covered path with a view over the entire garden when she stops to ask her what's wrong. Rachel looks solemn. "Lady Aileen. You do understand what attending to him at night means, don't you?"

"Of course I do. It will be a good opportunity to talk. I've finally found a lead that might help repair the man's relationship with his principal consort, too."

"Um, are you quite certain you understand? What are you going to do if, um, *that* happens?"

Realizing what Rachel is worried about, Aileen nods. "True, men will sometimes settle for any partner. Never fear; I'll break it."

"You'll break it?"

"Unlike Master Claude, if he's never able to use it again, it won't pose any sort of problem for me." But perhaps that would be doing Roxane a disservice. Thinking she'd like to talk to her as well, Aileen turns to face forward again. "Never mind that, how are Lady Lilia and Serena faring?"

"Quite well, it seems. General Ares has begun to consider

removing Lady Lilia and Lady Serena from the harem and having them serve Lady Sahra."

"Even though it's only been three days since I sent them?!"

Aileen had ordered them to conquer Ares—or rather, to become his allies—so that they could gather intelligence about the holy sword and civil war. At that, the two of them had cheerfully begun putting together a strategy. First, in order to make him relax his guard, they'd approach on the pretext of being infatuated with Sahra. What that sort of man needed was complete affirmation of his work, a show of brave frailty, a passion for justice—etcetera, etcetera. She hadn't told them to romance him, but they'd set out to do just that as if that were completely natural. Not only Lilia, but Serena as well.

Two heroines, plotting a honey trap. In terms of *otome* games, it seemed like a dubious proposition… Then again, the prime objective in *otome* games was romancing the hero, so perhaps they were right after all? In any case, after just three scant days, Ares has begun to trust them enough to consider making them Sahra's attendants.

It's possible that Ares is a pushover, but Aileen has only one thought on the matter.

Otome *game heroines are terrifying!*

"…For the moment, impress upon them they are to do nothing that will make it hard to look Prince Cedric or Auguste in the eye."

"When I say that, they both give me the most outrageous looks…"

"Assume that means it's effective… If anything happens, I'll take responsibility…"

With a distant look in her eyes, Aileen cuts across the courtyard. It's a tranquil garden: A fountain sits at its center, with water flowing from it in four directions. It's designed in such a way that no matter which angle she views it from, what she sees is as lovely as a picture.

"Oh!"

Aileen has been hurrying, but the wind blows harder, as if it's trying to detain her. She's distracted by the garden, and the silk gauze wrap she's wearing loosely around her shoulders slips away from her. It floats elegantly, and then someone catches it.

Time stops.

Beauty like a fair-skinned work of art, and not a drop of sweat under the hot sun. Black, lustrous hair sways slightly in the wind. The wide eyes he fixes on her are a beautiful, jewel-like red.

"........."

".............."

It's a mirage of her husband. Yes, that must be it— But she doesn't even have the chance to escape reality for a moment.

"Oh— Lady Aileen?!"

She whirls around at once. Discretion is the better part of valor. Unless she regroups first, she won't be able to fight.

...Or so she thinks, but reality isn't so kind. Wordlessly, Claude follows her. She'd love to believe this is a dream, but it isn't.

Eeeeeeeeeeeep!

She's running, while Claude is only walking briskly, and yet the distance between them keeps shrinking. Fighting the urge to scream, she runs desperately, but it's obvious he'll catch up to her soon.

I have to hide somewhere...!

She turns corner after corner, breaking his line of sight. As she does so, she looks around, then spots a door that's standing slightly ajar in a building that seems quiet. It's a treasure house. She slips inside and sets a hand on the door, trying to close it before Claude appears. It's heavy, but unless she hurries, he'll catch up…

"Aileen."

Wham. A long leg blocks the door she's attempting to close. Stifling a shriek, she tries to retreat deeper into the building, but slips and falls on her bottom. She scoots away, but her back promptly runs up against something, blocking her escape. When she twists around, trying to get up, Claude's long leg stomps down, blocking her way. He's standing on the fabric of the long kaftan that's fanned out between her legs— There's no escape.

"Why are you running? Your husband's come to take you home."

In the gloomy treasure house, Claude slowly looms over her, giving her a smile that goes no further than his lips. His eyes are terrifying.

Growing desperate, Aileen screams. "You have the wrong woman! I bear a strong resemblance to your wife, that's all!"

Claude's face turns serious. Tugging at the fabric of her robe in an attempt to free it, she keeps talking. "I—I also happen to be named Aileen. Isn't that an incredible coincidence!"

"……"

"A-and so, would you release me?"

"…I see. So you are not, in fact, my wife. Is that what you're saying?"

"Y-yes, that's it. After all, your wife would never be in Ashmael's royal harem."

"True. Now that you mention it, you're right. There's no possible way my wife would have been granted the Sea Palace and been made a high-ranking consort in the Kingdom of Ashmael."

He's absolutely onto her, but at this point, what is there to do but laugh. "Th-that's very true... Hoh-hoh-hoh-hoh-hoh-hoh. Um, I would really appreciate it if you'd move your foot."

"I'm afraid I've been terribly rude, then. By the way, don't tell my wife, but I'm a surprisingly bad man."

She has a nasty feeling about this, but by the time she tries to act, it's too late.

Claude is on his knees, holding her firmly around the waist. His face is right in front of her nose. His smile is like a potent poison that's been mixed into honey, and it paralyzes her. A voice that's far too sweet breathes on her earlobe. "May I examine every inch of you to see how you differ from her?"

"I am your wife!!"

She surrenders the moment his fingertips skim the nape of her neck. Claude shrugs. "Sometimes you put up this pointless resistance."

"Th-that's because you—"

"I'm glad you're safe."

She's lost track of what she meant to say. Instead, she presses her forehead against Claude's shoulder. That's all, and yet he gently strokes her back, as if he understands everything. She just can't win against this man.

"Rachel was there, too. Are all of you here?"

"...Yes."

"All right. Just leave the rest to me."

She almost nods on reflex, but then she comes to her senses— *The holy sword.*

"No, Master Claude, you mustn't! There's something I must finish in this kingdom."

"Oh really now? You can't possibly mean becoming another

man's consort, can you?" While Claude's voice is still kind, its pitch abruptly drops, and she cringes.

"Nuh, n-n-no! I'd never, I couldn't possibly—"

"Then why won't you come home with me?"

"Because— Yes, because I must play Cupid!"

If she's able to steal the holy sword, that would be great. If she fails, though... If Baal is possessed by the fiend dragon and Ares becomes king, he just might attack Imperial Ellmeyer and come for Claude's head. To keep that from happening, Baal must remain the holy king, which means she needs the power of love. However, she can't possibly seduce a man other than Claude, so she's going to support that man's principal consort instead—that's the current situation in a nutshell, or so she explains.

Claude freezes up with that mild smile still on his face. It's probably because he hasn't understood any of it. However, he promptly recovers. She'd expect no less of her husband.

"For the moment, would you tell me what brought all this on?"

"I'll omit the details, but if the holy king and his principal consort can be joined by love, I see a way to resolve everything. That's why I'd like you to please leave the country at once and let me handle this, Master Claude. It isn't safe here."

If anyone were to find out who he was, they would strike off his head and everything would be over. He must understand, and yet he came anyway. Aileen knows this is no time to swoon. "You didn't come alone, did you?"

"...Isaac and Auguste and... Well, there are others."

"If Isaac's here, then there's no need to worry." She sighs with relief. Claude's eyebrows twitch.

Without paying them any heed, she catches both his arms,

pulling him to his feet. "Master Claude. Hurry and leave this place. Please go home. I'm all right."

"...You're all right. I see."

"It's really nothing." *Not compared to losing you*— But before she can say that bit, she's interrupted by the sound of a fist striking the wall.

"......"

She suspects she's stepped on a land mine.

Belatedly realizing her error, Aileen freezes up, holding her breath. Claude has hit the wall right beside Aileen's cheek, and he's looking down at her with a perfectly blank face. "I'm glad this happened here, in this kingdom. No matter how I feel, I won't cause trouble for others."

"Th-that's...very true...?"

"I understand what you've told me, quite clearly. In other words, you want me to make you cry."

Overwhelmed by the anger in his words rather than the content, Aileen trembles. "H-how did you come to that conclusion?"

"What happened to your wedding ring?"

His tone is incredibly low, and her anxiety builds. If she tells him it was taken from her, he may very well go straight to Baal, fully intent on retrieving it. "Umm, it— I, i-it's fine! I'll make sure—"

Bam. He strikes the wall on her other side. "I take it you can't say, my sweet precious Aileen?"

"Th-that's right." She's completely boxed in, with that sweet voice speaking directly above her, and she shrinks back.

"Very well. I understand perfectly." As she trembles, wondering what's going to happen next, Claude turns on his heel. "If you won't come home, then do as you please."

"...M-Master Claude?"

"In exchange, I will also do as I please."

Claude sets off, his heels clicking sharply on the floor. Hastily, Aileen runs after him. "What? ...W-wait! Master Clau—"

"My name is Claw here."

"You took a liking to that name, hmm?! No, that's not what I—"

"What's this? We thought we heard voices, and look who we have here."

The door to the treasure house opens, and light abruptly streams in.

"We were told a guard had gone missing, and here he is, dallying with our consort."

The holy king's figure is more suited to light than gloomy darkness. At the sight of him, Aileen impulsively steps in front of Claude.

Baal has filled the treasure house with sunlight. He glances at Claude, then laughs. "We won't ask who you are. After all, the demon king himself would never saunter into an enemy nation disguised as a guard."

"......"

"Black hair and red eyes. You're just as the legend says, yet our kingdom failed to notice you. Their ignorance is grave indeed. Granted, they must have been utterly certain you'd never come here, since you aren't able to wield your power inside the sacred barrier."

Suddenly, Baal catches Aileen's arm and pulls her toward him.

"Just a—"

"Still, this woman is our consort. We won't tolerate assignations."

"Excuse me?! You have no right to give me an order like th— Mmph!"

Baal's big hand covers her mouth, and his arms restrain her tightly. Claude gives them a cold glance. Then he slowly walks right past them.

Baal calls after him, sounding entertained. "Are you sure? We won't give her back."

"Your principal consort's name was Roxane, wasn't it?"

"Huh?" Baal doesn't seem to have expected that. His grip slackens.

Aileen grabs the opportunity to shake her head, freeing her lips. "M-Master Clau… No, I mean— Um, at any rate, wait!"

She calls for him to stop, but Claude leaves the treasure house without even looking at her.

Don't tell me… No, he wouldn't, he can't!

Aileen feels the blood drain from her head.

"What, did his courage fail him because he couldn't win? And he calls himself the demon k—?!"

When she slams a fist into his solar plexus, Baal crumples and sinks to the ground. Aileen's fists tremble as she fights the urge to stomp on his back. "You don't understand the gravity of this situation at all, do you?!"

"—Why, you… Who hits kings in earnest?!"

"I know you saw his face! He'll steal Lady Roxane from you!"

Baal looks up at her with a dazed, foolish expression. *Aaaaaaah!* Aileen clutches her head. *I'm such a fool! I made him angry…!*

If this were a game, she'd immediately opt for a redo. She's chosen so, so wrong.

While trying to achieve marital happiness, she somehow triggers their first marital fight instead.

At the shabby inn where they've gathered to make their reports for the day, the demon king abruptly speaks up. "My Aileen is as adorable as ever."

"Never mind that. You mean she was in the harem. Okay. So—"

Not a day goes by without him bragging about his wife. Isaac tries to let it go in one ear and out the other, but then he notices Auguste. The young man is standing behind the demon king's chair, flailing his arms, before using them to form a big X. Isaac looks puzzled.

"She's too adorable, and that's why I want to hold it against her all the more. Heh-heh. What should I do to her? Just thinking of what will happen next makes my heart leap."

"……"

The demon king is positively glowing. Isaac looks at him, then at Auguste. Holding his gaze, Auguste nods solemnly.

Aileen finally went and stomped on the demon king's land mine, huh.

He'd heard that a high-ranking consort named Aileen had been given the Sea Palace. He'd suspected the news would stun the demon king, but apparently it's made him explode instead.

"I thought if I killed anyone, I would probably begin with your group."

"Coming right out with 'kill'? Isn't that a little too direct? At least make it 'eliminate.'"

"I was wrong, though. I should have taught Aileen a lesson first."

"Listen when people are talking."

"I haven't felt this energized in a long time. I want Aileen to really witness this love."

"Like I said, listen. Your brother hasn't come back; that doesn't worry you?"

"Oh, come to think of it, do you know what Aileen told me? She said if you were here, there was no need to worry. Do you mind if I kill you?"

"Please, Your Majesty, carry on with whatever you were saying."

The king is smiling, but he's also reaching for the sword at his waist, and for some reason, Isaac can't laugh it off as a joke.

"And so, to punish her, I've become the guard of the principal consort."

"...The principal consort?"

"Yes. She's suspected of having ties to the fiend dragon; I'll be observing her. The general ordered it."

The fact he's like this and still works efficiently is one of the demon king's most unpleasant traits.

"First, that Ares fellow will probably plot to usurp the throne."

"Huh...? What, really?! He didn't look like the type at all..." From behind him, Auguste finally speaks up.

Without turning around, the demon king continues. "If he isn't intentionally planning it, others will spur him on, and he'll attempt it soon. If not, a mere general would never have the principal consort placed under observation at his own discretion, without orders from the king. Unease regarding the fiend dragon, discontent over the holy king's failure to order military action, his own claim to the throne, the righteous cause of the demon king's subjugation, and his trump card, the Daughter of God: All the conditions are in place. Has he taken Cedric's bait yet?"

It's less a genuine question than a request for confirmation. Isaac sighs. "...Yes. The second prince of the Ellmeyer Empire, here to request help in freeing his nation from the demon king, has been sheltered by a friendly noble, and will be shown to General Ares's mansion soon. The holy king will not be informed."

"Probably because the holy king would refuse to shelter Cedric."

"That doesn't necessarily mean he's our ally."

"However, Aileen is protecting him. She would only do so if it benefited me. In other words, the holy king won't choose to oppose me."

The very thin basis of his theory could easily be construed as bragging about his wife. It may be a little late to care, but Isaac is fed up with it. The fact he suspects the king is probably correct doesn't help.

Behind them, Auguste looks as if he doesn't really get any of this. For his sake, Isaac speaks again. It's important for them to be on the same page.

"...So here's how things stand: Right now, this country is gripped by fervor due to the Daughter of God, and they're ready to go to war with Ellmeyer, using the fiend dragon as justification. It's likely that the holy king is the one who's holding them at bay. As a result, people are grumbling."

"Huh? You mean the citizens are the ones who want war?"

"The country has always been protected by the holy king's barrier. They don't think they could lose."

They must have been afraid of the fiend dragon at first, but the Daughter of God has stripped that fear away. The prevailing mood is that the demon king has threatened them, so they're more than ready to respond in kind.

"Some are probably against war, of course. The house of Fusca, for one; they're the principal consort's family. However, they're a rich, distinguished bunch. Regular citizens tend to think that people like them don't have their best interests at heart. With the atmosphere as it is, there's no way anybody else can speak up."

"I get that. Everyone's all 'Three cheers for Lady Sahra,' and it made today quite a slog... Does Aileen think there's going to be a civil war, too? Maybe she's trying to do something about it."

"She said she was going to play Cupid for the holy king and his principal consort."

"Huh? What's that supposed to mean?" Auguste looks puzzled.

Ignoring him, Isaac crosses his arms and mutters to himself. "I heard they don't get along, because of some messy love triangle with the Daughter of God. Is that what she's scheming? True, being at odds with her in this situation is a bad move. Besides, the fact that the holy king is still besotted with the Daughter of God is hurting his reputation. And because of that, the general who married her has more influence than the king..."

"......"

"The principal consort must have a good head on her shoulders. There's no way Aileen would suggest this otherwise. In that case, taking them down from the inside is our best bet... But without the Daughter of God, the fiend dragon would... Oh, the holy sword, huh? That's a danger to the demon king, too, so there's no way Aileen would leave that out of her sight. But if she still needs to steal it...that's gotta mean she hasn't found it yet... Auguste, where did you see Serena?"

"Oh, um... She was with General Ares, I guess, yeah..." Auguste falters, averting his gaze slightly.

"What, was she hurt or something?"

"No. She seems fine, it's just... She suspected something extremely humiliating..."

"—Oh, that you'd become a eunuch? Why didn't you just show it to her?"

"How could I possibly do that?!" Auguste yells in response to the demon king's outrageous suggestion.

The demon king nods back gravely. "You're right. I wouldn't have the courage to do it, either."

"Please don't casually tell your subordinates to do things you can't...!"

"So she's split up her group. Man, with Lilia Reinoise involved, that's really gutsy. She's always skating on thin ice... I wish she'd think about the people who have to cover for her."

"Isaac."

When he looks up, the demon king is smiling at him a little coldly.

"Your guesses are correct. I met the principal consort, and when she saw me she seemed startled. She knows who I am, or at the very least suspects it... In this country, where practically no one knows me."

"Meaning she actually has intel about other countries."

"Yes. However, when she heard that the holy king had given his permission, she fell silent. She's a discreet, intelligent woman. Even though having the demon king as a guard must frighten her. She's far better than that Daughter of God, or whatever that other woman is. I can see why Aileen likes her. Anyway is it all right if I kill you?"

"Why?! How did we get from that to this?!"

"It's probably because you understand Ailey *too* well, Isaac...," Auguste mutters. Isaac stiffens. He hadn't meant to give that impression, but the demon king's eyes are fixed on him, and he feels as if he's being tested.

"...I've just known her for a long time, that's all."

"Well, never mind. Killing you now would be a poor move. The important thing is exercising discretion."

Isaac doesn't ask, *Discretion in what?*

"Your interpretation of the situation is probably sound, Isaac. And so, I will play Cupid as well."

"Sorry, but you've completely lost me."

"It's nothing difficult. I'm merely going to teach Aileen a lesson, while simultaneously granting her wish."

After thinking for a few seconds, Isaac gets it. In spite of himself, he tells the king off. "That's low. She's extra vulnerable to that sort of thing. Or what, do you want to make her cry?"

"That's where we differ. The idea of Aileen crying makes my heart race."

That's not something to get excited over, he thinks, but realizes that really is what sets them apart.

"...Do whatever you want, but do you even have a shot at this? You said the principal consort was wary of you."

"Look at my face and say that again. As a matter of fact, I'd like to see what it's like to lose— Oh, don't tell Aileen. She'd say she understands, but it would weigh on her."

I hope you do lose. Internally cursing him, Isaac mentally switches gears. It's not as if he doesn't understand the demon king's anger. It's an emotion the men around Aileen feel over and over again.

It's just that this man is the only one who can confront her with that anger directly.

"So that's how things stand," says the king. "Auguste, you stay and guard the harem with me."

"Oh— Yes, sir!"

"Isaac, I want you to be our liaison. Use Cedric as you see fit."

"There's no way his princely highness is going to listen to me, and you know it."

"Just add 'says your brother' to the end of every statement. Cedric is a good boy."

"...Is that right?"

"The other one, uh... What was his... The instrument. I'll leave him to you as well." Marcus isn't even human anymore. "Oh, I can't wait to see Aileen's face."

"Really? I'm so happy for you."

"Oh, that's right. Rachel seemed well."

The attack comes out of nowhere, and Isaac's reaction is delayed. The demon king gets to his feet, smiling triumphantly.

Isaac *tsks*, irritated. "...I didn't ask. If Aileen's fine, she probably is, too."

"That's your fatal flaw. Auguste's prospects are better. Yes, all that's lacking is the courage to whip it out and show it..."

"Look, here's some friendly advice: Steer clear of that particular topic."

There are a ton of other things he wants to say, but that warning is the only genuine remark Isaac allows himself.

✦ Fourth Act ✦
When the Villainess Is Involved, Imbroglios Ensue

The day when she first came to this country and thought *Why did this happen?* feels like the distant past.

His black hair ripples, and the heels of his shoes click. That alone is enough to draw sighs of admiration from all quarters. His posture is elegant no matter which angle it's viewed from, and his tall, well-muscled physique seems modeled on the golden ratio. At the sight of the new guard, everyone naturally clears the way, and the principal consort who follows him is gathering envious gazes.

General Ares has chosen and assigned a guard to the principal consort. At first, everyone felt that he was a guard in name only and was really there to keep an eye on her. Now, any thought of pity or disdain has evaporated. They're simply jealous. It's almost palpable.

And this is all because of the taciturn, beautiful, faithful, kind, strong, well-mannered guard who's rumored to smile at no one but the principal consort. The only fly in the ointment is the fact his name is Claw.

"Your hand, milady."

He addresses her gracefully, extending his own hand. Roxane takes it, climbs the steps to the pavilion, and seats herself. The sight paints a lovely scene.

Aileen, who's hiding and watching from a distance, grinds her teeth. *Milady! He called her "milady"! I'm so jealous… I want Master Claude to wait on me and call me milady, too!*

If only a knight like that were to treat me like a princess—Claw, or rather Claude, had made that maidenly dream a reality in grand style.

On his very first day as a guard, when lower-ranking consorts had shown veiled contempt for Roxane, Claw held them at sword's point and demanded an apology. On the second day, there had been another attack believed to be the work of the fiend dragon, but he'd beaten it back without trouble, protecting Roxane. On the third day, he'd knelt before Roxane and slipped her shoes onto her feet. On the fourth day, when Roxane had fallen and the holy king insisted on ignoring her, Claw swept her into his arms and tended to her— At this point, Roxane isn't "under observation." She is the principal consort who's come under the protection of a knight and the envy of all.

Why is Master Claude so needlessly perfect…?!

She's so jealous, jealous, jealous.

Out of frustration, Aileen digs her nails into the wall of the building. Beside her, a man wearing the same expression mutters, "Why did this happen?"

"It's because your face is weak…!"

"Is that really a word for describing faces?! No, we're supposed to be one of those handsome types, so there shouldn't be a problem."

"You're awfully confident for someone who doesn't have a charming personality or a dashing demeanor!"

"Enough! The longer we watch, the more we start to suspect it might be true…!" Baal is clutching at his chest, but it serves him right. At any rate, no one who's hiding in the shadows grinding his teeth could be considered dashing. Not by a long shot. "Why does this pain our heart so?"

"No doubt because you're being forced to see that you're in a completely different class as a man."

"Even if that's true, Roxane looks a little different as well. That can't be right."

"Women shine brighter depending on the man they're with. You didn't even know that? If Lady Roxane looked dim and hazy before now, it is most definitely your fault."

"What?!"

"If you think I'm lying, just take a look for yourself!"

In the pavilion where songbirds twitter, Roxane is drinking tea. Gently, Claude holds out a book to her. Roxane gives the smallest of gentle smiles and says something to him. She's probably thanking him.

Baal watches them in a daze. "...The woman smiles? We've never seen that before."

"I imagine you haven't...!"

And Claude is doing this in order to force him to see it. In other words, he's helping Aileen. She hasn't lost his love. She knows that.

But he doesn't have to go so far, does he?!

There's no way he needs to get that close. He doesn't have to be so kind. He doesn't need to cherish her like that. And why does he look so gentle!

"—Hmph! It's none of our concern. Why should we have to care about Roxane?" Baal turns his back and walks away. He's spoken coldly, but his footsteps are angry. Not only that, but since he isn't looking where he's going, he walks smack into a tree branch at face height and ends up writhing in agony.

If she's on his mind, that's progress. Aileen's sure of that. However...

"Consort Aileen. Did you need me for something?"

When she suddenly hears a familiar voice behind her, she almost shrieks. Claude has joined her in the shadows and is smiling down at her coldly. "I've felt your eyes on me for a while now, so I wondered."

"I-i-i-it's absolutely nothing, nothing at all!"

"I see. I thought you might be jealous."

"Wh-why would I ever be—?!"

She huffs, turning away with the greatest degree of indignation she can muster. Ignoring her display of ire, Claude bends forward, drinking in her face deeply. From the look in his eyes, he's clearly amused by all this. That only makes her angrier, so she turns her back on him once more. Claude promptly circles around until he's in front of her again. The two of them go on turning pointlessly in place like that, until on the third round, Aileen finally explodes.

"For goodness' sake, what on earth do you want?! You are on guard duty, are you not? Why don't you hurry and go back!"

"May I?"

"Well, of course..."

If she asked him not to, would he stay? For just a moment, her weak heart makes her steal a glance at Claude. Instantly, she regrets it.

"Don't look as if you're about to cry. I'll enjoy it so much I won't be able to exercise proper discretion." With an expression that couldn't possibly be more triumphant, Claude whispers sweetly in her ear. "There's no need to worry. I am devoted to my wife."

"I—I know that..."

"And so, if my beloved wife asks me for anything, I fear I'll grant her request without a second thought. It's a real problem."

It's all right to ask me to stay. He dangles that temptation right in front of her, and Aileen bites her lip. It's a love trap: If she reaches out for it, she'll end up drowning.

Claude caresses Aileen's face like it's the most precious thing, and there's a hint of poison in his smile. "You're stubborn. Granted, that's appealing in its own way."

"……"

"I love you, my Aileen."

Dropping one gentle kiss on her cheek, Claude spins on his heel. Naturally, he's returning to work. No doubt he'll go right back to perfectly protecting Roxane.

The sense of defeat is crushing, and she clenches her fists. *Calm down. This is work and nothing more; that's right. I won't be the sort of asinine woman who pressures Master Claude with questions like "Which is more important to you, your job or me?!"*

However, Claude is kind, and Roxane is a very lovely woman. *What will I do if something* does *happen?*

"Why must I feel the same as the holy king, Rachel…?!"

"Because you angered Master Claude."

Aileen persisted in following Claude and Roxane around, irritated all the while, but now night has fallen, and she's returned to her palace. As befits an outstanding lady-in-waiting, Rachel flatly tells her the truth. "When Master Claude came to rescue you, you should have avoided wording things in a way that gave no consideration to the pains he'd taken."

"…Perhaps so, but—"

"At times like these, the first one to get angry loses. Calm down, please."

"I know that as well! But in the extremely unlikely event that anything untoward were to occur, what then?!"

"...Frankly, since you've become another man's consort, I'm not sure you are in a position to say much of anything..."

"I am Master Claude's wife! I've done nothing to be ashamed of!"

"No doubt Master Claude would declare the same thing..."

"Oh, Lady Aileen! Is it true that the demon king has cast you asi—?"

Lilia manages to drive her into a fury the moment she opens the door. Aileen hurls a small fruit knife at her to silence her, then hauls her up by her bodice for good measure.

"Say one more word and I'll kill you."

"My, my, Lady Aileen, you're quite lively when you're truly angry."

"Enough of that. There's no time." Already tired of their bickering, Serena yanks the knife out of the door and locks it from the inside. Then she turns and smiles down at Aileen. "Congratulations on your divorce."

"Lady Aileen, control yourself! And you, Lady Serena: Simply make your report, please...!"

"Yes, yes, all right. We've become Lady Sahra's attendants without trouble. We haven't found out where the holy sword is, though."

When she hears that proper report, Aileen gets her breathing in order, shifting her thoughts to another track. "Lady Lilia, can you sense the holy sword's presence?"

"Of course I can't. Perhaps I could if it were in its prime, but the holy sword is practically broken." Lilia flops down onto a cushion on the rug. "I did hear something entertaining, though. They say we're getting a guest from Ellmeyer."

"...From Ellmeyer? I wonder if that's Isaac."

"No matter who it is, it must be a trap set by the demon king. And come to think of it, I wonder why the kingdom's citizens haven't discovered him yet. Are they stupid? Oh, it could be a game spec—"

"Thank you for your report, Lady Lilia. Here, have an apple."

She shoves a whole apple at Lilia, successfully shutting her up.

"What about you, Serena? Did you meet Auguste?"

"Yes, we met. Has he lost his manhood?"

"...Can you please be a little more concerned with anything else? Poor Auguste. He came all this way because he was worried about you, you know."

"Worried? I heard he lost to that general. *I'm* worried he may hold me back."

"You really show him no mercy, do you...?"

"Oh, that's right, Lady Aileen. It sounds as though an envoy from the Queendom of Hausel arrived just after the fiend dragon's revival and stayed here as Lady Sahra's visitors. They've secretly been in contact with Ares ever since."

After finishing the apple, Lilia mentions something crucial with shocking nonchalance.

"—The Queendom of Hausel and General Ares?"

"That nation fancies itself the organizing body behind all women with holy power, so it's only natural that they'd concern themselves with the Daughter of God. And since they're mediating between Ashmael and Ellmeyer, it makes sense, but still rather suspicious."

"...Yes, it is."

"Lady Aileen, you'll have to be careful. The envoys from the Queendom are bound to recognize the demon king." Aileen gives her a sharp look, and Lilia smiles as if she's terribly entertained. "There's one other thing that concerns me. Do you think the fiend dragon is really with the holy king?"

"...What are you trying to say?"

In the game, that would have been the case, but Aileen hasn't checked. Lilia tilts her head sweetly. "Well, you know, it sounds as if the fiend dragon only ever appears near the holy king or the harem."

That had been true in the game as well. However, it was because the game had been presented from Sahra's perspective. There was no need for reality to follow suit.

"It's almost as if someone is manipulating the fiend dragon using demon snuff and making it attack those places exclusively, don't you think?"

A terribly sensible hypothesis. *Tsk*ing in irritation, Aileen gets to her feet. "Rachel, I'm going to the holy king. Get ready."

"What? —Um, at this hour, that may not be wise. Particularly if Master Claude catches wind of it."

"There's no time. I need to see whether the fiend dragon really is tied to the holy king."

At night, the dragon's presence will be stronger. Lilia raises a pointed chuckle, rising to her feet as well. "If I learn anything, I'll come and report. Serena, let us return."

"Lady Lilia, you know something, don't you?"

Lilia makes a show of opening her eyes wide and smiles. "Goodness, Lady Aileen. Don't make me repeat myself. I'm on your side this time."

"Could it be that you're intentionally trying to get the fiend dragon to possess someone?"

Lilia stares at her. Unlike a moment ago, her emotion is real.

As a rule, the fiend dragon targets Baal. By using the body of someone who possesses strong holy power, it gains strength that transcends both good and evil. However, in reality, not only has the Daughter of God awakened, but Aileen and the others are present. Under the circumstances, there's no guarantee that the dragon will target the same person.

"Hee-hee, hee-hee-hee." Lilia laughs, hiding her face.

Aileen takes a step forward. "Enough of that. Answer me. Depending on what you say—"

"There's no need to worry. I only have a hunch about who the dragon will go to in the end."

"...You *what*?"

"If you think about it, you'll see it, too. But that's exactly why I'm not worried. It could never win against the power of love, after all. Besides, the fiend dragon doesn't matter. And since we're already on the subject, I don't care about that trifling Daughter of God, either."

Lilia takes a step closer, peering up into Aileen's face. "I am enjoying myself, though. Do your best, Lady Aileen. I'm sure the action will speed up soon, as the end draws near."

Still irritated, Aileen kicks the door open. As she barges in, Baal blinks at her. He's already in bed, reclining against a generous stack of pillows. "If you're here to seduce us, make a more alluring entrance."

"No one is wooing anyone. I simply need to talk."

"What happened to the guards?"

"I put them to sleep. I can't have anyone starting odd rumors."

"How?"

"My lady-in-waiting is extremely well prepared."

Luc must have given her the substance. Rachel had taken some powder out of an inner pocket and set it alight, and the guards stationed outside the holy king's bedchamber had been asleep in moments.

"Well, that's incredibly pathetic."

"...If you'd had a few more people, it wouldn't have been this easy," she says, insinuating that there aren't enough guards protecting the royal bedchamber.

Baal gives a wry smile. "There's no telling when the fiend dragon may appear. No one would guard this place willingly."

"So the fiend dragon *appears.*"

"That's right. Just as the rumors say. Every night, it comes just as we're settling down to sleep."

Which means that, unlike the game, the fiend dragon isn't *inside* Baal.

I should have made sure of it first thing. It's all because I carelessly became this man's consort; it made me wary of approaching him...!

The fact she hadn't sensed the fiend dragon's presence in Baal wasn't because it had yet to overtake him. It never possessed him in the first place.

"Would you tell me about when the fiend dragon resurrected?"

"Why would you ask about that?"

"So that I may locate the dragon," Aileen answers immediately.

Baal props his chin on one hand, forcing a smile. "Unfortunately, it isn't much of a story. It happened about three months ago, right after Sahra brought the holy sword back from the sanctuary. Even though it was day, the world went dark, and a black dragon—the fiend dragon—raced up into the sky."

"The dragon appeared outside? It didn't possess anyone?"

She doesn't recall anything so flashy happening in the game. Why would the fiend dragon have left the demon realm and— As she thinks this, the words *three months ago* hit Aileen like a sack of bricks.

Was it because Master Claude lost his memories…?!

The demon king's control had relaxed. That was why the dragon had left the demon realm without Claude's permission.

"A-and then what happened?"

"It struck our barrier and turned into black rain. However, Sahra's prayer called the sun. To be more accurate, it was the holy sword she held aloft that did it."

"The holy sword… And what happened to the sword?"

"We can't tell you any more than that, Crown Princess of Ellmeyer."

Naturally, that reply leaves her at a loss, but she promptly regroups. "I am your ally. At least when it comes to avoiding needless war."

"Our ally, you say? Sit here, then." Baal lightly pats the side of the bed next to him.

True, standing isn't conducive to clandestine conversations. Without suspecting anything, Aileen seats herself—and then her world spins until she's facing up.

"You're tragically short on caution."

He says the words as if he feels them keenly, even though he's the one who pushed her down.

She scowls at him. "Don't toy with me. Go on with what you were saying."

"Fiend dragon, fiend dragon. We're tired of that subject. While we're at it, we're also love-starved. Because of the dragon, we can't call anyone to our bed. Keep us company."

"That isn't even funny! I am Master Claude's wife!"

"Even though you're a virgin?"

She stiffens, and then her lips begin to tremble. She feels her cheeks grow hot. *Wha, wha-wha-wha-wha, wha...!*

Looking as if everything's going his way, Baal pushes his face right up to hers and grins. "We can tell. You don't have the scent of a woman who's been fully immersed in love."

"I—I am loved!"

"Can you hold your head high and say that? You're just a wife on paper."

She doesn't have a good counterargument: It's true she is a wife in name only. That thought leads straight to an idea she's been trying to avoid, like a sore spot.

Why, Master Claude? What am I lacking? Don't tell me you regret making me your wife...

Do as you please. His words echo coldly in her mind. Now, of all times...

"...Well. Apparently you can look adorable after all." Baal's fingers touch her chin.

She glares straight at his face. "Don't talk nonsense. I'm well aware that I am not an adorable woman."

"No, you *are* adorable."

Adorable. If she's adorable, then why...? "...Am I truly?" She searches Baal's eyes for the answer.

Baal gives a meltingly gentle smile. "Yes. You are. There is absolutely nothing wrong with you."

It's probably because he has a lot of practice at this sort of thing. His words go straight to Aileen's heart.

The flame of the candle beside the bed flickers, and the lengthened shadows cast by man and woman slowly melt together.

"There's no need to worry. We'll make you forget that sorry excuse for a man. On the other side of a night without end— Bwuff?!!"

The sound of a sharp slap echoes in the bedchamber.

Baal wobbles, then topples over to the side after getting clapped in the face.

"I am adorable… In that case…"

With her hand still raised from the slap, Aileen murmurs earnestly, "In that case— Could something be physically wrong with Master Claude ?!" At this entirely unexpected development, Aileen bolts up, clutching at her neckline. "How can this be…? Good heavens. I am Master Claude's wife, and yet I tried to tempt him without even noticing—! Oh, I must have caused him such trouble. But, I mean, with that face, you'd never dream there was a problem… In fact, you'd think it was his forte!"

"W… Woman… How could you ruin the mood like that…?!"

"If he'd confided in me, I could have attempted any number of… No, but I hear that men are delicate. Perhaps Master Claude was too embarrassed to say. Oh… Whatever shall I do?"

"Hey, are you listening?!"

"First, I'll consult with Luc and Quartz and commission a remedy… But the issue may be emotional. That's right, that face— Who was it?! Which vixen traumatized my dear Master Claude?! No, more than that, what I really need is that secret art. If I had that, Master Claude would be able to relax and entrust himself to me…!"

"—You…" Apparently weary of yelling, Baal flops over sideways, burying his face in a pillow. "We've begun to sympathize with the demon king…"

"Sympathize?! He may be slightly dysfunctional below the belt, but I won't forgive you if you insult Master Claude."

"You're doing a perfectly fine job of that all by yourself. Why, oh why do none of our loves ever go well?"

"I have no idea why you'd suddenly bring that up, but the answer is obvious: It's because you love the wrong people."

Lowering her feet to the floor, she stands. Baal is lying faceup on the bed, and she looks down on him. "Thinking you're fine as long as the other is happy is simply irresponsible. In love, you decide that you will bear the responsibility for making your beloved happy, no matter how tiresome or painful it is."

"Duty... That's incredibly unromantic."

"You must know love and romance can't exist without responsibility."

A man of his rank in particular, who bears the country and its people on his shoulders, cannot love irresponsibly.

Even if love was something one fell into despite that understanding.

"You are king, so love a woman who possesses proper rank, education, and supporters, and who doesn't belong to another man."

"There is no such woman."

"I believe you're simply not looking for her hard enough."

He gives no answer. This man really is tiresome. As she's feeling mildly disgusted, Baal gets to his feet. "You won't be spending the night here, we assume? We'll escort you back. Be grateful to us."

"Well done. That's a passable first step toward becoming a fine man. However, the way you phrased it—"

"No nitpicking... You are our ally, aren't you?"

"Yes, that's right. You may count on me."

When she throws her chest out proudly, Baal narrows his eyes and mutters something rude: "The demon king has our sympathies."

Desert nights are cold. Even so, her footsteps have slowed of their own accord.

"Then even though you can teleport, you've never sojourned in another country?"

"Right. There are many who worry that if the holy king leaves the country, the sacred barrier may vanish. It won't, but the kingdom's closed off anyway, and we haven't had any reason to stay in another land. What about you?"

"When I was small, I traveled to several of the major nations! My father tossed me and one of my older brothers into the castle town of each without a penny, saying it would be a good learning experience. He told us we had to devise our own means of getting home."

"—Hang on a minute. How did that work out?!"

Baal is aghast. It amuses her, and she laughs. "I always had a brother with me, so it wasn't that trying. My third brother promptly negotiated with the owner of a passenger ship and worked as an interpreter in exchange for our passage back to Ellmeyer. My second brother earned money by working as a bodyguard and took me home by train. With my eldest brother... The next thing I knew, someone had come to pick us up..."

"What happened with him?"

"I don't know. It was fun, though. I got to learn words from all sorts of countries and really feel the differences between our cultures. Simply staying in a foreign country for a few days can be surprisingly instructive."

To that end, that father of hers had given his young sons and daughter the best possible education— He certainly hadn't done it merely to entertain himself, or so Aileen would like to believe.

"...You really were raised to become empress, weren't you?"

"Yes. I was even engaged to the crown prince."

"The second prince, the one they say was ousted by the demon king? That was quite a wasteful thing he did."

"If you think so, then take care you don't do the same."

Baal frowns, irked. "Don't tell us you've been talking about Roxane. Don't recommend her to us. It's unpleasant."

"Why?"

"We can't trust her. There's no telling when she may betray us. After all, she loves Ares."

Is he serious? Rather appalled, Aileen responds with a question of her own. "Then why did you make her your principal consort? Was it for Lady Sahra's sake?"

"That, too, but...Ares raised a commotion about executing her. The things Roxane had done could only be considered harassment at worst. Executing her would have been going too far, especially when Sahra was declared innocent and set free even after becoming Ares's lover while she was a harem attendant. If we'd done as Ares wanted, we would have incurred the wrath of the house of Fusca." Impassively, Baal continues; it's only at times like these that he possesses the face of a ruler. "When we asked Ares if he would offer Roxane in exchange for letting Sahra leave the harem and marry, he handed over his betrothed readily. Even though it would have been rather satisfying to us if he'd been a little reluctant."

"......"

"However, the biggest reason we made her our principal consort was because we pitied her. When she was spiteful to Sahra in petty ways, when she brandished sound arguments that no one bothered to hear out, when she tried to catch Ares's attention, she was too wretched to bear looking at."

"—Because, in truth, you also wanted to use your authority to eliminate General Ares and take Lady Sahra for yourself?"

Baal dons a wry smile, but he doesn't deny it. "And so we let her choose whether she would become our principal consort. Well, one hardly needs to wait for the answer to a question like that."

"...And Lady Roxane accepted?"

"Of course she did. What woman would refuse a position like principal consort? Aside from Sahra, we've never seen... No, you would refuse it as well, wouldn't you?"

Baal laughs weakly, then peers up at the twinkling stars. "However, even now, she picks quarrels with Ares and Sahra. She may still dream that she can steal Ares back. It's irritating, and we can't stand it."

"Because it feels like looking at yourself? Or is it because she won't look at you, instead of General Ares?"

"That's..." As if the idea's never occurred to him before, Baal's eyes wander uneasily. His gaze skims over the galleries of the dark harem—and then, abruptly, it stops.

"Master Baal?"

"Apparently our sympathy was unnecessary... We really have no luck with women."

The next thing she knows, Baal has begun to walk. When she sees where he's going, her eyes widen.

The Sun Palace is built to run parallel to this corridor, and in its passageway…

Lady Roxane and Master Claude…?!

Roxane has peeked out of her bedroom. She opens the door, and Claude enters. Then the door swings closed, hiding the interior, although it hasn't shut entirely.

"No… Master Baal, wait."

"She's finally shown her true colors. Adultery. If Ares won't do, she'll try for the demon king? She's constantly making a mockery of us."

"We don't know for certain that's what—"

"Your husband has betrayed you, too. Or maybe it's only natural for the demon king to be immoral."

There is a path, but it's a circuitous one, and Baal doesn't take it. With a scornful smile, he tromps right through the garden between the gallery and the palace. He's clearly lost his head.

Why must this happen now…? I have to stop him!

He still isn't conscious of the reason Roxane's smile irritates him. He's only just managed to tear his attention away from Sahra. No man in that situation would act reasonably.

"—Roxane!"

Bursting through the door, Baal strides in, bellowing. Then he gasps. Aileen, who's followed him, also peeks inside, and her eyes widen.

The two of them aren't in bed. However, they are holding hands.

To be accurate, Roxane is seated, holding a quill pen, and Claude is standing behind her, leaning over her shoulder and covering her hand with his own. In a corner of her mind, Aileen understands he's helping her write something, but under the circumstances, no doubt that will sound like nothing more than a weak excuse.

"What are you doing?"

Especially because the moment Baal notices, Roxane hides her hand and what she's writing. She may as well have confessed she's been doing something worth hiding.

"...Nothing. He was simply teaching me how to write letters. Never mind that; did you need something? It's very late."

"Oh, we happened to be passing by when we saw our principal consort inviting a man into her chambers."

"I see."

Roxane is probably responding the way she always does. However, Baal is not. Granted, that could be considered progress, but...

"You seem to be on very friendly terms with your guard. How pleasant for you."

"Your Majesty, it was you and General Ares who decided that he should guard me. I—"

"—*The Formation and Mechanism of Magic Circles*? What's this? Planning to curse us to death and elope?" Picking a book up from the table, Baal looks taken aback. "After we made you our principal consort. How capricious."

"......"

Roxane presses her lips together, falling silent. This seems to irritate Baal further. "If there's something you want to say, out with it."

"...No..."

"Out with it!"

"Stop this—"

"The principal consort is frightened."

Baal starts to slam the book down onto the table, but before Aileen can stop him, Claude has caught it. "If you're going to talk, perhaps you should calm down first."

Baal's eyes narrow. He's no longer looking at Roxane. "You would gainsay the king, you wretch of a guard? Shall we have you beheaded for adultery along with Roxane?"

"That would be a problem. I have a wife who's very dear to me."

Aileen has been watching the scene play out anxiously, but at that, her eyebrows twitch.

Baal gives a mocking laugh. "A wife? You have no wife. You must be dreaming."

"No, she exists. A very adorable, lovable, precious wife who's mine and mine alone."

At any other time, that line would have made Aileen writhe with embarrassment. In this particular moment, however, it irks her mightily.

"She would never disregard what her husband says, of course. She'd never become another man's consort. And she certainly wouldn't be alone with him this late at night. She's a virtuous wife, and she's waiting quietly for my return."

He says all this without a blush, and Aileen clenches her fists. *How dare he when he's alone with another woman in her room late at night…!*

Baal grimaces. Glancing at Aileen, he mutters. "…Uh, are you sure that wife isn't a figment of your imagination?"

"No, she wouldn't say anything selfish like 'I don't love you,' after suddenly proposing to me out of nowhere. She wouldn't surround herself with men and say it's for work, and she wouldn't dress as a boy and acquire more lackeys. She wouldn't sleep like the dead on our first night together, either. I have a wife who treasures me and always puts me first."

"That's…uh… I see you've had your share of troubles."

The sympathy in Baal's voice makes something inside Aileen snap. "My, what a marvelous wife! By the way, where is she now?"

"I really couldn't say."

Her husband feigns ignorance, although he's looking right at her. Aileen gives a pointed sigh. "I have something similar: A husband whose face alone is perfect."

"…His face…alone?"

"He's a lot of trouble. One little comment from me, and he makes it rain. Everyone around him indulges him constantly, and if I weren't hard on him, I believe he'd be spoiled rotten."

"……"

"Why, the other day, he selfishly developed amnesia and babbled nonsense about breaking off our engagement. I can't even tell you how difficult it made things for me."

"—The amnesia was beyond my control."

"My situation was unavoidable as well."

As quiet sparks fly between them, Baal takes an involuntary step back. Roxane looks bewildered as well, so Aileen smiles at her. "Lady Roxane. Don't you feel that married couples must say what they wish to say, precisely because they are married?"

"……"

"Yes, the ability to listen is vital."

"I still have a few choice things left to say."

For now, she picks up a nearby chair. Baal looks oddly anxious. "H-hey, Aileen. Put the chair down."

"P-please calm yourselves, both of you." Even Roxane is flustered, poised to dodge.

Claude responds gently, "There's no need to worry. This is adorable."

"My, how kind. Hee-hee-hee. Men with composure are splendid, aren't they? I envy your wife."

"And I envy the husband you vilify. It's proof that he's loved."

"Hee-hee-hee-hee-hee-hee, my goodness, how dare you—!" She brings the chair down mercilessly. However, he cuts it apart, moving so rapidly she doesn't even see it happen.

*Tsk*ing, Aileen picks up a side table, hurling it with all her might. Claude dodges it very casually. The table strikes the wall and smashes, making an incredible racket.

"My, my, how strong you are. What a reliable husband! Your wife must feel very safe."

"Hey— Whoa, Aileen, no, wait!"

Snatching the sword from Baal's waist, she slashes at Claude. Claude parries without raising an eyebrow. "Actually, no. My wife is stubborn and won't rely on me."

"Isn't that at least partially your fault?!"

"No. The problem lies with you."

This time, Aileen really snaps. She sends a shelf flying, throwing Claude off-balance, and strikes at him from the side. "I will not apologize!!"

"Of course not. If you're going to whine because I'm showing a little kindness to another woman, then I wish you'd avoid constantly miring yourself in trouble in the first place."

Every time their blades clash, silver dishes roll around, and mirrors fall to the floor and shatter.

Baal is clutching his head; he's retreated to a corner so he won't get dragged in. "Y-you'd start a domestic spat in a place like this...?!"

"M-Master Baal. We must stop them. The national treasure, over there—"

Roxane is pointing at an incense burner, an item presented to the principal consort. Said to be made of the same material as the holy sword, it's a treasure in which evil-quelling incense is burned. Unlike the holy sword, it has no function beyond burning incense, but even so, it has existed since the nation's founding. The vibrations from the sword strikes and the wind pressure have it teetering on its pedestal.

"All this, merely because I became another man's consort?! Master Claude, with that face, you must have an illegitimate child somewhere!"

"Why is that twisted jealousy the only kind you're capable of?"

"I'm so very sorry I'm not adorable!"

"I didn't say th—"

"Wait, you two! Stop!"

The incense burner falls from its pedestal.

Baal hastily reaches for it, but it slips through his grasp. Roxane throws herself onto the floor in a desperate attempt to catch it, but it skims past the tips of her nails—and with a loud crash, the national treasure of the Kingdom of Ashmael smashes right in front of the king and his wife.

"How are you going to make up for this?!"

Claude has lowered himself onto the ground alongside Aileen.

He looks dubious at Baal's furious yell. "'How'? You can't unbreak an object, not usually."

"You destroy a national treasure, and that's all you have to say...?!"

"Everything physical must break someday, you know."

"So you'd say the same thing if one of Ellmeyer's national treasures were broken?"

His voice is low and threatening, and it makes Aileen feel rather uncomfortable.

Claude sighs wearily. "This wouldn't have happened if you'd behaved."

"...You're saying it's my fault?"

"No, I'm not saying that. You are the one who struck first, though."

"Goodness... Master Claude, you're completely unrepentant, aren't you?"

"What should I have to repent of?"

Aileen has set the sword on the floor, but now she picks it up again. Wordlessly, Claude rests a hand on his own hilt.

They begin crossing the floor—although there's really no place to walk, covered as it is with scattered shards of glass, pottery, and what remains of a national treasure. Baal gets between them and cries. "Enough of this! You never learn!"

"—It's finished," Roxane says. She's been writing something at a table whose broken legs have made it slant toward the ground. She rises, displaying a paper to Aileen and Claude.

Everyone looks at it. It's a bill for an amount featuring a very long row of zeros.

"Compensation for damages. Pay it, if you would."

"This much?!"

"It was a national treasure, you know."

"This much... And it's all your fault, Master Claude!"

"No, it's yours."

"If you feel you can't pay it, you may cancel it out by waiving the compensation we owe the crown princess for the trouble we've caused her."

Although Aileen has been glaring at Claude, Roxane's words make her blink.

Baal is wearing the same expression. "...Roxane, you knew?"

"I noticed only recently," Roxane says impassively. "It's just that, when the demon king—His Highness the crown prince of Ellmeyer—arrived, I suspected that might be why." Retrieving the bill, she tears it up. "Now neither of our nations has committed any transgressions. Will that do?"

"Yes. That's more than acceptable." Impressed, Aileen nods.

"Wait," Baal stops her. "We haven't agreed to this. Don't just settle it on your own."

"I'm not satisfied, either. You kidnapped my wife and made her your consort."

"Then you two talk amongst yourselves, over there." Dismissing their husbands with a word, Roxane turns back to Aileen. "First, to avert any misunderstandings, I will tell you: I invited Master Claude into my rooms so that he could teach me how to draw this magic circle." She holds out a book and the paper she'd been drawing on earlier. The book contains a patently ominous design. However, the attempted copy on the paper is as shakily executed as a child's drawing.

Baal and Aileen both look at Roxane. Her cheeks flush, and she clears her throat. "...I—I have no talent for art."

"I couldn't just stand by and watch. She was making a copy, and yet somehow ended up with something completely different." Claude has casually said something quite mean.

Aileen's shoulders slump. "I understand your reasons and the circumstances... But why were you drawing a magic circle?"

"Since we had the opportunity, I thought I would have the demon king take the fiend dragon home with him."

"What, as if it were a souvenir?!"

Through her shock, Aileen realizes the idea had merit. *That's right. This magic circle was in the game as well. It's the one Roxane used to summon the dragon...!* She wonders idly whether the game version of Roxane had any artistic talent.

"Initially, I simply assumed the demon king had come to retrieve the dragon. I wasn't certain whether he wanted to stop its rampage or simply cover it up, but I thought either would be fine. However, when I spoke with him, it turned out he didn't know even where the fiend dragon was..."

"And so you drew a magic circle to summon it...?"

"Yes. If I managed to produce the dragon, he agreed to remove it for us."

"Why would you do a thing like that?!" Baal yells, as if he can't help himself.

Roxane is calm and collected. "You feel that fighting Imperial Ellmeyer would be a poor move, and it would be. Our nation must not be used by the Queendom of Hausel in a proxy war."

"...How did you pick up on that? Who told you?!"

"No one. If anyone considers the intent of the orders you've been issuing, it's patently obvious. In any case, if you meant to fight, you would have declared war long ago. However, you postponed the restoration of the holy sword, and you've been conducting yourself so as not to provoke Master Ares and the others unnecessarily. I can tell by looking at you… But even though I knew, all I could do was find the women the Queendom had sent here to incite war and expel them from the harem…"

"……"

Baal starts to say something, then stops. No doubt he can't find the words.

"Either way, unless we do something about the dragon, dissatisfaction with your refusal to fight will continue to build. That is why I asked him to retrieve the demon, but…"

Roxane glances at Claude, and he finishes the sentence for her. "It looks as if the fiend dragon has gotten lost."

"Lost?"

"The poor child has never been outside before," Claude says tenderly, as if he's talking about a hopeless child. "In a rush of excitement, the dragon flew off. However, after ramming into the barrier and losing its power, the poor thing's lost and all alone. I don't think the dragon can return to the demon realm without help."

"…Wait a minute. You're talking about the fiend dragon?"

"Yes."

"And you aren't trying to deceive us?"

"Why would I need to do such a thing?"

Planting both hands on the floor, Baal writhes in agony. Out of nowhere, the demon that threatens his kingdom has been reduced to a lost child who can't get home. Aileen understands his feelings.

"No— Wait, we refuse to be tricked. It appears to us, every night. That malevolence, that ominous air. It can't possibly just be lost."

"Are you sure that isn't someone else's fiend dragon? Mine wouldn't do that."

"You can't be serious! They're *all* yours!"

"When you put it that way, you have a point… I think the child's probably irritable. The dragon's been imprisoned, after all."

"'Imprisoned'?" Aileen asks.

"Yes." Claude nods. "I call, but there's no answer. If I were beyond this country's borders, I'd understand: the sacred barrier would naturally interfere. However, we're both inside the barrier now. The fact that we haven't met yet is proof that the dragon is locked up somewhere."

"You can't use magic here. Isn't that why?"

"No. Even without magic or my memories, I am the demon king."

That's right. Even when Claude had lost his memories and his magic, if he'd wished for something, the demons obeyed.

Of course. That's why Lady Lilia— Gracious, even Serena said it!

It's obvious where the fiend dragon would go: to Claude. There's no reason to manipulate people and attack them. The dragon was attacking because of the machinations of a human—someone using demon snuff!

"Oh, but wait, the supply of demon snuff is controlled by the church…and they don't get along with the Kingdom of Ashmael."

"However, the church and the Queendom of Hausel get along very well," Claude says, as if he's read Aileen's thoughts. When she turns around, their eyes meet. "In short, it's a trap. It probably began back when you boarded that ship."

"What…?"

"The Queendom of Hausel is a nominally pacifist nation. Even if they're dealing with the demon king, declaring war of their own accord would go against their principles. As a result, when Ashmael came to them with a request for mediation, they began trying to steer them into a proxy war. They sent women who have sacred power to the harem as personnel to fight the fiend dragon, then had them stir up support for war among the populace, loudly claiming it's a fight they could win. Holy King, as a condition of Hausel's mediation, I imagine you were told to accept the women who were fleeing to the Queendom on that ship into your harem. That's why you seized the entire vessel. Am I wrong?"

"We don't have to answer that."

"And this time, the crown princess of Ellmeyer was on the ship. The Queendom of Hausel orchestrated that, most likely without your knowledge or that of the general, in order to sow the seeds of conflict. If it came down to it, they planned to pin everything on Ashmael and abandon you. Either that, or to say Imperial Ellmeyer had slipped her in as a spy."

Baal doesn't answer. Leaning back against the wall, Claude shrugs. "Well, don't worry. If I'm here, they're sure to release the fiend dragon. They'll want to make Ashmael and Ellmeyer fight each other—to make the holy king slay the demon king. Or else to run me through with the holy sword."

"—If you knew that, then why did you come?!" Aileen shouts at him. Claude has spoken about the very apparent danger to his own life as if it were no great concern.

Aileen rises to her feet. Gazing at her, Claude answers mildly, "If I didn't, the fiend dragon would be killed the moment an incident occurred in this kingdom… And that would become yet another convenient justification to act against us."

His conclusion could not be more correct. At the very least, it's an answer Aileen couldn't have produced, desperate as she is to protect Claude and only Claude.

This man is a true king. And Aileen is his wife.

She takes an unsteady step forward. Then, giving in to her impulse, she grabs Claude's shirt and pulls him toward her.

She knows of no other way to express her emotions.

"……!"

Claude's wide, red eyes. The sensation of their lips colliding.

They melt violently, yet more softly and sweetly than anything.

"—I am still very cross with you." She glares at Claude's face, which is so close to hers she can clearly make out the tips of his eyelashes as he blinks. It's partly an attempt to hide her embarrassment. "That said! I am your wife. Let me help you!"

As Aileen gets fired up, Claude's eyes widen again. "Help…? You knew…?"

"Please don't say a word, Master Claude. I understand everything!"

"I see… I suppose it's impossible to hide things from one's wife. It's safe here, though. I'm getting by without losing control."

"L-losing control, hmm? So you do, erm, lose control… U-um, in cases like that, what should I do…?"

She has no experience with this sort of thing, after all. Her spirit may be willing, but she's frightened, and she fidgets uncomfortably.

Claude is endlessly gentle. "It's all right. If there's something I'd like you to handle, I'll ask. Please don't do anything reckless."

"Master Claude… A-all right. I'll show you I'm serious; I'll accept everything…!"

"What is this farce? And what's more, we have an intense hunch that you two aren't on the same page."

"I don't really understand what's going on, but I share your hunch, Master Baal."

Remembering that Baal and Roxane are present, Aileen comes to her senses. This is no time for her and Claude to deepen their mutual understanding.

"For the moment, let's consider what we're going to do about this predicament. We may have our own separate circumstances, but it would be irritating to fight simply because the Queendom of Hausel desires it. Don't you agree?"

"We refuse. We don't like his smug face."

"And I'd prefer not to cooperate with the sort of man who tries to steal another's wife."

"Even now, you two are still— Both of you! Who do you think you are?!"

"We are the holy king."

"And I'm the demon king."

They're in sync only where they don't need to be. Feeling a headache coming on, Aileen calls for help. "Lady Roxane, say something, please!"

"Someone's coming."

In a lovely gesture that makes her look like a model noblewoman, Roxane gets to her feet. Aileen checks the clock. It isn't yet dawn. However, she can hear several sets of rough, hurried footsteps. The occasional metallic clinks are the unmistakable sounds of swinging swords. This seems far too ostentatious for a normal visit to the principal consort's bedchamber.

Claude, who's been quietly scanning the area, murmurs, "...They've surrounded the Sun Palace."

"What?" asks Baal. "What's the meaning of this—Roxane?"

Roxane whirls around and gropes under the bed. There's a

clunk as something falls into place, and then the floor opens to reveal a stairway, leading underground.

"This way, Master Baal. If you take this secret passage, you'll emerge near the palace."

"We are the king. You're telling us to run? Why?"

"They may have learned about Master Claw— I mean, Master Claude. If they discover that you are in communication with Ellmeyer now, it may give rise to unnecessary suspicions, such as the idea that you intend to betray the nation. Public opinion favors General Ares and Lady Sahra, who are calling for the demon king's subjugation."

Dexterously, Roxane fastens the door's inner lock, drops the bar into place, and begins moving furniture. "If they've come here, there's no doubt they're planning to find incriminating evidence. However, fortunately, our relationship couldn't be colder. If you cut me off, they won't be able to drive you from the throne just yet."

"You…"

"No doubt they suspect me of summoning the fiend dragon. My jealousy of Lady Sahra was so great that I tried to borrow the dragon's power and kill her. That's probably what this is about. After all, *that is how they planned it.*"

"Roxane. Are you there?" There's a subdued knock on the door. The voice belongs to Ares.

Baal is standing there in a daze. Aileen grabs his arm and pulls him toward the stairs that lead underground. Stumbling, Baal starts down. Then he turns back. "Roxane, why?"

"Lady Sahra's power is splendid, and it's likely that General Ares is correct. However, you are the one who is best suited to be king. We must not let civil war break out."

"But... But you and Ares..."

In his bewilderment, her husband lets a stray thought slip out. Roxane acknowledges it unwaveringly, her face still expressionless. "I did admire him. I believed I was loved, and yes, I harassed Sahra in an attempt to keep her from taking him. It was the ugly, disgraceful act of a jealous woman. But I—"

"Roxane! I know you're in there. Open up."

Behind her, Ares bangs on the door. Roxane offers a thin smile. "I was passed on to someone else, with no regard for my feelings or position, as if I were an object."

"Isn't the key here yet? Hurry up!"

"He considered it a matter of course. He didn't ask me my thoughts on the matter. He gave me no choice. He sneered at me, telling me I was fortunate."

"I can hear voices. She has to be in there."

"The thought that I'd been in love with a man like that filled me with despair."

"—But in that case, we aren't much different. We thought making you our principal consort would keep you quiet."

"No." Roxane shakes her head. "You asked me whether I would be your principal consort. I know you were confident I wouldn't refuse. Still, you did ask... And so, when I agreed, I did so of my own free will."

Slowly, Roxane puts a hand to Baal's cheek. Baal's eyes widen, stunned, and he lets her do as she pleases.

There's no love there. Their romance hasn't even begun yet.

However, whatever she's trying to grasp with that hand exists—it's there.

"I thought I'd rather die than remain the fiancée of a man like that, and I chose you of my own accord."

Her determination to crawl up from the bottom is the same feeling Aileen once experienced.

"That is why I am your principal consort— Now go, please. You mustn't show me mercy. As things stand, you've done no wrong. Thank you for all you did for me."

"Roxane."

"I'm sorry I don't have time to love you."

Roxane shoves Baal's shoulders hard. He falls down into the space below, but the sound is camouflaged by the pounding on the door.

"Lady Aileen, Master Claude, you hurry as well. I won't ask you to save me. Please escape to a place that has no connection to any of this. That's all I ask."

Ashmael's dignified principal consort raises her head, straightening up.

Baal begins to shout something, but Aileen covers his mouth. Above their heads, the door slowly closes, blocking out the light.

"Come, let us move quickly!"

"—Wait, what's going to happen to Roxane?!"

"Lady Roxane is innocent, which means whatever proof General Ares produces is falsified. For now, a tactical retreat is in order; we'll use this chance to find out who's behind everything!"

A principal consort in name only, respected by none, treated coldly by all, and suspected of summoning the fiend dragon. No one will protect her. Using that fact as her weapon, she's transformed herself into a decoy.

"I won't allow you to squander Lady Roxane's feelings. If you do, I'll take her away from this country myself!"

"Aileen."

"You should conceal yourself quickly as well, Master Claude. I imagine the palace isn't safe anymore. Once you're outside—"

"You don't have to put on a brave front." In the darkness, he gently traces her lip; she's bitten it so hard there's a little blood on it. "I should always be the only one who makes you cry."

"Is this any time to say that, Master Clau—?"

He puts an arm around her waist, pulling her close, and covers her lips with his own. She knows this because it feels the same as the kiss they exchanged a moment ago—or so she thinks, but then an unfamiliar sensation slips into her mouth.

"Nn, nnuh?!"

When her eyelids open, she can just make out a pair of red eyes in the shadows.

So intense they seem to see through everything.

"They're more likely to take the bait if a man believed to be the demon king is with her."

Her head is reeling; he seems to have stolen her very breath. He pushes her toward Baal. "I'll loan her to you. As collateral, I'll hold on to your consort."

"...Master Claude...?"

"This is a good opportunity. Aileen, you should see how I feel once in a while."

Light streams in from overhead again, dazzling her eyes—and then the bed falls onto the hatch, blocking it.

"Wha—? You're...!"

"Unhand that woman."

"Don't shrink back, surround them! Whatever you do, don't let Roxane escape!"

Clashing swords, angry shouts, the sound of many feet. Dazed, Aileen stares at the path of retreat Claude has cut off. Clenching her fists, she speaks quietly over her shoulder to Baal. "We're going. If you complain any more, I'll end you personally."

Her eyes have begun to adjust to the darkness, and she sees Baal get to his feet. "...Right. We won't let Ares do as he pleases any longer."

Baal grips Aileen's hand. Sacred power flows into her.

It's the same. Power that's meant to protect.

"We have the holy sword. We can win." He wouldn't have told her that if he didn't trust her. Aileen nods firmly as he continues. "Work with us, in order to rescue your husband."

"Yes. In order to save your wife."

Before she knows it, they're back in Baal's quiet bedchamber.

Less than an hour later, they receive word that General Ares has arrested Roxane, the principal consort, and her guard Claw for the crimes of adultery and summoning the fiend dragon.

Slowly, Lilia opens her eyes.

The clock tower that marks time in the harem is located at the very center of the barrier. Sacred power flows in the night wind. She's seen something very, very good, and her lips curve in satisfaction. However, the two holding her hands—the ones she's just shown that scene—don't seem to share her feelings.

"Lady Aileen..."

"Ares is absolute scum... Who ties up their ex-fiancée like that?!"

"What will become of Lady Roxane and Master Claude?"

"Shh, you two. You mustn't. You have to pretend you don't know. Lady Roxane was in communication with the demon king; they're villains who were attempting to destroy this nation."

"Don't you have any thoughts about this at all?!"

"It's a gripping story!"

Insolent wretches. That was what the dauntless villainess had said, as a throng of soldiers surrounded her. She'd been lovely. The demon king had tried to protect Roxane even though he couldn't use magic, and had challenged them with a sword. He'd been splendid as well. So splendid, in fact, that when Ares had slashed him from behind, she'd been infuriated by the man's cowardice. What a beautiful scene.

"That's why I showed it to you. I thought you'd be moved."

"'Moved'? Look, you... Nevermind, I'll let that slide for now. Isn't there anything we can do?"

"Let's see..." She puts a finger to her chin, thinking hard.

The heroine and villainess of Game 2 watch her attentively. Their eyes are alive. Everyone who gets involved with Aileen ends up like that. Not bad at all.

"I did promise Lady Aileen that I would help her... But are you sure? Particularly you, Serena."

"Huh? Why me?"

"Because you won't be able to go back."

She asks because she genuinely wants to know.

She wouldn't mind choosing for her. The player gives a cruel smile, and the heroine flinches. However, she promptly returns the smile. "It's a little late to be worrying about that."

"Um, you don't intend to make Lady Serena do anything dangerous, do you...?!"

"What's with you? Don't tell me you're worried about me."

"Th-that isn't why..."

"You, too, then, Rachel. You're sure about this?"

"I've been prepared ever since I made up my mind to serve Lady Aileen."

The villainess never has any power, and yet she tries to put up a fight anyway. The sight makes Lilia's heart tremble uncontrollably. She's entranced.

"Good. Then let's all give it our best together."

To think the day would come when she'd say something so ridiculous to characters! How entertaining.

"That power you used just now sure is handy. If you watched Ares that way, couldn't you find out where the holy sword is right away?"

"Oh, no, that's not possible. I don't have the sacred sword right now. I managed that because of you."

"—Huh?"

"Well then, time to go."

She has no further use for the Daughter of God. Characters who aren't chosen by the player have no reason to exist.

✦ Fifth Act ✦
The Villainess Conspires with the Final Boss

The Queendom of Hausel's envoy, who has been staying in Ellmeyer in order to exert diplomatic pressure, is rattled by the report of the demon king's arrest in Ashmael.

"That's ludicrous. The demon king is definitely here."

"Then the one in Ashmael is an impostor?"

"That's right. It isn't possible to use magic in Ashmael. There's no way he'd go there. If he did, there's no telling what would happen to the fiend dragon—"

"Ah, envoy. Has there been a new report from the Queendom?"

The demon king emerges from the depths of the corridor. At the sight of him, the messenger who's just brought the report looks dumbfounded. *There, you see?* Bottling up those bitter thoughts, the envoy steps forward.

The demon king approaches, his steps graceful, his black cloak billowing around him. Hair like black silk thread, eyes like red jewels. The beauty of his face makes the sunlight that streams in through the windows pale in comparison.

"No, Your Majesty. I was just reporting the progress of negotiations here. Such as your claim that the crown princess has not run away."

"I see. You have it rough as well. I'm sure simply staying here must be dull for you."

The sarcasm is clear, and the envoy's jaw clenches. *Know your place, Demon King.* However, the two guards behind the king seem to pick up on that faint trace of displeasure, and they curb their visitor with a single look.

They're Nameless Priests: church-made weapons who exist to slaughter demons. These two were once said to be their finest masterpieces, talent the Queendom of Hausel would have given its figurative right arm to get. How in the world had the demon king managed to snatch these two from the church and domesticate them?

"We are also actively working to clear up the misunderstanding regarding the crown princess," replies the king. "Be patient."

"Sire...!"

On his way past, the man casts a red glance at the envoy, who hastily bows to him.

No matter how repulsive the envoy found him, the demon king had a presence that instinctively made humans kneel.

Watching the three of them move on, the envoy sighs heavily, shoulders slumping. The demon king is here. He couldn't possibly be in Ashmael.

As soon as they're inside the room, the spell comes undone with a *boomf.*

Walt hastily shuts the door. Keith, who's been waiting inside with a pocket watch, grimaces. "As we thought, it doesn't even last five minutes."

"I'm...sorry...but this is the best...I can do...!"

Elefas topples over backward, gray-faced. Kyle catches him, refusing to let him fall. Luc promptly comes over, checks his pulse, and nods. "He's alive. It's all right; he can keep going."

"No... I can't do it anymore... It's not just my magic... It feels like this is wearing my life force away..."

"...Drink this. We made improvements. It may let you stay transformed longer."

"You're absolutely experimenting on me, aren't you...?!"

"There, open your mouth and tip that medicine down the hatch. You have a meeting to attend."

"No, I mean it, I really can't—"

Working together, Luc and Quartz pinch his nose and manage to pour the hot medicinal decoction into his mouth. A ferocious bitterness he'd really prefer not to get used to makes him feel faint.

"Hey, Elefas? You alive?"

In theory he is, but he feels half dead. He can't respond.

"Well, I suppose we have no choice. Lay him down on that sofa. We have a little time."

"Why is he this worn down when he's borrowing Master Claude's magic?"

He was considering just dying right here, but Walt's skeptical voice annoys him, and he musters his strength to respond. "As I've said before, many times... Changing the color of one's hair and eyes is taboo, a violation of the laws of this world! I'm doing something that ordinarily can't be done, making the impossible possible by channeling Master Claude's unreasonable magic with my own skill! And as a matter of fact, borrowing the demon king's magic is a fairly reckless endeavor to begin with. Do you understand now?!"

Desperately, he highlights his own brilliance and efforts, but the demon king's servants show no mercy.

"But Master Claude is having you do it because he thinks you can."

"Yes, and I am doing it! Frankly, it's taking years off my life!"

"It's all right. Master Claude will do something about your life as well." There's a trace of sympathy in Kyle's eyes, but his words are less than comforting.

Elefas flops over sideways. He wants to go home. He doesn't want to work anymore.

"Still, is this meeting about what I think it is? The thing about the demon king being captured in Ashmael?"

"Not the demon king, Walt. Someone who looks exactly like the demon king."

"Shouldn't we go rescue him?" Kyle sounds worried, and Elefas opens his eyes a crack. He's been wondering the same thing.

Keith, their highest-ranking superior, pushes his glasses up and speaks flatly. "No. It would make him happy, and he'll acquire a taste for it."

"Wh-what's that supposed to mean?"

"He'll be delighted we came to save him, and he'll start getting captured on purpose. That's the sort of person he is." They can all visualize it, and no one argues. "We'll have to let him suffer a bit. After all, we tried to stop him from going, and he shook us off. In fact, if he loses and comes back home in disgrace, I'm not letting him into the castle."

Realizing that the calm-looking attendant is actually the angriest of them all, Elefas quietly averts his eyes.

"Respond to any inquiries from the Kingdom of Ashmael with firm denial. Prime Minister Rudolph is doing the same."

"Um, but then what will happen to Master Claude…?"

"Oh, perhaps they'll execute him or something. It's fine, just let him be."

"That's fine?!"

"Yes, it is. After all, he probably got caught because he was trying to show off for Lady Aileen, or because he thought it would be entertaining. And so the man in the Kingdom of Ashmael is an impostor. Our demon king isn't that much of an idiot. Is that clear?"

Elefas, Walt, and Kyle all exchange looks. Seeing this, Keith sighs. "—We already have instructions for what to do in a situation like this. It was an anticipated scenario."

Oh, it was? Elefas feels a little relieved, and the tension drains from his shoulders. This strikes him as odd.

Before, no matter what sort of master he served, he never felt worried or uneasy for them.

"I'm counting on you, Elefas. Until I return, you're the only one I can rely on."

All because the king said such words to him. In that regard, he and his wife are exactly the same.

"All right, break time is over. Elefas, get up, please."

"I—I can't yet."

"You are Master Claude's mage. Make the impossible possible."

But he does still want to go home. He hopes the king will forgive him for that.

In this world, what's right isn't always allowed. Ares knows that.

"Roxane won't confess to anything?"

"No. She denies summoning the fiend dragon and committing adultery with the demon king. Even when we show her proof, she feigns ignorance. It's pointless."

However, it isn't in his nature to resign himself and admit defeat. He wants to rectify mistakes. He's irritated by people who don't correct their errors, or refuse to admit them. Even if that person happens to be his own ex-fiancée—in fact, that makes it all the more irritating.

"She must not understand her position," the holy king says, toying with the drawing of the magic circle used in the fiend dragon's summoning. The drawing on the paper is extremely precise; it's the proof Ares fabricated in order to charge Roxane with her crimes.

I thought she'd give up and confess if we had that, but...

Roxane had definitely been attempting to summon the fiend dragon. The harem attendants had testified she had borrowed a suspicious book from the library, and she had been off by herself, absorbed in studying spells of a dubious nature. The house of Fusca was covering for their daughter, saying she had been conducting research in order to subjugate the fiend dragon, but it was obvious to everyone her goal had been harming Sahra. Ares had no choice but to act before his wife's life was endangered.

That was why he'd made his move before she actually summoned the dragon. The dragon was imprisoned, and Ares had known Roxane wouldn't be able to summon it. Even so, she'd been plotting to do so, and as far as he was concerned, that was more than enough to condemn her.

"I hate to do it, but shouldn't we extract a confession from her even if it takes torture? If it turns out that the demon king tempted her, we could grant her lenience."

He'd assumed that if they confronted her with proof, she would confess in order to protect herself. However, Roxane obstinately insisted that she knew nothing about the demon king or summoning the fiend dragon. Even when they asked her leading questions—such as whether it was the demon king's fault she'd soiled her hands with such misdeeds, or possibly Baal's fault—she'd given the same answer. He hadn't expected that. He'd assumed she was bound to deflect the blame onto someone else, but he'd been proven wrong.

Ideally, he would take this opportunity to firmly establish that the demon king had used the fiend dragon to target Ashmael, but the woman is being thoroughly useless. He really doesn't feel like showing her mercy.

"Speaking of the guard you say is the demon king, we've just received an answer from Ellmeyer. Or rather, it came via the Queendom of Hausel."

"I see. What did they say?"

"That they know nothing about this. They claim the demon king is definitely in Ellmeyer."

"Huh?"

Ares wasn't expecting that answer, and he looks up. "That's not possible. Black hair and red eyes. Those are the hallmarks of the demon king."

He knows because the envoy from Hausel who's secretly staying in his mansion told him as much.

"Well, that's true, but there could easily be other men with black hair and red eyes."

"No… No, that is the demon king! I'm positive."

"How can you be so sure?"

Ares almost answers truthfully, then presses his lips together tightly. Unconsciously, he touches the band on his right arm. *Ever since that man appeared, the fiend dragon has been putting up a ferocious resistance. Even when it's under the influence of demon snuff, it tries to go to him.*

However, there's no way he can say, *Because this armband I used to seal the fiend dragon is telling me so.*

"If you want us to declare war on Imperial Ellmeyer, then produce conclusive proof that guard is the demon king and link him to the fiend dragon."

"...Yes, sire. I swear I will."

Now may be the time, he thinks. Time to strike the finishing blow.

A blow that will expose the fact the spineless holy king can't protect this kingdom.

Maybe I'll use the proposal that one fellow made.

"On that subject, Your Majesty. I believe it's high time we repaired the holy sword. May I have permission to conduct the ceremony?"

He's suggested this many times, and every time he's been rebuffed, but this time Baal agrees easily. "Yes, we'll leave that to you. Ensure that it succeeds— By the way, Ares. Did you know that Roxane can't draw to save her life?"

"Huh?"

Ares looks up, wondering where this is coming from all of a sudden. Baal smiles back at him thinly. For a moment, those violet, noble eyes overawe him, and he gulps.

"It was a joke. Don't worry about it. Just go."

As if embarrassed that he's flinched, he bows his head again and leaves the throne room.

The attendant he employed a short while ago is waiting for him just outside. The man has absolutely no skill with a sword, but Ares has plenty of that himself; he hired this fellow for his quick wits.

This adviser is the one who came up with the plan for arresting Roxane.

"Isaac. The holy king has finally given his permission. We're going to hold the ceremony to repair the holy sword."

"I see. In that case, let's do it as soon as we can. Tomorrow, even. We've already procured weapons, and the other preparations are complete."

Ares, who'd begun walking down the corridor, is so surprised he stops. His eyes narrow. "But then there won't be time to get Roxane's confession. What will we do about that?"

"We don't need her confession. What's important is the perception of it all. The people want to know once and for all who's protecting this country, and who saved it."

Isaac raises his index finger. "First, we'll have the fiend dragon possess the demon king's body and barge in on the holy sword's restoration ceremony. We can make him tell us about his relationship to Roxane then. That way, everyone will see that the demon king is using the dragon in an attempt to destroy the kingdom, and that the principal consort led him here."

He goes on, putting up a second finger, and then a third.

"Then we'll give the holy sword to the holy king, so he can kill the demon king. It won't be the real sword, of course. We'll use the copy the Queendom of Hausel made."

"—The demon king can't be killed by something like that."

"Exactly. That will prove the holy king isn't fit to hold the sword. He'll lose his legitimacy as a ruler. And that includes the fact he wasn't able to stop the principal consort. We'll expose him as a weak king who can't defend his kingdom. Then we'll make it look as though Lady Sahra has restored the holy sword a second time, at which point you'll wield the real one, seal both the fiend dragon and the demon king—and the legend will live again."

Legend. That word thrills Ares to the depths of his heart.

"We should hold the ceremony in the harem. If we allow the scope to increase any further, we'll end up with too many victims, and that would come back to bite us."

"What do you mean?"

"The greater the damage, the more certain it is that people will blame the new king later on. It's best to limit your stage to the harem in the first place, so that the only victims will be the former holy king's relics. The only one to lose everything will be the previous king: It will be clear poetic justice."

Ares nods; that makes sense. Even if sacrificing innocents was a necessary evil, too much of that would probably make things tiresome later.

"The preparations are all in place. If there's any cause for concern— Yes, I suppose it would be the demon king. Even if he can't use magic, let's hit him three or four times and weaken him."

As Isaac makes this proposal, he's wearing a very refreshing smile.

Ares nods. "Good idea. I'll let you handle that."

"Just leave it to me, sir. I swear I'll make a success of it."

And on the day it succeeds, I'll be the one seated on the throne.

Suppressing the exultation welling up from deep inside him, Ares nods again, emphatically.

Lovely golden hair and gentle green eyes. When he smiles lightly, his features are sweet and elegant. He looks exactly like a prince from a story or a picture book. He actually is a prince, as a matter of fact, which makes her feel very nervous indeed.

"Thank you very much for your invitation, Damsel Sahra."

Being called a damsel is quite novel to her, and she's flustered. "Oh, n-no. I-I'm sorry for asking you to come here. I wanted to hear more stories of other lands..."

"Gladly. After all, I have nothing to occupy me at the moment."

Still nervous, she encourages him to take a seat. Has she used the proper words? She hasn't made any strange movements, has she? Her guest is Cedric Jean Ellmeyer, second prince of Imperial Ellmeyer, and the more polished his behavior is, the more awkward she feels.

When she moves to sit down as well, the man who's waiting behind the prince promptly comes around and pulls out her chair for her. She thanks him, and he tells her not to worry about it. He's wearing a very serious expression. Then he straightens up, standing tall, and unlike the guards at the door, there's a dignity in his bearing that can't be missed. Apparently, he is what's known as a knight. There is no such profession in the Kingdom of Ashmael. He behaves quite differently from their guards and soldiers.

People like these really exist... I feel like a princess. Come to think of it, even that man...

She recalls a certain guard. She hadn't been able to take her eyes off him, either, probably for the same reason: He was different from the men she knows. When she heard he'd become Roxane's guard, she'd been disappointed and angry at the same time. It would never do to envy Roxane.

However, Roxane is in prison now, and there are rumors that her guard is in fact the demon king. It's a good thing she didn't go near him. The Daughter of God can't be involved with anything nefarious like that—although if he sought her help, that would be a different matter.

The Daughter...of God.

The thought sends an anxious twinge through her heart. Pretending she hasn't noticed it, she smiles.

It should be fine. It will be; both Ares and Baal said so.

Sahra is the Daughter of God. There's nothing to fear.

"Oh, Prince Cedric, your tea... Wh-what are Serena and Lilia doing?"

"—Lilia?"

"Y-yes. She's a girl who came to work for me just recently... Um, is something the matter?"

For a moment, she thinks Cedric looks stern, and her voice turns timid. However, his kind expression promptly returns. Sahra's sure her eyes must have been deceiving her.

"No, I was just a little startled. She shares a name with my fiancée."

"My... Your fiancée? Um, is she not with you?"

"No. This is a covert visit, and it would have been dangerous."

"So you've been separated... That must be hard."

"No." Cedric shakes his head; his eyes are sad. "There's something I must do. I'm told you will also be performing an important ritual soon, Damsel Sahra."

"Oh yes."

"A delicate woman like you... God is very cruel sometimes."

Cedric's sympathy makes her feel better. "No. This is my duty."

"If there's anything I can do, please tell me. You will be risking your life, after all."

Her eyes widen. Then her mind catches up and begins to race— *What?*

Cedric lowers his eyes, as if he's seen something heartrending. "I heard that the holy sword will be restored in exchange for your own life force."

Her heart thumps heavily. No one told her about this.

"However, if the fiend dragon truly revives, there are bound to be victims...particularly if the demon king is conspiring with it. We need the holy sword, no matter what. I wish our Maid of the Sacred Sword had been genuine, but...as you know, she became the demon king's pawn."

Yes. And so there is no one but Sahra who can raise the holy sword that will exorcise the fiend dragon and the demon king, and save the world. That's why everyone treasures her. Sahra is the one and only savior.

"However, the idea that you'll lose your life as a result... It's a truly heartless affair."

Except she's never heard that before. Not from Ares, and not from Baal.

It's a lie... If I repair the holy sword...I'll die...?

But would a second prince who'd defected from a neighboring country have any reason to tell such a lie?

Of course; it must be some sort of mistake... If I ask Ares, I'm sure he'll laugh and say I'm being silly...

Hardly remembering either the conversation or the flavor of the tea, Sahra leaves the room, making her way down the corridor on unsteady feet. At a turn in the hallway, she stops. Some of the attendants are having a casual conversation.

"—Did you hear about Lady Roxane?"

"Yes. They say she won't admit to her crime..."

If she is the Daughter of God, she bears commensurate obligations. Those were the words of someone whose attitude toward Sahra hadn't changed, no matter how the people around them flattered her.

"General Ares has decided to use torture."

"I imagine she'll be executed soon… The general can't abide dishonesty."

"Know your place. You and I live in different worlds."

Ares is going to torture Miss Roxane to death…?

Sahra's world really is different from Roxane's. She had always thought the other woman lived in a world that was sordid and dirty and unkind.

But it occurs to her, belatedly, that Roxane's former fiancé and Sahra's husband are the same man.

"—Was that satisfactory?"

Stripping off his sweet princely mask, Cedric checks with his fiancée, who's been waiting in the corridor. They've only just been reunited, and she offers him her usual charming smile. "Thank you, Cedric and Marcus. I couldn't have said it better myself, I think."

"…Is it true? If she repairs the holy sword, will she, um… Will she really die?"

"It's true. Awful, isn't it? No one told her. Poor Lady Sahra…"

She knits her brows as if she pities the girl, but Cedric doesn't miss the fact there's a smile on her lips.

Their reunion hadn't been the least bit moving. The second prince of Ellmeyer had arrived on a secret visit in order to discuss how willing Ashmael might be in supporting a bid to overthrow the demon king, and when he'd been welcomed into General Ares's mansion, they'd run right into each other. There hadn't been time to mentally prepare.

Cedric and Marcus had been so startled they couldn't even process the situation. Before they could say anything, Lilia had smiled, said, "Perfect timing!", and arranged for a tea party with Sahra. They haven't even had a chance to fill each other in on their respective circumstances.

Even so, when Lilia said "Hurry!" he'd set all of that aside and done what she told him. He'd been whipped like this ever since they'd first met.

"But Cedric, 'If anything happens, you can flee to Ellmeyer'? I didn't ask you to tell her that."

Still, if he only did whatever Lilia told him, he wouldn't be able to keep her. His wife would lose interest in him. That's what his brother had told him.

"If they really are forcing her to be the Daughter of God when she doesn't know anything, we'll need to take her under our protection. Can those arrangements be made, Marcus?"

"Yes. I know a few people I can ask, but... Are you sure?"

"It's fine. My brother wouldn't tell us to just hand her over to the Queendom of Hausel, either."

She'll probably be an important witness, capable of testifying to Ashmael's crimes. Either that, or a thread they can follow to unravel the Queendom's plot, which may very well be responsible for everything.

"...I'd expect no less of you, Cedric. I hadn't thought that far!"

And so he doesn't mind playing along with this woman's farce, or the contrived smile she turns on him. "Right. That's our job. Don't worry about a thing; you can just leave it all to us."

As he tells her that, he's careful to keep looking her straight in the eye. Lilia gazes back at him as if she's seeing something that doesn't make sense. She looks at him that way a lot lately.

Lilia hasn't picked up on it.

The joy a man feels when he manages to make a woman who seems to know everything look at him that way.

"...It sounds like they'll hold the ceremony tomorrow. What will you and Marcus do, Cedric?"

"I'm not sure. What do you want to do, Marcus?"

"Well, obviously, Lilia's—"

Cedric gives his straitlaced, unsubtle friend a good hard kick in the shin.

Looking at Marcus, who's now crouching in the hall, Lilia giggles. "Well, there are things I need to do, so I'll be going. Give it your best, you two."

"What are you going to do, Lilia?"

"It's a secret between girls. I can't tell you." Giving him a precious wink, Lilia sets off down the corridor, stepping lightly.

"H-hey, Lilia, wait. We need to talk— Why aren't you going after her, Cedric?" Marcus, who's finally raised his head, looks at him accusingly.

Cedric sighs. "This is what's wrong with you."

"What?"

"Just try telling her point-blank that you're going to guard her, then follow her. She'll lose you before you know it." Marcus must have experienced that before; he falls silent. "If you're going to keep an eye on her, be discreet."

"I don't know if that's such a great idea, either... Besides, what do you mean, 'keep an eye on her'?"

"Quiet down. If we call it 'keeping an eye on her,' my brother will let it slide. Hurry up and figure out when to say what you mean and when to use tact. If you've understood, then go after Lilia. You're going to lose her."

"—No." Getting to his feet, Marcus shakes his head firmly. "I'm your knight. I'll prioritize your safety."

"...Huh?"

"I can't say it all that well, but...I think I had that wrong at first. If I'd kept my head a little better, you might still be crown prince."

The unexpected confession startles Cedric.

"Lester and the others say all sorts of things...but ultimately, the demon king let us go free because you bent the knee. I may be your friend and I may have known you for ages, but I'm also your knight. I shouldn't have let my liege lord feel compelled to do that."

"It's nothing to worry about. You know being crown prince was...too much for me."

"Yes, but I also know how hard you worked. And that Aileen didn't pick up on what you really meant... I'm the only one who knew. I'm the only one who had the chance to do something about it."

They've lost that relationship with their childhood friend forever. This is the first time he's heard Marcus's regrets.

"Looking at General Ares makes me think that 'being right' is terrifying. It lets you do awful things without minding a bit... Just like what we did to Aileen."

I'm not the one who's being awful. The other person is forcing me to do this. That mindset makes it easy for people to cross unthinkable lines.

"There's no point in saying that now, though. I don't intend

to repair my relationship with Aileen. It's not something she could forgive anyway. And it's probably best not to apologize… At least for another three years or so."

"Why three years?"

"You know why. She's the type who insists she feels no pain even when she falls down and hurts herself. If we apologize, she'll just say it doesn't bother her and brush us off."

Cedric is right. It's probably inappropriate, but Marcus laughs.

"Besides, Aileen wouldn't accept an apology that's just talk in the first place. She definitely holds us in contempt right now. She'd scoff and say nobodies like us couldn't possibly hurt her, and that would be the end of it. In that case, we should start by doing our job properly."

"You've put…a lot of thought into this." Marcus is impressed, and yet the remark earns him a ferocious glare.

"…I can't become emperor anymore, you know."

"Probably not. You don't seem like you even want to."

"They may use us, then throw us away."

"I'm well aware of that."

In that case, there's nothing more to say, and Marcus's inflexibility isn't anything new.

"Then don't mention this conversation in front of my brother. You really will end up being reborn as an instrument."

"I know. And Aileen may not look it, but she cries at the drop of a hat."

She'd boldly attempt to charge down an unfamiliar road, then trip, fall, and cry. She'd cry about not being able to lift a sword that was as big as she was. She'd fight with her brothers and cry. She'd get yelled at by her parents and cry. She'd read a sad story and cry.

"In every memory I have of Aileen, she's wailing. I really don't understand why the demon king would want to make her cry…," Marcus says, as if he feels it keenly.

For the first time in quite a while, Cedric laughs out loud.

The sound of footsteps joins the sound of dripping water, and Claude's eyes open a crack.

He's hanging by his chained wrists, and his body aches. His hair and the wound on his cheek are caked with dried blood; it feels disgusting. His skin has been whipped raw.

"Yikes… They did a bigger number on you than I thought they would."

"…Isaac, huh? …That figures."

Every time he moves his mouth, he tastes blood. His cut lip hurts. It's almost as if he's human.

"What do you mean, 'that figures'?"

"The plan I overheard… It sounded perfect, but it had this…clear flaw that practically screamed 'If you take advantage of this, we're finished, so go right ahead'…"

"Are you complimenting me or running me down?"

"It was so convenient for us that I thought…it might be a trap. You've infiltrated and are manipulating the general, hmm? I see… As always, you…can't do it if you don't try."

"Right, got it, you're not complimenting me." Gingerly, a light illuminates him. "…Are you okay?"

He probably looks awful. Isaac is being unusually solicitous.

It strikes him as funny, and he laughs. "...It hurt more than I expected. It still hurts."

"Well, yeah," Isaac replies. "...There had to be some other way. Why would you pull a stupid stunt like this?"

"When I imagined Aileen too worried and uneasy to sleep, it made my heart flutter, and before I knew it—"

"Okay, sounds like your head's fine. Business as usual."

"...Is the principal consort all right?" He's been concerned about that.

Isaac frowns. "She's safe. Her life isn't in danger... I had them go easy on her."

"...I see... I told them to leave her and just take me...but that man, Ares..."

He feels more pity than anger. The man's almost certainly not a bad person. How easily people fall.

Well, he's reaping what he sowed. Claude chuckles deep in his throat.

"I know where the fiend dragon is," says Isaac. "I made it so the demon'll head your way; was that the right move?"

"...Yes. Do as you see fit."

"Hearing that just makes me worry more. Don't tell me you could lose to the dragon."

"You don't need to worry about that... How is Aileen?"

He can sense that the question irks Isaac. "She's toughing it out. Obviously, since she hasn't come rushing in here."

"I see... Heh-heh. Apparently I win our little fight."

"I don't think any guy in your condition should feel like a winner."

"By the way, have you managed to see Rachel?"

"Now is really not the time for that. It's probably the same on her end."

Work takes priority, hmm? Claude's impressed, and at the same time, he sighs. "You'll never get anywhere that way. You can't do it if you don't try, so be a little more proactive."

"Shut up, all right? Just wait here quietly until help shows up!"

With that parting shot, Isaac leaves, taking the light with him. Apparently Claude's managed to make him angry.

With the light gone, darkness falls again. Under the cover of that darkness, a shadow nestles close to him.

"Oh… It's all right. Don't worry. He wasn't an enemy."

A black haze seems to crawl up from beneath Claude's feet, pleading with him. He gives a wry smile. "I know. Once this is over, I will, I promise. I see… You feel your sanity fading? Humans do truly terrible things…"

The haze slips around him smoothly, clinging to him as if begging for affection, but it's growing thinner. It seems they're out of time. The moment must be about right, though.

Possibly because he's taken Aileen's will into account, Isaac's plan is a kind one.

But what's needed is a clear villain. A story where everyone can see who's evil and who's on the side of justice… If possible, he'd hoped to avoid doing things this way. However, when he'd told that man not to hurt Roxane, he'd ignored him.

Aileen's going to be worried about somebody besides me.

That is a serious crime.

"Yes, it's fine. I won't be angry with you. Go ahead."

The fiend dragon: The former ruler of this land, who had been sealed into the demon realm by the holy sword—a copy of the sacred sword—and a woman known as the Daughter of God. An ancient demon who possesses the power to create a second demon king in the unlikely event of Claude's death.

Although the dragon had been captured, nothing dramatic had happened because the Daughter of God and the holy sword are both frightening.

It was because hurting humans would have violated Claude's orders.

"Go and teach those foolish humans a lesson."

Lifting his red eyes to gaze into empty space, Claude issues a gentle command.

The first blow comes at dawn.

In her bedchamber in the Sea Palace, Aileen is startled awake by the tremor. A demon's ominous aura instantly banishes her drowsiness.

Small ornaments rattle, then smash on the floor. Rachel dashes in from the antechamber. "L-Lady Aileen! Are you all right?!"

"Yes. Let's go outside. I can't believe it: a natural disaster, today of all days..."

The first shock was intense, but the trembling subsides quickly. Tossing the shawl Rachel has brought her on over her nightclothes, Aileen makes her way out the door. *I can't imagine they'll call off the plan, but...* There's someone she wants to rescue as soon as possible. Right this very minute, even.

However, impulsively doing so would mean squandering the wishes of the two who'd stayed behind. And so, both she and Baal have been desperately restraining themselves.

When she'd heard people arguing about whether it was really

the demon king if he bled when they wounded him, she'd clenched her fists so tightly her fingernails bit into her palms.

It's only been two days, but she doesn't want to endure this for a single day longer. Baal must feel the same.

The stage is set. She must lay the groundwork and ensure that nothing goes wrong— But the moment Aileen steps outside, she realizes she's misunderstood.

This isn't a natural disaster.

The dawn sky looks bloodstained.

An expanding darkness is seeping across it, and it isn't the last traces of the night.

"L-Lady Aileen… That…thing…is moving…"

Shifting like a sinister cloud, the thing gradually bleeds across the kingdom's sky. Abruptly, as if searching for prey, it opens its eyes.

Countless red eyes.

—The fiend dragon!

A demon with a host of red eyes, lurking in darkness and cloaked in an ominous miasma.

"The fiend dragon is supposed to go to Master Claude. Why fly over the harem?!"

"Lady Aileen, something's coming!"

As Rachel shouts, the dragon's eyes flash red. Attacks streak toward the sky, trees, buildings, people—but a membrane of light repels them.

It's the holy king's barrier. Floating above the palace, all alone, the king of this land confronts the demon. In no time, the screams turn to cheers.

"Master Baal!"

Noticing Aileen, who doesn't look as delirious as the people around her, Baal descends to the ground. "Hey, this isn't the plan we heard about. Isn't that the fiend dragon's true body?"

"I believe so. But I haven't heard anything, either. Something unforeseen must have hap—!"

A roar rings out. This time a gaping hole—probably a mouth—opens between the clouds and spews out an enormous quantity of magical energy.

*Tsk*ing in irritation, Baal sweeps his right arm to the side. Layer upon layer of sacred magic circles fan out, repelling the fiend dragon's rays. Explosions soon fill the air.

...That's a shock. Apparently "holy king" isn't merely a fancy title.

However, as the wife of the demon king, she can't stand by and let him injure the fiend dragon. "Master Baal, until we understand the situation, could you refrain from attacking the dragon?"

"Have no fear. All we can do is defend!" He says the words decisively, and she catches herself gazing steadily at him.

"...Don't tell me that's why you made me your consort..."

"If we could attack, we would need neither the holy sword nor the sacred sword, obviously."

"How do you manage to be arrogant even about a thing like that...? At any rate, I'll try to make those attacks weaker!"

"Leave the defending to us!"

The way he says it—standing tall and bursting with confidence—irks her, but now isn't the time for that.

She must be delicate so that she won't end up killing the demon. The damage has to be kept to a minimum... Picking up on Aileen's intent, the sacred sword flies from the palm of her right hand, straight toward the fiend dragon. It goes right through, as if the dragon's body were a cloud—but the sword's power has clearly been repelled.

"...It didn't work! Why didn't it work?!"

"Hmm. So that isn't the dragon itself, then? —Or rather, the moment it slipped through our barrier, it could no longer be considered a mere demon."

Startled, Aileen looks up. The fiend dragon has begun to cover Ashmael's sky. This demon emerged inside the holy king's barrier, which even the demon king's power couldn't penetrate, and begun to attack, which means...

"It's attacking through some human intermediate. Only the holy sword can defeat it— Let's go."

"Go where?!" Aileen asks in confusion.

"Change of plans. We'll have Sahra repair the real holy sword."

"But if we do that, then our scheme to make her lose power won't—!"

According to Isaac's plan, Claude was supposed to take the dragon into his care, while the holy sword would be switched for a fake, forcing the restoration to fail.

If the fiend dragon didn't resurrect and the Daughter of God failed to repair the holy sword, they could corner Ares. On top of that, if they brought up the fact he'd been secretly communicating with the Queendom of Hausel and had forged the evidence he'd presented against Roxane, the man would probably give up. Most of all, Baal had hoped to avoid involving his citizens in a civil war.

"Not only will we be unable to curb Ares," Aileen says to him, "you'll be blamed for the fiend dragon's resurrection!"

"It doesn't matter. If the fiend dragon has truly revived, the damage will be far worse than anything a civil war could do."

"...! Let's release Master Claude at once! If we do that, this may still work out somehow."

"It's too late. If people learn that man is the demon king now, no matter what excuse we give, everyone will think he's behind the attack. Everything will be ruined."

Issuing evacuation orders to the people around them, Baal sets off for the palace, walking fast. "Even if Ares's power continues to grow, now isn't the time to worry about it. The holy sword, the Daughter of God, Ares's troops, the consorts with sacred power who've gathered in the harem: using all the resources at our disposal and sealing the fiend dragon comes first. As long as we don't kill it, you shouldn't have anything to complain about."

"Yes, but in that case, you'll—"

"What good is a king who fails to protect his people?"

Aileen has been following Baal at a trot, but at those words, she stops. Even at a time like this, she's smiling. *Lady Roxane. Your decision was correct.*

This man is a true king. Just like Claude.

"You're going to help us, too. You are our consort."

"Don't even joke about that. I most certainly am not your consort. I refuse."

"Are you telling us you won't help, this late in the game?"

"Rephrase it as 'neighbor.' 'Friend' or 'comrade' would also be acceptable." Drawing herself up to her full height, Aileen greets him, slowly and formally. "I am Aileen Jean Ellmeyer, crown princess of Imperial Ellmeyer."

The sudden introduction makes Baal blink. Looking up at him mischievously, she makes a vow: "I swear on the name of my husband that I will aid you, Holy King of Ashmael, Baal Shah Ashmael— As a matter of fact, after the demon king, I am the strongest in our land, you know?"

✦ Sixth Act ✦
The Villainess Wins with a Foul

"What is the meaning of this?!" Ares bellows.

That's what I want to know, Isaac thinks, privately gnashing his teeth. *Why would the fiend dragon choose now of all times to go out of control? Don't tell me the demon king did it?*

That's it. That has to be it, he decides half out of spite.

"What does the Queendom's envoy have to say?"

"All I've heard is that they know nothing," Isaac tells him honestly.

"Of all the irresponsible—!" Ares spits out the words bitterly. "The holy item they gave me isn't working. They told me that tool would let me imprison the fiend dragon and gain complete control over it!"

"There's no point in blaming them now. More importantly, please be quiet. At this point, it would be a bigger problem if anyone were to learn you'd had the fiend dragon in captivity, General Ares."

"Why? I was keeping it under guard until the holy sword was repaired. I even risked bodily harm to do my duty."

"It will look as if you were sheltering it until it grew to this size."

The warning makes Ares's eyes widen. He probably never dreamed he might be suspected of wrongdoing.

"Calm yourself. In a way, they've stolen a march on us."

"What do you mean?"

"Right now, the kingdom is being protected by the holy king's barrier. In that sense, this development is working in the holy king's favor." Isaac continues to explain, assessing the situation even as he details what might happen following such an unanticipated series of events: the results and possibilities. "Not only that, but I just received a report that the crown princess of Ellmeyer has arrived."

"The crown princess of Ellmeyer? What business does the demon king's bride have here? Has she come to grovel?"

"The Maid of the Sacred Sword has come to save this kingdom from the fiend dragon. At least that's how other countries will see it."

It isn't just Ares; everyone around him looks startled.

These people are hopeless.

This kingdom really can't hold their own in the world of foreign affairs. Even Ares knows only what the Queendom of Hausel has put into his head.

No wonder the holy king's concerned. If anything happens, the first blow will flatten them.

However, that worry won't matter unless they get through this situation.

"The fact that Ellmeyer has dispatched the Maid of the Sacred Sword is extremely significant. It signals their intent to save our kingdom from the fiend dragon. They've essentially announced that the demon king doesn't condone the dragon's actions."

In that sense, the fact Aileen has chosen this moment to reveal her true identity is very important. Isaac deliberately delayed his report to Ares, so his people probably won't be able to suppress the rumors at this point.

"S-so what? Ultimately, the fiend dragon can't be defeated without Sahra's holy sword. No doubt that's why Baal ordered me to bring her to him."

"That's right."

That's the weak point of this maneuver: No matter how much Baal and Aileen do, in the end, the Daughter of God is the one who'll secure all the glory. At the moment, the people are accepting this assistance from Ellmeyer with skepticism, and only because of their immediate fear of the fiend dragon. Unless Aileen manages to pull off something truly impressive, they'll just say she was trying to put them in her debt.

Aileen must have decided it doesn't matter, but Isaac can't afford to do the same.

What do we do? Should we get the holy king to remove that barrier and have the demon king shut down the fiend dragon? No, that would make it look even more like he'd intentionally resurrected a demon to cause havoc. If all we do is send aid after the battle, we'll be shooting ourselves in the foot. Argh! Push comes to shove, we can set up that second prince as the mastermind and execute him— Yeah, let's go with that. Wow, that's the demon king's little brother for you; he sure comes in handy.

They need the holy sword. That fact isn't going anywhere. *Think.* Isaac keeps on talking and racking his brain. "The Maid of the Sacred Sword may have joined the fight, but her sword hasn't worked on the fiend dragon. In other words..." The fiend dragon has already possessed a human. Abruptly, his lips curve upward. "As long as Lady Sahra is the Daughter of God, General Ares— You won't have to worry about a thing."

As he says this, he casually takes a piece of paper out of his pocket and jots down a note. He has to get this to Aileen.

Paying no attention to what Isaac is doing, Ares nods, looking satisfied. "True. However, if things go on like this, we'll end up giving the holy sword to Baal..."

"Have Lady Sahra proclaim that you are the one fit to wield the holy sword. Besides, you're a general. Under these circumstances, there's no problem with your fighting on the front line. On the contrary, if the holy king happens to disappear in the meantime—"

"Who's there?!" Auguste yells; he'd joined Isaac in Ares's camp.

A woman quietly steps into view. She's wearing a servant's uniform that's famous in Ellmeyer. It's Rachel.

Their reunion catches him completely off guard. He's sure their eyes meet, but Rachel doesn't let it show in her expression. She bows, deeply and courteously. "I beg your pardon for interrupting your discussion. General Ares and Lady Sahra seem to have been delayed, so I was told to go and see what was happening."

"One of Ellmeyer's agents, huh?" Before someone else can say it, Isaac takes a step toward Rachel. *Argh. This seriously bites. Considering what happened last time as well, we must have the worst compatibility ever.*

He brusquely shoves her slim shoulders. Rachel hasn't expected anyone to push her; wide-eyed, she stumbles back, hits the wall, and sinks to the floor.

"'Scuse me."

Looking down at her with a sneer, he takes out a folded handkerchief and tosses it at her. It lands on her knees; the note is sandwiched between its folds. "But we can't have the likes of you sneaking around. Let's get going, General Ares."

"...Right. What will we do with the woman, though?"

"She was kind enough to come all the way to us. Auguste, be a gentleman and see her back."

Putting a guard on an enemy agent so they aren't free to move around is a perfectly natural thing to do. Ares doesn't object to what Isaac is implying. It isn't clear whether Auguste has caught his meaning or not; he's wearing an indescribable expression, but he nods.

Now Rachel will be safely tossed outside. As he follows Ares out into the hall, Isaac exhales heavily, shoulders slumping, and looks up at the ceiling. *It's not my job to save that woman.*

...And it's not like I was hoping for a tearful reunion or anything.

As long as she delivers the note to Aileen, that's enough.

However, even if Aileen gets it, this is still a risky maneuver. Everything is as ugly as it could possibly get.

"Sahra. Are you there? We're leaving. It's finally time."

In response to Ares's call, Sahra emerges from her room dressed in her ceremonial robes. She's flanked by Serena and Lilia. Isaac doesn't consider these two allies. However, there's a rule that the Daughter of God must be attended by women who possess sacred power during the ceremony. These two are the only pawns he has to work with, so he's been forced to put his faith in them, even with the distinct possibility of betrayal.

"Everything is ready. Let's make sure that this succeeds."

"—Um...Ares...erm... What if...it d-doesn't...?"

"General Ares. Lady Sahra is nervous. She keeps saying the most incredible things." Like an older sister, Serena puts an arm around Sahra's shoulders.

Ares laughs. "What are you talking about? You are the Daughter of God. It's going to be fine."

"Um... Um, Ares? Th-there's something I'd like to ask you. Just...hypothetically..." There's an odd desperation in Sahra's tone. It tugs at him, and he focuses his full attention on her. "What if I'm not the Daughter of God? What will you do...?"

"What are you saying? You *are* the Daughter of God. If you're uneasy and can't believe in yourself, then believe in me."

Isaac can't see Sahra's face. However, behind her, he sees Lilia gloating and Serena sneering.

And so he understands, vaguely, that Ares's answer was *the wrong one.*

For some reason, the fiend dragon hasn't budged from the sky above the harem. There's no telling why, but for now, everyone is barred from entering the grounds, except those who can either resist the fiend dragon or fight. Row upon row of soldiers file in. However, people keep breaking ranks and fleeing from the rays of light that shoot sporadically from the dragon's red eyes.

Every time the fiend dragon attacks, they hear explosions. As power collides with power, the shock waves mow down trees and buildings alike.

At this point, the harem is a battlefield. The flower garden where a thousand beauties smiled has been shattered beyond all recognition.

"Bring out every sacred item we've got! Surround it with sacred power!"

"Y-yes, sire!"

Surprisingly, many of the people who've remained are low-ranking consorts. They pour their power into sacred stones, supplementing the holy king's barrier with a second barrier they've created as a group. A single attack from the fiend dragon could vaporize it instantly, but it's better than nothing. If Baal's strength runs out, there won't be anything else to shield them.

"If this keeps up, we'll have a battle of attrition on our hands. Isn't the Daughter of God here yet?!"

"Lady Aileen."

Rachel comes running up to her with a note. When she reads the hasty scribble on it, she's appalled. Apparently just getting through this situation isn't enough for Isaac.

"He's far too greedy."

"It is Isaac, after all." Rachel sounds rather proud, and that makes Aileen smile.

"Rachel, lead the evacuation from the harem, please. The fiend dragon shouldn't target any other locations."

That was how it had been in the game. It may have been because they were stingy with background art, but at any rate, right now she wants to believe in the game's almost neurotic design.

Rachel nods, seemingly without any doubts. "You're right. I'm sure Master Claude won't forgive a harem in which you became a consort."

"...What? That's why? This behavior is because of Master Claude's feelings?!"

"What? Is that not accurate?"

"I...suspect it isn't..."

In other words, it's very likely Aileen's fault that the fiend dragon is attacking the harem with such ferocity. Her cheeks stiffen.

"Lady Sahra and General Ares are here!"

When she turns to look, the group is just arriving with Ares in the lead. Ares and the soldiers around him are dressed in their finest. Lilia and Serena, who are attending Sahra, wear white silk robes and walk gracefully. Sheltered in the center of the group, Sahra is dressed so beautifully that she looks out of place in all this destruction. Her face is hidden, she's adorned with glittering jewelry, and a long train trails behind her.

Isaac and Auguste follow closely behind Ares. She glances at them, and they both respond with subtle nods.

"You're here, hmm, Sahra?" says Baal.

"Y-yes. Um..." Timidly, Sahra steps forward.

Baal faces her squarely. "We're sorry. We did all we could, but in the end, we're left with no choice but to entrust this to you."

It's probably the lingering remnants of Baal's love for her: He doesn't want to make the woman who's precious to him fight all alone. As if she's just realized this for the first time, Sahra looks up.

But it's too late. With the face of a king, Baal gives her an order. "Daughter of God. Save this kingdom—"

"Your Majesty," interrupts Ares. "Before that, there's something I'd like to ask you. Surely you aren't going to tell me that woman is the crown princess of Ellmeyer?" Aileen has been nursing a consort felled by an attack, but when Ares points to her, she rises to her feet.

She's wearing the same clothes from when they met on the ship. Even if he doesn't recognize them as being from Ellmeyer, they're clearly the costume of another land.

"Yes, General Ares. I am Aileen Jean Ellmeyer."

When she introduces herself boldly, Ares bursts out laughing, as if this is too hilarious for words. "That's... That's brilliant! Your Majesty, explain this, please."

"She's come from Imperial Ellmeyer to assist us. She may not look it, but she's apparently the Maid of the Sacred Sword. No wonder she had enough power to break the sacred item in the arena—"

"You made the crown princess of Ellmeyer your consort! That means you were in communication with the demon king!"

Several people are looking her way. Their reactions are varied: Some of them had apparently wanted to say the same thing but had been unable to, while others seem to think now isn't the time for this.

Turning back to face Aileen, Ares sneers. "You came to save our kingdom? No doubt you actually came to cover up the fact that you provoked the fiend dragon!"

"In that case, General Ares, would you be so kind as to explain the woman standing behind Lady Sahra?"

"What are you talking about?"

"That woman is the fiancée of the second prince of our empire: Lilia Reinoise, former Maid of the Sacred Sword."

Both Ares and Sahra turn back, startled. True to his feelings, Baal shouts. "She's what?! No one told us about this. Is it true, girl?"

Lilia has been waiting behind Sahra with Serena, head bowed. Slowly, she straightens up and smiles. "Aw, I wish you'd introduce me as your dear little sister-in-law, Lady Aileen."

"Be quie— N-no, I mean… I have also heard that the second prince himself, Cedric Jean Ellmeyer, is staying with you. What is the meaning of this?"

"Th-the meaning of… What are you even—"

The sky flashes red, interrupting Ares. It's happening again.

Baal looks up, shading his eyes with a hand. As more magical attacks rain down, Sahra screams and clutches her head. The world around them turns bright white and the harem attendants, unable to maintain the barrier, are sent flying.

"Ares. Our apologies, but we'll hear your story later."

Ares has frozen at the sight of the horrendous attack, but after a few seconds, he comes to his senses. "B-but this situation is your fault—"

"Can you not see what's happening?!" Baal bellows, and Ares gulps. Frightened, Sahra hides behind Ares, but Baal doesn't pay any attention to her now. "It's a miracle that no one's died yet. With the fiend dragon hovering like that, we can't even send the citizens out of the capital! Criticize us later. Right now, we need that holy sword at once!"

"That's, um—"

"However, under the circumstances, we can't trust you with it," Isaac cuts in.

Baal *tsks*. "Like general, like subordinate, hmm? All you do is quibble. We don't care; do as you please."

"Then General Ares will be the one to use the holy sword, once it's repaired. You don't mind either, do you?" Isaac gives Aileen a mocking glance, and she remembers that scribbled note.

Oh, so that's what he meant.

"—All right, Sahra. We entrust the holy sword to you."

Baal holds his arms out. A shining gold rift opens in empty space.

The first thing to emerge is the hilt. As if being drawn from an expanding ring of golden ripples, a naked sword appears, rusted and chipped in places.

...The holy sword. He did say he had it, but...

If he can store objects in empty space, the holy king is as

limitless as the demon king. No wonder she couldn't even sense its presence.

Softly, the decrepit blade drops into Sahra's hands.

Silence spreads. Sahra presses her lips together tightly. Ares puts an arm around her shoulders. "Go on, Sahra."

"It may be wise to step back, everyone."

Thinking that now is the time, Aileen speaks up.

Apparently she's guessed correctly, because Isaac responds, "What do you mean?"

"The fiend dragon has already possessed someone. This refusal to leave the harem alone means that person may very well be here."

An uneasy murmur runs through the crowd. Baal intentionally hadn't revealed that information in order to avoid causing chaos; he shoots Aileen a critical glance, but she doesn't care. She watches Isaac's eyes, confirming only that she's correct. "What are you trying to say? Conjectures like that will only make people jump at shadows."

Isaac's eyes are smiling, and so she smiles back. "I'm merely concerned. Will the person possessed by the dragon and those who've been in contact remain unscathed once the holy sword has regained its power? There's no guarantee that the person who's been possessed is aware of it. After all, the attackers manipulated previously by the dragon weren't aware."

Ares is clearly disconcerted. The guards around him—probably people who were involved in his plot and in keeping the dragon imprisoned—don't seem to know where to look.

Suggest that the holy sword is dangerous for everyone who's been in contact with the fiend dragon.

That was what the note had said. If she does that, those people are sure to attempt to flee.

Well, we hardly have to look. It's so obvious.

In fact, the holy sword will work on the person who's been possessed by the fiend dragon and no one else. However, only those with knowledge of the game will know that. The only information these people have are centuries-old legends.

Ares has already promised he will wield the holy sword. If he backs out now, he'll be admitting he was involved. If he runs, he'll fatally disgrace himself.

"Of course, it's only a possibility. Besides, I highly doubt anyone who was involved with the fiend dragon would hardly have remained here, where we will be confronting that very same dragon with the holy sword. I apologize for the interruption."

Smiling, Aileen wraps up her speech. Ignoring the fact Ares's face has gone gray, she turns to Sahra. "Now then, Lady Sahra. Restore it, if you would."

Wordlessly, the girl grips the holy sword in trembling hands. When Ares sees this, his lips quiver. He may be trying to think of an excuse to back out of using the sword. Some of the soldiers he brought with him seem restless, too. One of them may confess about the fiend dragon.

At the very least, this should ensure that Ares doesn't become a hero…

"—I don't want to! I can't!!"

The unexpected voice, joined by the sound of the holy sword falling, makes Aileen blink. It's Sahra.

She's tossed the holy sword aside and is backing away, shaking her head. Ares looks startled. "Wh-what's the matter, Sahra? What do you mean, you can't?"

"N-no! I don't want to die."

"Die?"

"Yes, die! —Repairing the holy sword will kill me, won't it?!"

The question has come out of nowhere, and no one is able to respond. Sahra takes this as affirmation. She screams again. "I don't want to die!"

As if timed for that exact moment, the sky flashes again. Baal's barrier blocks the fiend dragon's latest attack, but as the world around them turns white, Sahra takes to her heels. She's making a run for it.

"Wha— Wait just a—"

"Sahra!!"

"After her, catch her! Sa… Sahra's gotten the wrong idea!"

On Ares's orders, Auguste takes off after Sahra. Although Ares has managed to give the order, he's still stunned. As everyone is standing there dazed, someone giggles quietly.

"I knew she wouldn't do. They may call her the Daughter of God, but she's only a half-baked fool."

"Lady Lilia, you…!" Realizing what she's put into Sahra's head, Aileen glares at Lilia.

It's a choice in the game. When the heroine confronts the fiend dragon, she is asked whether she will repair the holy sword and slay the dragon, even if it means risking her life. In fact, risking her life at that point is the only real option. No other correct answer is possible. If she runs from her mission, she'll die; if she faces it squarely, she'll survive. It's a gaming classic.

However, if one intentionally confronts a real, living human being with that choice, the matter is far more complicated.

"What were you thinking?! Neither you nor I can repair the holy sword!"

"It's all right. If my idea is correct— Serena."

At the sound of her name, Serena turns. Lilia smiles at her; she's picked up the damaged blade. "It's your turn. The holy sword is still alive."

"Huh?"

Serena looks as if none of this makes any sense to her. Aileen can't follow what's happening, either.

Lilia glances at their faces, then flashes a sweet smile. "Lady Aileen, you never played the fan disc for 2, did you? Hee-hee, that's still no excuse, though. You should have suspected something when you played Game 2."

"What do you..."

"Serena receives the sacred sword from Lilia, remember?"

She does, and then she makes Auguste a holy knight. She gives him the sacred sword.

...Wait a minute.

Would that be possible for an ordinary human, one with no abilities whatsoever?

"The idea sounds a bit like a retcon, but in any case, the idea is fleshed out in the fan disc: Lilia recognized Serena's ability and lent her the sword. Or, to be completely accurate, a single fragment of the sacred sword's power."

"Hold it. What are you talking about?"

"But Serena turns that into the sacred sword, then gives it to Auguste."

Lilia catches Serena's hand and places the holy sword in it. Then she gazes into her face. "Now then, as in the game, I'll teach you. It's all right; the flags have all been tripped. You've worked very hard. Auguste waited ten hours for you, didn't he?"

"What?! What are you talking about?! Exactly what does any of this have to do with Auguste?"

"You can't do a thing by yourself. However, you amplify others' power. Your feelings are the most important thing, of course, but even your body fluids can be used to boost performance."

With that, Lilia brings out a knife she's been concealing and slashes Serena's arm, the one that's holding the sword. A thin cut opens in both the fine silk and the skin beneath it, and there's a little spray of blood.

"It works on both demonic magic and sacred power."

Serena is stunned. A red bead trickles down her arm, then falls onto the rusted blade.

"And even a holy sword that's nearly destroyed, as long as it still has some power left."

In the next moment, the holy sword flares with light. The rust flakes off, and the chips in the blade are filled in by sacred power.

It can't be... It's repairing itself?!

The hilt with the holy crest engraved on it. The bright silver blade. The Kingdom of Ashmael's shining, precious sword.

"The holy sword...," someone murmurs.

The blade has risen into the air, and now it descends, scattering glittering particles of light—

"Ah— Ah, Aaaaaaaaaaah!!"

The dreamlike sight is shredded by Ares's scream. Everyone turns to look and is shocked into silence.

Darkness is swallowing the light generated by the holy sword. Instinctively, everyone understands that it's the fiend dragon. The inky substance overflows from the band on Ares's right arm, gradually staining that arm black. Baal shouts, "Ares, take that thing off!"

"M-my body...won't...obey—"

"Goodness, did Serena's blood splash onto the armband just now?" Lilia giggles cruelly. "If it did, then of course the fiend dragon's true body locked inside would naturally grow stronger."

"Out of the way!"

Shoving Lilia aside, Aileen swings the sacred sword at Ares's armband. The moment it connects, there's a *crack*, and the band splits and falls, rolling across the ground. Ares sits down hard.

"...What does she mean, 'the fiend dragon's true body'? Why would a thing like that emerge from your armband?"

"Th-this is— She has it wrong, there must be some sort of mistake. It's not the fiend dragon— I mean, the dragon possessed me! So—"

As Ares is stumbling through an incoherent excuse, the miasma that's flooded out of the armband traps his arm. One bloodred eye opens, then swells. Before he can even scream, Ares is engulfed by the miasma as if he's fallen into a swamp.

"Eep...!"

"Th-the fiend dragon devoured General Ares!"

The dragon tangles around soldiers' legs and swallows petrified harem attendants headfirst. The attacks aren't random, though. Only people Ares brought in are being taken. Isaac *tsk*s. "Anyone who helped lock the fiend dragon up, run for it! You're gonna get eaten!"

However, his warning and the screams and confusion are all blotted out by the light rays the red eyes shoot toward the sky. As if they're conspiring, the fiend dragon in the sky roars. The two are attacking the barrier from both sides, above and below.

Instantly, with a sound like shattering glass, the barrier fails. To anyone who can see sacred power, those glittering fragments must look like the harbinger of despair.

Freed from the armband and having fed on humans, the true body rises into the air and merges with the dragon hanging in the sky.

Baal promptly recasts the barrier, and the fiend dragon strikes at it again. An incredible gale blasts from the gaping maw. The dragon's attacks haven't reached them yet, but those light rays are getting closer and closer. Baal is struggling.

"I thought your defense was supposed to be perfect!"

"The intensity of the attacks is clearly different from what it was a moment ago! That isn't just magic!"

"Yes, it's been amplified by Serena's power. That alone would be serious enough, but since it's taken in humans as well, neither magic nor holy power can slay it now," Lilia explains, her tone alarmingly calm.

Resisting the desire to strike her, Aileen shouts, "All of you, evacuate the harem! Master Baal, once everyone has fled, take down the barrier!"

"What are you planning to do? There's no telling whether even the holy sword will work on that thing now...!"

"I'll hit it with a cheat!"

She grabs the holy sword, which no one is attempting to take up at this point. With her other hand, she grabs Lilia by the scruff of the neck; the woman was about to evacuate with everyone else. "Where are you going? Take responsibility! You're the one who—!"

"I'll be cheering the dashing Lady Aileen on from a distance!"

"Oh, I see. In other words, you're saying you're more useless than Serena, and worth less than the Daughter of God, correct?"

Lilia's eyebrows twitch. Aileen pushes the holy sword into her hands.

She doesn't actually want to leave this to Lilia. She'd rather die than work with her. However, the fiend dragon has swallowed Ares and other humans, and thanks to Serena's blood or whatever it was, this has already gone well beyond the game's plot. On top of that, to Aileen, victory doesn't mean slaying the dragon.

"Ares and the others are probably still alive. After all, sacred power isn't supposed to work on a dragon that possesses living humans. On the other hand, if we drag the humans out, that'll just leave a regular demon that's just been boosted by Serena's power. The sacred sword ought to work then."

"......"

Lilia doesn't respond, but she doesn't deny it, either. In other words, Aileen's correct.

"I'm going to rescue all the humans who got eaten. While I do, you use the holy sword to stop the dragon."

"Anyone can use the holy sword. It doesn't have to be me."

"Whether they're using the sword or not, no one will be able to stop that demon except you or me! You can do it, can't you? I don't trust you, but I do believe in you."

Lilia sighs, and her shoulders slump. She pouts, tilting her head prettily. "...That isn't fair, Lady Aileen. Saying a thing like that to your enemy is terribly gallant."

With that, she picks up the holy sword. Once again, the blade shines.

It's a power that surpasses both the Daughter of God and the Maid of the Sacred Sword. The corners of the woman's lips rise in a devilish grin. "Just this once, all right?"

"I don't want to do this again, either."

"Hey, it won't hold up much longer! You're ready, aren't you?! We're leaving this in your hands!!"

At Baal's shout, Lilia steps lightly forward. Aileen comes up beside her, and they look up at the fiend dragon together. The barrier winks out. They haven't done anything, but that horde of red eyes roll down to focus on them. Apparently the dragon knows who its enemies are.

"Let's go. Try not to hold me back."

"And you, Lady Aileen. Do your best to finish before I kill the dragon."

Aileen holds up her hand. The sacred sword materializes, followed by something else. The holy king's barrier is gone now, and so, using her shadow as a medium, Aileen cloaks the sacred sword in Claude's magic.

There is nothing this blade can't sever.

After all, the title of this game is *Regalia of Saints, Demons, and Maidens.*

Just what sort of monsters are they keeping over in Ellmeyer? Two of them, at that. That's Baal's first thought when he sees them.

Even the holy king's barrier had trouble with the fiend dragon's attacks, but Lilia repels them easily, while Aileen charges ahead as if the miasma isn't even there.

"...We really were wise to avoid war, weren't we? —Whoops."

The fiend dragon fires light rays from all over its body in every direction. Blocking all of them, Baal sighs. He doesn't have to maintain a huge barrier anymore, but apparently the task of protecting the kingdom still falls to him.

"Good grief, there's no time to rest."

"Hey. Here."

Someone shoves the broken armband in front of his face. It's the man who was at Ares's side earlier. Baal looks at him, impressed he's picked up an object the fiend dragon manifested from.

"The armband's from the Queendom of Hausel; it was created to imprison the fiend dragon. There's some sort of magic circle drawn on the inside. That's evidence."

"We seem to recall that you were Ares's aide."

"Never mind that, just hang on to this thing. Auguste is...not here, huh. Hey, what's-your-name. Serena."

"...What?" The woman who's been wrapping her cut arm with a bandage glares their way.

"You can move, right? Head back to the general's mansion and collect some more evidence. Anything's fine."

"Who said you could boss me around? Can't you see I'm wounded?"

"Not that badly. You'll get a bonus for each piece of evidence."

"Deal." Summarily changing her mind, the woman climbs to her feet and sets off.

Baal, who's watched their exchange, looks down at the armband. So this means... "Hey, don't tell me all of you are—?"

"Your Majesty, something's coming!"

The scream of a lower-ranking consort snaps his attention back to the action. He's braced himself for a dragon attack, but then he sees a human arm protruding from the incoming black mass. Reflexively, he catches it with sacred power. A human smeared with mud-like miasma hits the ground. When the figure groans, the surrounding crowd lets out its collective breath and starts shouting.

"It's one of the people who were devoured! ...They're still alive!"

"Th-they're okay...?!"

"—Hey! Split up and go grab the people they've rescued from the dragon, right now," the man who was Ares's aide shouts. He emphasizes the word *rescued*, impressing the fact that they're protecting people onto his listeners. "I mean every last one of them. They're vital witnesses; don't let them die! They should get General Ares out soon, too. Catch him; don't let him slip past you! That's what we should do, isn't it, Your Majesty?"

"That's fine. We'll leave it to you."

The soldiers haven't had much to do until now, and they spring into action. This is probably easier than just holding their breath and watching the fiend dragon. Keeping an eye on them, the man gives an exaggerated sigh. It's as if he's thinking *That's one job finished*... Even though the fight isn't over yet.

"You're one of Ellmeyer's men, aren't you?"

The man doesn't nod, but Baal's sure of it. This fellow, and the second prince's fiancée, and the woman who just left for the mansion— How many traps has Aileen set here? The second prince, who's apparently at Ares's mansion, may be bait as well.

"...'Friends,' hmm? Making a friend of that woman is one hell of a waste."

The aide's eyebrows twitch. *Oh-ho*, thinks Baal, but the man promptly gives him a wry smile. "Go ahead and negotiate that with our demon king."

"Come to think of it, is that man alive?"

"Honestly, if there's a way to kill him, I'd like to hear about it... Although I guess you might be able to manage it."

"Never fear. We're through loving the wrong women." After he says that, Baal finds himself looking into the distance. He wonders what Sahra is planning to do, now that she's fled.

...She was...an ordinary girl.

She possesses slightly more sacred power than normal. People had counted on her, so she'd mustered up her courage and tried to give it her best. That's probably all there is to her, and yet, because he and Ares had fallen for her, her life had been warped.

She'd never been the sort of woman who could serve as the holy king's queen.

Would it be possible to simply let her escape? What would Roxane say, if he proposed it?

More than Sahra's excuses, he's dying to hear from Roxane. He wants to know what she's thinking. He wants to hear what she sees when she looks at him.

He wants her to tell him whether she'll love him. Whether she'll be his wife.

"—It must be all right by now. Would you go and rescue our principal consort?"

The man's eyebrows draw together slightly, and he chooses his words carefully. "Shouldn't you be the one to do that?"

"We are the king. We must defend this place."

At the moment, the fiend dragon's attention is focused on Aileen and the other woman, but there's no telling when the beast might attack the rest of them. The harem has been emptied out and half-demolished, but even so, someone needs to protect it.

"...All right. The demon king may have saved her already, but I'll go look."

"Please do."

"Be a good king."

Encouragement doesn't come any more insolent than that. The holy king blinks, then laughs in response.

★ ★ ★

On the way to the harem's dungeon, they run right into each other. It's completely out of the blue, and Isaac freezes up.

"I-I-I-Isaac." She's flustered, too.

Thanks to that, he recovers first. "What are you doing?"

"U-um, I thought I would go check on Lady Roxane and Master Claude..."

So that's why her arms are full of spare clothes and a first aid kit. Isaac nods. "It's okay to let those two out now. I've got the keys. Let's go."

"A-all right. Um— If, um, you'll give me the keys, I could go alone—"

Before Rachel finishes her suggestion, a strong gust of wind blows past them, buffeting her. She stumbles forward. Catching her, Isaac glares upward, *tsk*ing. "Can't they fight a little more quietly up there? Unbelievable."

"I-I'm sorry, I—"

Hastily, Rachel puts some distance between them. Isaac doesn't have any legitimate reason to stop her. He's able to take half what she's carrying, though. "The holy king asked me, so I'm going, too. It's my job."

He's freed up one of Rachel's hands, and at first she looks startled. Then she smiles, nodding. "All right. Oh, I gave that note to Lady Aileen. Did it go well?"

"—Yeah. Thanks. Uh... About earlier..."

"It's fine. I'm glad I was useful." And because she's gone and said something that plucky and sweet... "...What? Um, I, huh?!"

"I can't have you getting blown away again, can I? C'mon, let's go."

...He takes her hand and pulls, pretending it isn't a big deal. The girl is confused anyway; she's not going to notice he's flushed all the way to his ears, and besides, this is an emergency.

An explosion rumbles above them. As Isaac and Rachel look back, the fiend dragon gives a howl—the loudest one yet.

The moment she grabs the hand submerged in darkness, she's sure of it: This is Ares, the last one. His hand doesn't tighten around hers, but it's warm. He's still alive.

When she thrusts with the sacred sword in her left hand, the dragon flinches backward. She tries to take that opportunity to pull Ares up, but the enraged dragon forces her back with a blast.

She flips in midair, then lands. She isn't able to kill her momentum, and her heels skid across the stone paving. She really liked these shoes, and now the heels are ground down to nubs.

She's on the clock tower, the highest point in the harem. It's been damaged in the fighting, and its bell is missing, so she has a very good view. Aileen gazes up at the dragon. Judging by the noticeably lower height, they've definitely weakened the demon. However, those countless eyes are growing redder and redder with anger, and the roars are almost nonstop now.

"It doesn't look as if we'll be able to drag General Ares out, does it? Shall we give up and put an end to it with the holy sword?"

Lilia lands lightly beside her.

"After all this work? Don't even joke about that. Master Baal!" Calling his name, she descends to the ground.

Baal, who's saved her from several of the fiend dragon's attacks, turns around. "What?"

"Please lend me your strength. The dragon refuses to release

General Ares. Could you use a sacred barrier to keep our friend in place? Even a few seconds will do."

"Don't ask the impossible. Neither sacred nor profane power alone is enough to stop that thing now."

"Even if you feel it won't work, it's better to try than do nothing. If sacred power alone won't do, I shall provide support with magic—"

Behind her, the fiend dragon moves again, firing an enormous light ray at her. Baal blocks the attack squarely with a barrier, but it shatters in the blink of an eye.

"Oh n—"

As the light bears down on her, Aileen gets a better grip on the sacred sword. And in that moment, a black shape suddenly appears in front of her. After an incredibly loud explosion, the light ray dissipates.

"Good grief. Why don't you turn to me at times like these?"

Finding the grumble very familiar, Aileen blinks.

Claude is there, holding Roxane. Both his streaming black hair and his beautiful face are perfectly unmarred.

Oh...

The things she'd steeled herself to witness once all of this was over are nowhere to be seen, and the flood of relief makes her knees go weak.

There isn't a scratch on Roxane, either. As Aileen is feeling reassured, the woman abruptly vanishes from Claude's arms.

"That's our consort. Return her."

It seems that Baal has forcibly teleported her. Roxane looks dazed, but when she realizes she's in her husband's arms, a flush steals over her pale cheeks. They don't say a word to each other.

However, since they share the same resolution, perhaps there's no need.

That's true of Aileen and her husband as well, and so she only calls his beloved name. "Master Claude..."

"Why didn't you come to save us first thing? As soon as the barrier was gone, I recovered, and then it was too late. You'll practically never get another chance to see me whipped and bloodied, you know."

She expected this, but the laid-back way he says it turns her worry into anger. "This is an emergency! If you have time to say things like that, then stop the fiend dragon, if you would!"

"The dragon, hmm? ...Such a shy thing before all this, but look at how the little one's grown..."

"This is no time to be impressed! If this goes on, we'll be forced to kill—"

"I swear, humans are always so..."

At the sight of the demon king's cold eyes, Aileen falls silent. At this rate they'll have to dispose of the fiend dragon, but Claude will never agree to it.

"The dragon won't listen to me; that human who got swallowed is getting in the way. If we pull him out and calm the poor thing down, everything should go back to normal."

"Are you sure? Wouldn't it be safer to kill it?" Lilia says, intentionally goading him.

Claude gives her a thin smile. "If you wish to kill the dragon, go ahead. However, it may spell the end for this country."

"...Demon King. What do you mean by that?"

"This is, or was, a water dragon. Water dragons are weak to pollution—to human malice. Long ago, a water dragon that had been defiled by malice came to be known by humans as the fiend dragon. The true nature of the creature never changed, though. That miraculous water sprang from the dragon, didn't it?"

"You mean the holy water didn't come from the holy sword?"

"You know the sword doesn't have the ability to generate water. It only purified the water drawn from the fiend dragon."

Come to think of it, that's true. No one can argue with him, but nobody completely believes him either. Only Lilia shrugs and mutters, "That's a shame." She must have known already.

"Fine. Demon King, we'll believe you." Baal hands down his decision first. Claude gives him a mystified look. "More accurately, we'll believe in Aileen, who believes you."

"...I see." Claude's tone drops ever so slightly, but this is no time to worry about that. They've reached a consensus.

"Then Master Claude, you and Master Baal keep the fiend dragon still. Lady Lilia and I will mount another charge."

"Lady Aileen," Lilia calls out, "I don't think the holy sword will last much longer."

"Make do with sheer willpower!" Aileen counters.

"Aileen." Claude snaps his fingers, then opens his hand. When she looks closer, she sees a ring. It's the wedding ring Baal took from her.

Baal sees it, too. He pats down the front of his kaftan, then yells. "Hey! When did you—?!"

"It already has magic in it. Thirty times as much as before."

"Th-thirty...times...?"

She feels as if she can see a deep-seated grudge—or rather, "magic"—rising from the ring...or perhaps not. She nearly draws back, but Claude doesn't give her a chance to refuse: He takes her hand and slips the ring onto her finger. Then he drops a gentle kiss in the same spot. "Give it your best, and don't worry about watching your back. I'll protect you."

"Y…yes, of course!"

Claude's words clear away any unease she feels. She turns back, fixing her eyes on the dragon. The strength of a hundred men is hers to command. With the power of love, there's no way she can lose. "Let's go, Lady Lilia!"

"What? No, talk amongst yourselves a little longer, or we could take a little break—"

This is getting tiresome, so Aileen grabs her by the scruff of the neck and hurls her at the dragon. The woman is complaining about something or other, but there's no need to listen.

"Master Claude, Master Baal!"

Red and violet eyes flash. The fiend dragon gives a roar that sounds like a scream.

Caught in an enormous net of magic, the demon struggles, attacking in all directions. The sacred barrier contains the wild rampage. Lilia runs the shining holy sword through narrow gaps in it. "Really! What does Lady Aileen think I am?"

Evading all the fiend dragon's attacks without turning a hair, Lilia makes a precise horizontal slash through the dragon's middle. Aileen slides between the two halves and grabs Ares's hand again. As if the dragon means to swallow Aileen as well, the wound begins to close around her. Lilia, who's gone in behind her, slashes it open again and laughs. "If you don't hurry, you'll end up dying with me."

"That isn't even funny! —!"

A multitude of eyes have appeared on the inside of the gaping wound. Just as she thinks *No—*, the dragon gives another roar, freezing as if bound in place. Claude has begun his assault, drawing the dragon's attention to the outside, while Baal focuses on containment.

"My, the demon king and holy king are doing surprisingly well, aren't they?"

"—Let go of this thing, dragon...!" Aileen yells, hauling on Ares's arm. "If you eat someone like him, you'll make yourself sick to your stomach!!"

Just then, as if all their struggles had been some sort of illusion, Ares slips free. She tosses him out, then makes her escape from the howling fiend dragon's interior.

In what seems to be a final show of resistance, the fiend dragon's entire body begins to glow. The attacks are completely indiscriminate now. A light ray slips through the barrier and blows the harem's clock tower away. However, Claude has struck the dragon in the back of the head, and that mist-like form is gradually coalescing into the shape of a dragon again. The demon is returning to normal.

When dragon feet appear on the ground, Lilia skewers one of them with the holy sword, pinning it in place. It turns out that was the final gasp because the sword shatters right after.

"Now, Lady Aileen!"

All those red eyes come to bear on Aileen. She meets them squarely. Claude's barrier is at her back. She has nothing to fear.

"Be a good little one and go to sleep!"

Pouring all the power she has into her attack—Claude's magic from the ring combined with the power of the sacred sword—she slashes at the top of the dragon's head.

There's a light, audible crack, as if a shell just broke. Then the mass of miasma crumbles away, flaking off like caked dirt.

Aileen felt a clean hit land. Right then, a burst of light appears right in front of her.

"Aileen!"

The last thing she sees is a world of white blasting away all impurities. However, as she falls backward, she knows the arms that catch her are her husband's.

The fiend dragon is no longer in the sky. Listening to the distant cheers as if they've nothing to do with her, Serena checks the sheaf of documents one more time, then hugs them to her chest and leaves Ares's mansion.

I told Prince Cedric to make a quick exit. I didn't expect Sahra to be here, though.

Foolishly straightforward, the Daughter of God had returned to her own room, packed up her things, and tearfully begged Marcus—who'd been passing through—to let her go. She doesn't know what they plan to do with her, but apparently Cedric had been the one who convinced her to go with them. That second prince is constantly plotting something or other... Although it's possible that Lilia was pulling the strings.

"......"

Your power.

Remembering what she's been told, she clenches her fist and opens it again.

If I can't do anything personally, there's no point.

In other words, she's still herself, and nothing has changed. The wound on her arm is just a cut; it will probably heal up soon. She's been put through plenty of awfulness, so she's going to make sure she gets her just reward. Of course, she'll be charging separately for the Queendom of Hausel guard duties.

In the end, the one to use the holy sword and defeat the fiend dragon had been Lilia or Aileen. She hadn't been involved at all—or so she thinks.

"...?!"

"Don't make a sound."

Someone has grabbed her hair, set a knife against her throat and dragged her into the bushes. As everyone else is rejoicing over the now-empty sky, this man's face is gloomy, and he's wearing an unpleasant smirk. "I've been waiting for you."

"General...Ares..."

His looks have changed so drastically that it's taken her a moment to recognize him. With the tip of his knife at her throat, Serena looks around. Ares, and—one, two others. They're all men who were devoured by the dragon. They're grimy, and there are no bright futures waiting for them now.

"General Ares, this woman has the account book! The one with the record of bribes and contraband weapons from the Queendom of Hausel."

"I don't care. She'll be a souvenir. A present from us to the Queendom."

Serena had assumed she'd be used as a hostage while they made their escape, and the unexpected remark makes her eyes widen.

Ares puts his face right up to hers. "You're the one who repaired the holy sword, aren't you?"

You won't be able to go back.

The words she heard on the clock tower echo in her mind.

"I've never heard of the ability to amplify others' power. If

I've got you, the Queendom of Hausel is sure to treat me as an honored guest."

"...And Lady Sahra? What about her? She's your wife and the Daughter of God—"

"Enough about that woman! Never mind her. You're worth more now."

Sahra. She certainly hadn't liked her. The girl had manipulated people by acting cute, thrown her weight around, and gotten an inflated ego over being worshipped as the Daughter of God.

However, when she'd run from this man because she didn't want to die, she'd made the right choice.

"I could make you my wife, if you want."

"No thank you!"

Slipping a small knife out of her sleeve, she slashes through her own trapped hair. She's caught him off guard; now's her chance to make a break for it. She doesn't have the power to fight several people head-on and win, especially not if they're trained men.

But Ares reacts faster. As if he's predicted her movements, he strikes her back with the hilt of his sword, then sweeps her feet out from under her.

"Agh...!"

"Don't struggle. I don't want to hurt you any more than I have to. Your body's fluids are valuable."

She's collided with the trunk of a tree, and she sinks down. Her ankle is hot where he tripped her. She may have sprained it. Her back hurts, and after ramming into that tree, so does the rest of her.

"I won't waste a single drop of blood. Or any tears."

It's a purely physiological response, but her eyes have begun to well up. When he sees that, Ares smiles. He grabs her chin, tilting her face up, and licks them away. It's disgusting. She grinds her teeth in frustration. *Don't cry! Crying won't help, and you know it.*

No one will save her. She's the only person she can rely on. It was the same when her cousin hit her, and even when she'd obtained the demon snuff— She must have been born unlucky when it comes to men. The thought actually makes her smile.

"You know, you've got a pretty face," Ares says out of nowhere. His eyes look exactly like the ones her uncle once turned on her. "If your fluids can work miracles, what would happen if I put a baby in y—?"

She can't move very well, so instead she spits in his face.

"There, have some fluids. Be grateful and lick that off."

"You bitch—!"

He slaps her across the face. Then he rips her bodice open. She gives a short, sharp laugh. Everything men do is simpleminded. She clenches her fists. She isn't scared. Make him angrier, she's not scared—if he's angry he's sure to get careless—she's not scared, it doesn't matter if nobody comes to save her, she can fight.

But for how long, all by herself...?

"Serena?"

That voice is painfully out of place here. She sees a stupid-looking face.

Of all people, she thinks, just as the weight that was bearing down on her vanishes. She hears a groan, and the men who were keeping her pinned sink to the ground.

"—What are you people doing?"

Auguste has taken down two men just like that, and he straightens up slowly. He seems like a different person. Ares, who had apparently put some distance between them on reflex, draws his sword and levels it at him.

With a gasp, she remembers: Auguste has never won against Ares in hand-to-hand combat.

"Don't! You can't beat him!"

By the time she tries to stop him, Auguste is already in motion. Flawlessly, the tip of his sword precisely darts toward Ares's neck. Ares evades that strike, but Auguste drops into a crouch and lashes out with a kick, which catches his opponent in the side. Ares goes flying, and as he rolls over the ground, Auguste stabs his sword down right next to his face.

The entire battle lasted only a moment. Ares is stunned, unable to grasp what happened.

"...They tell me you're an important witness." Auguste's voice is flat; all of his usual cheeriness is gone. "But if you ever do anything like that to Serena again, I'll kill you."

Yanking his sword out of the ground, Auguste mercilessly strikes the side of Ares's head, and Serena's eyes squeeze shut. When she opens them and sees how still Ares is lying, she turns to Auguste nervously. "Did you...kill him? You can't have..."

"He's alive; I just knocked him out. Um... Serena."

When Auguste turns to look at her, a shudder runs through her. Seeing it, he hastily scrubs his hands on his clothes as hard as he can. Once they're clean, he slowly holds them out to her. "Um... Uh, your hair."

"......"

"A-are you o—?"

"I am obviously not okay! And you're late!"

When she yells at him, Auguste looks stunned, then flustered. "I-I'm really sorry! I was late, wasn't I?! I'm sorry!"

"How are you going to make it up to me?! My hair— I'd grown it out so nicely... Lend me your jacket!"

"Yes'm!"

"I can't get up, I can't walk...!"

"I'll carry you on my back! So, um..."

The world is warping. Even so, she can clearly see Auguste's thoroughly troubled face. "Don't cry. I won't know what to do if you—"

Irritated by his total lack of consideration, she smacks her forehead into his shoulder. She's certainly not clinging to him. She's also not crying. She just has dust in her eyes. Apparently her tears are expensive; there's no way she'd just give them away for free like that.

But she's sure this man would never say her tears were valuable.

Auguste freezes up for a moment, but then he puts his arms around her and holds her close.

See? He can do it if he tries. The thought relieves her, just a little.

Every morning, the first thing she should see when she wakes is her husband. And so, when her eyes open, she isn't quite sure where she is.

"—leen, Aileen...!"

"Master Claude... Is it morning already...?"

Claude blinks. He looks around. "Morning... It, uh, might still be morning."

"...Of course, the fiend dragon!"

As everything comes rushing back, Aileen leaps from Claude's arms. Then she blinks.

The sun is high in the sky, and a beautiful white dragon gleams in its dazzling rays. The stunning creature is just a little larger than a human, and as soon as their eyes meet, the dragon ducks behind Claude to hide from Aileen.

However, being larger than Claude, it's adorably failing to stay behind cover.

"...Master Claude. That dragon..."

"Yes, this is the fiend dragon. Or rather, the water dragon."

Dazed, Aileen looks around. Apparently, she was only unconscious for a moment.

Baal is close by, with Roxane at his side, and they're both looking at her with concern. The others aren't around, but the sky holds no trace of the fiend dragon.

It's over. The moment she realizes, the fatigue hits her and she collapses back into Claude's arms. "Th... This was just as exhausting as last time."

"Guests from Ellmeyer." Slowly, Baal steps forward. Roxane takes her place beside him, and behind them, their citizens kneel.

Claude begins to pick her up, but Aileen stops him and gets to her feet on her own. This is diplomacy.

The king of the neighboring country bows his head to them. "You have saved our kingdom, and we thank you. I hope we will remain good neighbors."

"We couldn't ask for a more welcome proposal," Claude replies.

"We would like to express our gratitude somehow. Granted, we do have a kingdom to rebuild, so we won't be able to part with anything valuable."

"Master Baal, you shouldn't say it like that." Roxane frowns, reproaching him.

Claude smiles at her. "In that case, it just so happens I have a request for you. Provided Queen Roxane doesn't mind."

"...Me? Might I ask...?"

"Could you let this little one—the water dragon—live in the harem?"

The request is completely unexpected, and Baal's eyes fly open. Aileen blinks, looking back and forth between Claude's profile and the hiding water dragon. Roxane's eyes are wide; she sounds bewildered. "...Let this live in the harem... You mean you would like the dragon to be a consort?"

"Wait a minute, it's a female?! Wait, more importantly—Make it a consort?! You want us to marry that?! What brought this on?!"

When Baal points at the water dragon, she curls her tail up as if she's embarrassed and buries her face in her sharp claws. She's actually pretty cute.

"She says that while she was visiting you every night, she developed feelings for you."

"We don't understand this at all! Or rather, we don't even want to...!"

"You talked to her every night, didn't you? About how unrequited love was painful, and how you were lonely all by yourself."

"Aaaaaaaaaaaaaaaaaaaaah?!"

Baal screams into the sky, then crumples to his knees. The dragon's long whiskers twitch, and she watches Baal, looking flustered.

"It made her sympathize with you."

"That's...just...ridiculous..."

"She says that, if it's your kingdom, she doesn't mind ensuring it never runs out of water."

Startled, Baal looks up. Aileen hasn't been able to interrupt this preposterous development either, but she finally understands what Claude is trying to do.

In this arrangement, as long as Ashmael remains a good neighbor to the demon king, they'll never lack for water.

Once she realizes this, the king's principal consort doesn't hesitate. "Very well. I will welcome her into the harem as the holy king's consort."

"Roxane?! Listen, even we aren't up to making children with this!"

"Resign yourself."

"You... What...?" Baal totters.

Ignoring him, Roxane looks up at the water dragon, who's still hiding behind Claude. "Lovely dragon princess. You are like a daughter to the demon king, the crown prince of Ellmeyer. I am the principal consort, but no doubt that rank would be insufficient in this case. In order to ensure that you remain a consort of this kingdom for a very long time—I will create a new title for you. You shall be the one and only holy dragon consort. You are welcome to live anywhere you wish in this harem, nay, in the kingdom."

"...Thank you." Lowering his eyes, Claude gives the water dragon's back a gentle push. "If things ever get hard for you, come home anytime."

"—Do you think you can gloss this over by talking like you're giving your daughter away in marriage?! Look, I know you're enjoying yourself! Is this payback because we took Aileen?!"

Baal tromps forward, discarding his regal expression, and hauls Claude up by his shirtfront.

Claude responds impassively. "You never took my wife."

"Oh-ho, is that right? Yes, we suppose you can't yet call Aileen your wife anyway, can you...?!"

"—What's that supposed to mean?"

"Exactly what it sounds like. For a husband who doesn't perform, you sure talk big."

Aileen feels as if she's heard a crack form in Claude's impervious blank expression. It isn't her imagination; he proves as much by setting a hand on the hilt of his sword. "And you have a mountain of consorts, but you're still lonely. So lonely this dragon pities you."

"Why you— You're bringing that up now?! Fine, then... We're keeping Aileen."

"What?!"

"Since you're a coward, we'll take over for you and make her moan every night! Ha! Ha! Ha!"

The crash of swords echoes through the harem, where the fighting had supposedly ended. The demon king has fully drawn, and the holy king blocked with his own blade.

"Magic won't work on us."

"Fine words from someone who can only defend."

"We never said we couldn't use a sword!"

True to his words, Baal raises his blade against Claude in style. The blast wind is probably from the magic and sacred power they're both using to supplement their skills.

"W-wait, you two! Don't!"

"Aileen is my wife!"

"No, she's ours!"

The two slash away at each other. Neither looks like they are about to start listening. War has suddenly erupted between the demon king and the holy king— Put that way, it sounds impressive. However, this is just a brawl, and the people around them have no idea what to do.

If the kings keep this up, we won't get anything resolved!

Someone taps her on the shoulder. When she turns around, Roxane is standing there, holding two buckets. "This is holy water. I drew it over there. Please take one."

I see. Nodding, Aileen accepts a bucket from Roxane. Between the two of them, they may have enough to make a river.

Then they promptly slosh it over the brawlers.

"..........."

"..........."

Soaked from head to toe, the two turn to look at them. Tossing her bucket aside, Aileen speaks up. "It appears that neither of you is sufficiently conscious of your position as king."

"If you must continue this, please indulge yourselves out of the public eye."

"...Wait just a minute, Roxane. Don't tell us this is holy water—"

Before Baal can finish his question, the ground sinks under their feet. Water floods away from them in a muddy torrent, mingling with the canal, and washes the pair downstream.

In the blink of an eye, they're out of sight. After she's seen them off, Aileen turns to Roxane. "Shall we get the terms hammered out while we have the opportunity?"

"Yes, let's. Someone bring us tea."

"Sweetened with sugar that isn't sand, if you would," Aileen says, and Roxane gives the faintest hint of a smile.

It may be holy water, but it isn't harmful to humans. He'd let the current take him because he was startled, but when he uses magic, getting out is easy enough. Watching the water rush under him toward the canal, Claude pushes his dripping hair out of his face. "What a thing to do to her husband..."

"We couldn't agree more." The remark comes from a short distance away; Baal has climbed up onto the bank. He shrugs. "Well, it probably means one shouldn't defy one's wife."

"Yes, there's no telling what that wife of mine may do."

"Apparently our wife is also frightening if we anger her. We didn't know that until today."

For some reason, laughter works its way up from Claude's insides. Then, the same happens to Baal.

The two kings laugh on the riverbank for a while, looking like a pair of drowned rats. Then they both sneeze dramatically.

✦ Final Act ✦
The End of the Villainess's Journey

James is at the demon king's desk, buried in paperwork, when the door opens. He glances up. "What, you're back, Auguste?"

"Uh-huh. The holy king can use teleportation, so he sent us back instantly."

"How did it go?"

Isaac has given him a report already, so he knows the rough story. However, unusually, Auguste has worry lines between his eyebrows. In the middle of signing his name with the quill pen, James pauses, puzzled. "What's the matter? Did something else come up?"

"Oh, um. Everyone's safe, and they're going to ratify an official treaty…? Or something like that. The holy king and his wife are going to visit Ellmeyer one of these days, and we caught the bad guys, so that went well, but… James? Can I ask you something?"

"Ask me what?"

"You and I are friends, right? —Do you ever want to hug me or touch my hair or hold my hand?"

James's fingers snap the quill pen. Auguste has good instincts, at least, and he straightens up.

"So you're trying to get me so angry I turn into a demon, hmm? Is that what this is?"

"Oh— Sorry! You don't think those things, of course you don't! I knew that. I just thought I'd ask…!"

"Even getting a question like that is extremely unpleasant!"

"I said I was sorry! But… Yeah, you're completely right… Haaah…"

Auguste is so dejected that he crouches down on the spot. That cools James's temper, but he isn't nice enough to try to draw him out.

"What am I going to do? I really don't think I can be friends with Serena."

So it *was* something stupid. He feels like grumbling *Finally*, but he changes the subject instead. "Never mind that. When are Master Claude and Aileen coming back?"

"Oh, probably by next week or so? Come on, James, help me out. I don't know what to do."

"No. Go ask Walt."

Auguste whines about it, but just then they hear footsteps out in the hall; someone's heard that Auguste is back. It's a familiar sound, part of their daily routine.

To James, the fact that life is returning to normal is far more important.

"…Don't you think that's just mean?"

Claude sounds unusually despondent.

Aileen, who's left the after-dinner cleanup to Rachel, gives him the same answer she's given him several times before. "Well, you did make Master Keith angry."

"But telling me not to come home for the time being? He's gone too far."

"There's no help for that. Your fever's come down, but if you leave the holy king's barrier while you're in poor health, there's no telling what will happen to the weather."

"That's true, but…"

Claude, who's sitting up in bed in his nightclothes, doesn't seem convinced. He sighs, looking at the response from Keith.

The words on the paper say, *Take it easy in the Kingdom of Ashmael until you recover.* However, interpreted rather freely, it means *Dimwitted fools who'd visit the Kingdom of Ashmael without permission and then catch a cold aren't welcome home until they're better.* Keith is probably mad he's been forced to run around trying to make sense of the fact that Claude, the crown prince of Ellmeyer, aided the Kingdom of Ashmael. His anger is palpable in every word of the impeccably polite letter.

Aileen herself has received a heartwarming message from her father, Rudolph, the prime minister, telling her to come have dinner with the rest of the family once she's back. If she doesn't prepare herself thoroughly before going home, she'll probably die instantly.

"Just take your time and rest, Master Claude. There will be work waiting for you when you get back. After the incident in Ashmael, there's no longer any need to visit the Queendom of Hausel, but we do have to deal with them as well in due time. There's a mountain of problems… Yes, think of this as our honeymoon and relax, please!"

"Our honeymoon…? This ridiculous, chaotic mess…?"

Claude looks at her as if he doesn't want to believe it, but she nods firmly. "Yes. We should have had the others stay here as well, instead of just Rachel. Isaac and the rest returned without even sightseeing. A change of location can often result in a change of mood, too…"

"Ah… Well, that's all right, isn't it? They held hands and embraced. Really, Cedric's the only one who made no progress. And he calls himself my little brother. Pathetic."

"…What are you talking about?" She blinks at him.

Claude shrugs and changes the subject. "I should be able to get out of bed by tomorrow. How's the holy king?"

"Much the same as you, Master Claude. He tried to sneak out of bed, saying he was well enough to move around, but was discovered by Lady Roxane and sent back. Still, he seemed rather pleased to have her caring for him."

"She'll have him firmly under her thumb before he knows it. Is the holy dragon consort being a good girl?"

"Yes. She was enjoying a bath a little while earlier. Master Baal seems to have given in and allowed her into his bedchamber. I'm told they're going to expand the current room and make a place for her to sleep."

"I'll order her to be sure to get into bed with him. That's a wife's duty," Claude declares, with an oddly invigorated smile. *If she does that, Master Baal may never be able to sleep with anyone again*, Aileen thinks. However, if she points that out and the two start fighting again, they'll have an epic war between good and evil on their hands, so she decides to not mention it.

"The rebuilding also seems to be going well… The harem consorts are putting in a surprising amount of effort. They're also taking meticulous care of the water dragon."

"They are, hmm? That's good to hear."

As a matter of fact, many of them are motivated by the belief that if the dragon takes a liking to them, the crown prince of Ellmeyer may fall in love with them at first sight, but she doesn't tell him this, either.

"So the remaining problems are how to handle the Daughter of God and the Queendom of Hausel, hmm? …I assume it would be best to coordinate our efforts on both fronts with the Kingdom of Ashmael."

"Yes, I believe so."

"Either way, there can be no specific support, trade, or policies unless the holy king and I sign a treaty. If possible, I'd like to get at least that done by tomorrow."

"I thought you would say that, so Lady Roxane and I have been making preparations."

"...You and the principal consort get along well, don't you?"

"It's less that we get along and more that we both have troublesome husbands."

"That's the other one. I'm not a troublesome husband."

Baal is probably saying the same thing to Roxane. Giggling, Aileen checks to see how much water remains in the pitcher on the nightstand, then lowers the lights. Ordinarily, she would leave these things to Rachel or the servants, but she wants to nurse Claude herself as much as possible.

Once they leave this place, it's going to be hard to relax and spend time with him again.

"Tomorrow will be a busy day. Please hurry and go to sleep."

"—Aileen."

He's caught her hand. When she turns back, the sight of the red eyes smoldering in the dim light makes her freeze up.

"You should sleep here tonight."

She's fully aware of what he means by that.

"...B-but, this is... I mean, we are guests..."

"It doesn't matter. Actually, the fact that they gave us separate rooms even though we're married made me murderous... Besides, this may not be the best way to put it, but because of the holy king's barrier, it's a sure thing here."

"But I haven't bathed yet."

Both physically and emotionally, she's completely unprepared for this. Should she call Rachel and get ready as quickly as possible? But she feels as if doing so may spoil the mood. While she's dithering, he pulls her toward him, and she falls onto the bed. Claude's mischievous red eyes are laughing at her. "You kissed me, remember? What happened to all that courage?"

"Th-that was the heat of the moment..."

"Thanks to that, my plan was ruined. I'd intended to make your first time something you wouldn't forget as long as you lived, and then you stole away my opportunity so callously."

The way he phrases it embarrasses her so badly she feels as if flames may shoot from her head. "I-if you put it that way, um... I—I was startled, too."

"Oh, I startled you, hmm? —In that case, let's practice. Your hands, Aileen."

"P-practice?"

"Yes. Kissing."

The honeyed mood has dulled her wits, and as she's trying to puzzle out what he means, Claude takes both her hands and pulls her arms around his waist. "Hold on to my shirt. That's right. Now close your eyes."

Obeying his pleasant voice, she closes her eyes, and he gently covers her lips with his own.

Oo-ooh...

The embarrassment makes her want to scream, but she squeezes Claude's shirt and endures it.

"Breathe. You don't have to be nervous, Aileen. We're still just practicing."

"P-prac...practice... I-I'll, do my, best, but..."

"Good girl. Don't be embarrassed, just—open your mouth."

"Y-yes...?!"

When his tongue slips between her lips, her voice cracks. *I—I can't, I can't, I can't, this is too much, I'll die!*

His tongue seems to steal her very breath away. The back of her head tingles, and that sweetness is the ultimate poison. She tries to shake her head, but it won't budge. As if he's picked up on Aileen's faint resistance, Claude whispers between kisses. "Aileen, relax. It's all right, you're doing well... And now for the real thing."

"I—I can't, Master Claude. I'm not, c-confident I can manage more than—"

"I love you."

He'd say that now? Not only that, but he pushes her down, and his kisses grow deeper. Even so, because she's grabbing at his shirt for dear life, she can't push him back.

Not being able to breathe properly makes tears well up in her eyes. She doesn't know what she should do, or how. She's simply at his mercy, and she calls his name, as if asking for help. "Master... Claude."

"I won't do anything frightening. I'll cherish you. Only you, for as long as we live." In a husky voice, Claude implores her. "I want you."

In the dim bed, his red eyes beseech her desperately. If she rejects her beloved husband when he tells her he wants her, when he begs, simply because she lacks confidence, she doesn't deserve to be his wife. Besides, to truly become husband and wife is what she's been wanting this whole time.

Women must be bold. Mustering up her courage, Aileen nods. "A-a-all...right... B-but, Master Claude, please promise me one thing."

"What is it?"

"I-if you don't feel well..."

"If you mean my cold, it won't be a problem."

"B-but you, erm… You have another issue, don't you?"

Claude blinks at her, once. When he responds, he seems to be sounding her out. "…As I said before, we're inside the holy king's barrier. Right now, I'm no different from a normal human."

"I—I know that. These symptoms are precisely because you are a normal man." These are the times when a wife must put her best foot forward. Aileen makes a firm request. "And so, even if it doesn't work this time, please don't lose confidence!"

"……"

"I promise I'll help you! …Master Claude?"

"…I'd like to check on one thing. Just to make sure we're on the same page."

What could it be? It seems late for a question like this, and she's perplexed, but she nods.

With eyes so mild that their earlier passion seems like a dream, Claude strokes her hair gently. "What issue of mine do you mean?"

"…Oh, n-no. Are you asking me to say it aloud?"

"It's the sort of thing you can't say?"

"O-of course. I…I couldn't possibly speak of a man's, erm, you know what, in explicit terms."

"—Is that what this is? Do you think I have trouble functioning as a male?"

He's speaking about it quite directly. She tries to get mad about that, but his smile is oddly intense and overawes her. She blinks.

Claude lowers his head. His shoulders are quivering. He's laughing. "I see… I see, yes, so that's what it is. I'm so glad this happened in Ashmael." But his eyes aren't smiling. She has a bad feeling about this. "If this were Ellmeyer, the shock would have made me blow the castle away."

"U-um, actually, let's not do this tonight after all!" Shuddering, Aileen tries to get up, but he promptly pins her shoulders down.

"I take it back. I'm going to get a little rough. You just stay beneath me and moan all night long."

There's anger mingled with his passion now, and his red eyes glitter ominously. A shiver runs down her spine. "M-Master Claude, don't tell me…um…"

He smiles back at her, and while she doesn't understand what's going on, she does realize that she had the wrong idea. In that case, this anger of Claude's is— When it hits her, she feels the blood drain from her head. "W-wait, Master Claude! Calmly, let's discuss this calmly!"

"I am extremely calm. Now then, where shall I savor you first?"

"I am not food— Ouch! Please refrain from biting me! Wait— Don't— Then what was this physical issue of yours?!"

"We can think about that later. Right now, you're so precious it may drive me mad. You did say you would accept my everything, didn't you?"

"A-at least hold back a little! Control yourself, please! I'm begging you, Master Claude…!"

He steals her lips, and her head reels. *It's no use*, she thinks, *I'm going to be swept away*, but just then—

"Demon king! You wretch! What order did you give the water dragon?!"

Baal abruptly materializes over the bed, and Claude stops moving.

"Things were just getting good with Roxane, and that thing jumped in and ruined it! How dare you get in our way...!"

"...Can't you see what's going on here? You've taken the words right out of my mouth."

"Ha! You got in our way, so there's no need for us to stay out of yours!"

Laughing in the face of Claude's anger, Baal folds his arms. He's quite impressive. Claude gets up, moving with menacing slowness. Quietly, Aileen slips out from beneath him.

"It looks as if I really will have to settle things with you once and for all."

"Bring it on. We'll make it so you can never get in our way again."

"And as I said, that's my line!"

With that, swords begin to clash, and Aileen heaves a deep sigh.

"Wh-what is this, Lady Aileen?! Master Claude, Master Baal..."

"Let them be, Rachel. This palace is going to be demolished shortly, so have everyone evacuate, if you would. I'll sleep in Lady Roxane's room tonight."

"I—I see... I-is that all right?"

"It's fine."

Behind her, the clang of sword blades are punctuated with the sounds of smashing windows and furniture. Angry yells and cursing fly this way and that, but it's basically just a scaled-up children's squabble.

Listening to the lively noise behind her, Aileen smiles, half in disgust and half fondly.

"After all, seeing Master Claude act like this is rather novel."

★ ★ ★

Claude Jean Ellmeyer's first achievement as crown prince was the restoration of diplomatic relations with the neighboring Kingdom of Ashmael, which had historically been unstable. There are many interpretations of his relationship with Holy King Baal, who is famed for vanquishing the fiend dragon. Some say they were good friends, while others say they were rivals in love. However, the water dragon presented to the holy king by Demon King Claude was granted the rank of holy dragon consort and became Ashmael's constant protector through the years.

Subsequently, Ashmael's harem was transformed into a garden of women who cared for the holy dragon consort. The child of Holy King Baal's principal consort Roxane later married into the Ellmeyer Empire, and the two nations headed by the holy king and the demon king forged a steadfast relationship as friendly neighbors.

However, one fact has been neatly omitted from the records by considerate scribes: On the day the treaty that would serve as the foundation of all this was signed, the holy king and demon king were dragged to the table by their respective wives, looking very ragged indeed.

✦ Encore ✦
The Final Bosses' Tea Party

"Our wife is adorable."

As he says this, the holy king is resting both elbows on the table, his face deadly serious.

Bragging about his sweetheart, hmm? Claude frowns over his cup of tea. "What are you saying? My wife is adorable, too."

"It's a different sort of adorable. We don't understand it, but she seems about fifty percent more beautiful than she did before. We can't get enough of that awkward smile of hers. How can a principal consort be so precious? Isn't it a crime?"

"I think the exact same thing about my wife. It seems that's known as 'love seeing no faults.'"

"It really is, then? But how can we say it… Even so, we don't want to let other men see her."

"That probably won't be possible. As principal consort, no doubt she'll choose to be in the public eye." Roxane and Aileen are very similar that way. It's likely they have the same type of strength.

Baal knows this. He rests his chin in his hands and sighs. "You're almost certainly right. Good grief; we've fallen for yet another troublesome woman. But she is adorable."

"Did you come here to go on and on about how lovable your queen is? Does the holy king have that much time on his hands?"

"Roxane is still insisting that we take it easy. When we told her we wanted to discuss things with you ahead of the conference in Ellmeyer, she allowed us to do that. It makes no sense."

"What a coincidence. Aileen gave me permission to get out of bed as long as I was going to talk to you..."

Is it possible they're both being neatly managed by their wives? The thought does occur to him, but Claude pretends he hasn't noticed. He can't have Aileen drenching him with holy water again.

"Still, what sorts of things does one talk about at a time like this? Should we mention the fine weather?" Folding his arms arrogantly, Baal jerks his chin at the garden around them.

Bright sunlight streams down into their surroundings. The pavilion technically isn't suited to confidential talks, but a thin, membrane-like barrier has been cast to keep others from overhearing their conversation. It's very sophisticated: Although their conversation won't get out, sounds from outside can still filter in, so they are able to hear birdsong and the murmur of running water.

Whatever else, he is still the holy king, Claude thinks.

"Talking about the weather is an all-purpose greeting. I read as much in a book of some sort."

"Hmm. Then let's say we've gotten the greetings out of the way and get to the discussion. We were technically told to ask, in a roundabout way, how you would prefer we handled Sahra and Ares, the Daughter of God and the mastermind of the rebellion."

"It doesn't interest me. It wouldn't be a decisive blow to the Queendom of Hausel in any case."

"True. As far as we're concerned, having the water dragon stop by our bedchamber every night to make a nuisance of herself is a bigger problem."

"Take good care of her."

"Fine. In that case, we'll continue to make a nuisance of ourself after you've returned to Ellmeyer."

"Let me ask again. How much free time do you have?"

"Have no fear, we'll teleport. It will be instantaneous. Destroying the mood for you every single time will be a simple matter. By the way, is it true that you have a demon king's castle there? Show us around. We've always wanted to see demons."

The holy king could eradicate all demons, but his eyes are sparkling like a child's. Finding that peculiar, Claude leans back in his chair. "As long as you don't menace them... You're a strange one. Demons don't frighten you?"

"We are the holy king. Why should we fear demons? Even you, their king, are merely human in our presence."

Logically, he understands it, but it just doesn't feel real.

In the first place, I'm not sure how to treat a human who is my equal.

As that absent thought crosses Claude's mind, Baal nods, looking smug. "You can't believe it, hmm? Quite so; we can't believe it either. To think that a human who was our equal existed in the world."

"If it doesn't feel real to you, either, why are you so confident?"

"Well, it's entertaining, isn't it? Come on, the holy king and demon king are having tea. Nothing good can come of this. Listen, will you be all right if you go back to Ellmeyer?"

When he hears that question, for the first time, it sinks in.

This is what it means to have someone who is his equal.

"Is that the main topic of discussion?"

"Of course. What in the world is going on? You lost your memories, your control slipped, and the fiend dragon ran amok. Hmm, yes, that's understandable. But you also said this: Whether you had your memories or not, you were the demon king. In that case, something doesn't add up."

"......"

"We'll overlook the fact that you're deceiving your wife. That's one facet of love. However, we won't let you trick us, Demon King. Tell us everything. Who was it that slipped through your guard and released the fiend dragon? Does it have anything to do with the fact that the demon king was born into the imperial family of Ellmeyer, descended from the Maid of the Sacred Sword?"

"—Do you think a hopeless love is something one should carry forever?"

He's derailed Baal's interrogation, and the man seems irritated. However, he sighs, then shakes his head slowly. "Some loves can never be, and some never should. Certainly, giving it up is no easy task, but the love that is meant to succeed lies beyond it."

"You're right... I think so, too. At least *the current me does.*"

They'd wagered on the future that, one day, they were sure to be united. She and he, together.

"What...?"

"It's a very common story. The demon king inherits power and memories. I suppose you'd call them memories of my past life. Before now, they were all someone else's affair, mere knowledge...but it seems I've recovered some unwanted memories along with my magic."

He looks up. Baal doesn't look away.

"Holy King. I love Aileen, from the bottom of my heart."

"...Yes. We know that."

"However, the me from long-ago who loved the Maid of the Sacred Sword seems to consider it a betrayal."

★ ★ ★

Once upon a time, there lived a pair of twin sisters.

The beautiful younger twin vanquished the wicked demon king with her sacred power, saved the world, married the prince she loved, and created a happy, prosperous country where humans could live.

"Hee-hee... Lady Aileen. This was the first and last time we'll fight side by side. After all, in a game, one is supposed to enjoy the protagonist's exploits, correct?"

From the Kingdom of Ashmael's demolished clock tower, she can see the ocean. Far over the horizon is the Holy Queendom of Hausel. The next stage.

Her smile vanishes. Narrowing her violet eyes, the Maid of the Sacred Sword murmurs.

"You are the protagonist. And *I* am the player."

The ugly elder twin had an affair with the demon king and plotted mankind's downfall, but the Maid of the Sacred Sword defeated and killed her.

And the rest lived happily ever after.

Afterword

Hello, this is Sarasa Nagase.

Thank you for picking up my humble novel. The story of Aileen, the demon king, and their merry friends has reached Volume 4. I hope you enjoyed it.

This volume is based on the fourth section of the online edition. I've made some additions and corrections, and then there's what I've termed an "encore" at the end: I've designed it to look like an aside, then used it to drop a bomb. I think I wrote about twenty pages of new material in all. The online version also has anecdotes that didn't make it into this version, so feel free to read and compare both editions if you'd like.

True to the title, this is another story in which the villainess tames a final boss. You'd think we'd be close to running out of final bosses, but I'd like to keep plugging away for a while longer. I wonder how many final bosses I can create!

This was also a "couples' installment," so I worked with different combinations of characters than I usually do. Writing conversations (or rather, talk about love interests) between groups of all girls or all guys was a whole lot of fun.

And now for the thank-yous.

Mai Murasaki, who draws beautiful illustrations for every volume. Anko Yuzu, who draws the terrific manga version of this story for *Monthly Comp Ace*. My supervising editor, who gave me guidance. The proofreaders, the members of the *Kadokawa Beans Bunko* and *Comp Ace* editorial departments, the designers and marketing personnel, everyone at the printer, and all the people who were involved in the making of this book: Every one of you has my deepest gratitude.

In addition, I'm always encouraged by the kind words people send me in letters and on Twitter. Thank you very much.

Finally, to everyone who picked up this book: It's because of you that this series has been released up to the fourth volume. Really, thank you so much. Please continue to give Aileen and the others your support.

Now then, with prayers that we'll meet again…

Sarasa Nagase